D0889987

TERROR

TERROR

Conor Gearty

faber and faber
LONDON · BOSTON

First published in 1991
by Faber and Faber Limited
3 Queen Square London WC1N 3AU

Photoset by Wilmaset, Birkenhead, Wirral
Printed by Clays Ltd, St Ives plc

A CIP record for this book
is available from the British Library

ISBN 0-571-14450-0

Contents

Acknowledgements   vi

Introduction   1

1 The Trance of Terror   8

2 Sparks   17

3 The Spiral of Brutality   27

4 The Dispossessed   45

5 A War with Words   58

6 War with the Shadows   73

7 The Pseudo-colonials   97

8 The IRA   112

9 The Price of Victory   131

Conclusion   147

Notes   155

Bibliography   160

Index   165

Acknowledgements

I am grateful to many people for helping me with this book. It has its origins in a proposal, made some years ago, for a documentary series for Channel 4 television. The idea for these programmes came from Peter Flood, and without his drive and determination they would never have got off the ground. The three-part series, entitled *Terror*, was eventually broadcast in autumn 1990, and I was fortunate when preparing the book in having access to the research that was generated by the team making the series at Antelope Films. In particular, I would like to acknowledge the help and support of Peter Montagnon, Clive Syddall, Clare Elliott, Tony Stark and Jo Ralling. Tom Roberts worked on the TV series with me in its first development phase, and his enthusiastic and sharp mind helped me to shape my ideas on the subject. At Faber, I was given great support by Will Sulkin and, after his departure, by Susanne McDadd and the rest of the staff at Queen Square. I am grateful to them all. At home, Diane Wales was – as ever – a source of encouragement and constructive criticism; the book could not have been written without her. Finally, I would like to acknowledge the influence of my parents. Without their support and confidence in me over the years, and the atmosphere of intellectual inquiry that they generated at home, I would never have reached the point where a book such as this would have been contemplated, much less written. The book is dedicated to them, for their unfailing interest and love through the years.

Introduction

Political terror is the ugly wonder of the modern world. The explosion in the bar, the shoot-out in the airport lounge and the mid-air blowing apart of the jumbo jet are typical examples of its carnage. In such indiscriminate attacks, the innocent are dispatched to immediate death or branded for life with physical or psychological scars. The bloodshed is in the name of a political goal unknown to many of the victims and irrelevant to them all, but the purposefulness of such acts makes them chillingly different from the road accident or the natural catastrophe.

The success of these atrocities lies in the way they compel our attention. We follow with horrified interest the fate of the hostages in each new hijack or kidnap drama. We wonder not only at the terribleness of the deeds but also about the personalities and the causes that underpin them.

Paradoxically, acts of terror thrive in the relative freedom offered by mature democracies. These societies share a dedication to the peaceful absorption of political ambitions through the ballot box. They will often have spent centuries and expended many lives in squeezing the inclination for subversive violence out of their culture and traditions. The terrorists' bombs and bullets blow open doors which society has long believed not only shut but locked and bolted as well.

The Breadth of Terrorism

Violence is unequivocally terrorist when it is politically motivated and carried out by sub-state groups; when its victims are chosen at random; and when the purpose behind the violence is to communicate a message to a wider audience. These elements are what unite such disparate terror acts as the IRA's Birmingham pub bombings in 1974, Black September's assault at the Munich Olympics in 1972, and the blowing up of the Pan Am flight 103 over Lockerbie in December 1988.

Since its emergence in many places in the late 1960s, terror has provoked a remarkable reaction from the governments against which it has

I

been directed. Huge sums of money have been spent in making embassies, public buildings and political leaders safe from attack. Parts of the travel infrastructure have been redesigned to account for the possibility of assault. New counter-terrorist laws in many countries have transformed the relationship between the individual and the state, while the battle against terrorism has forged extensive new links between national police forces, involving the sharing of technology, intelligence and surveillance duties. Many of these developments directly threaten civil liberties.

Politicians have not been slow to talk of terrorism in a vocabulary of fear previously reserved exclusively for communism. In the first twenty years, the subject shared its language with the old enemy. General Gadaffi may have been the 'mad dog', but the Soviet Union remained firmly entrenched as the 'evil empire'. Now, however, the death of communism in eastern Europe and its imminent decline in China has left the field of fear clear for terrorism. Recently an undercurrent of anti-Islamic and anti-Arab senti-ment has crept into the debate. The Muslim faith stands out as the one remaining alternative to Western values. So it is hardly surprising that it – or the terrorists it is said to sponsor – should have drifted into the space once filled by Stalin and his advocates of world domination. If Senator McCarthy were alive today, his questions would be about mosques, not membership.

It is clear, however, that terrorism hardly compares with the threat once posed by the expansionary communism of the cold war era. The Soviet Union had an ideology of world domination, with money and troops to help realize its aims. It had successfully penetrated the higher echelons of Western society and had a record of imperialism in eastern Europe and parts of the developing world. In contrast, terrorism has achieved little of any consequence. No government has fallen because of its attacks, comparatively few casualties have been sustained, and no terrorist group has achieved anything more than a fraction of its long-term aims. The effects of two decades of terrorism has been irritating, not fatally poisonous.

Deeper reflection on the subject introduces further complexities. The public may continue to connect 'terrorism' with evocative and symbolic places like Lockerbie, Birmingham and Munich, but it is clear that the word is also used in a much wider sense than these tragedies would suggest. The death of a police officer in Northern Ireland is routinely designated a 'terrorist outrage', as is the killing of a government official in the Basque region of Spain. A frontal assault by the IRA on a British Army patrol would also be labelled a 'terrorist' action, despite the nature of the chosen victims and the military connotations of the tactic adopted. All the activities of groups engaged in acts of terror are automatically classed as terrorist, even when many of those activities, such as fund-raising and political campaigning, are conducted in a peaceful manner. In extreme cases those who merely share the political goals of subversive groups may find themselves described as terrorists. This has been the fate of members of legal political parties in both Northern Ireland and Spain, such as Provisional Sinn Fein and Herri Batasuna.

Terrorism and Subversion

The subject becomes yet more impenetrable when it is realized that these expanded meanings of 'terrorism' have drifted beyond the liberal democracies, and have found a home in countries where the authoritarian or totalitarian nature of the ruling establishment raises difficult questions about the morality of violent subversion. In the 1970s, South American military regimes committed many of their worst atrocities under the protective cover of 'robust counter-terrorism', while successive Israeli authorities have managed to present their control over the occupied territories as a battle with a gang of international terrorists who threaten the West as a whole. It is clear, too, that the South African government enjoyed a degree of success in its attempt to affix the label 'terrorist' to the ANC, at least that is until it decided (to the shock of those who had believed them) to talk to the organization on equal terms. The strategic value to the ruling authorities of such linguistic opportunism is considerable. If successful, it appears to deprive these insurgent groups of their history and traditions. Moreover, it unsettles Western opinion, which is broadly sympathetic, by equating such groups with the IRA, the Red Brigades, the Baader-Meinhof gang and all the other marginalized and despised advocates of Euro-terrorism. Even where such associations are not successfully made, the charge of terrorism usefully distracts attention from the violence perpetrated by the government's own forces. There was always something faintly ridiculous about discussing the rights and wrongs of an ANC bomb in an empty shopping precinct, or stone throwing in the Gaza strip, while the authorities in both places were shooting unarmed civilians with alarming regularity – in the name, of course, of the struggle against terrorism.

The inadequacy of the West's understanding of the term terrorism has made it vulnerable to being packaged off on such ethical tangents. At times, particularly when discussing the ANC and the Palestine Liberation Organization (PLO), it has seemed as if the idea of terrorism has reached the point where it can now be said to embrace subversive violence anywhere in the world. Such an approach, however, is impossible. Many of the great advances of the past have been rooted in violent subversion, and few countries can condemn all political violence without disowning the heroes that brought their own nations to life. If this interpretation of terrorism were rigorously applied, the German opponents of Hitler in the 1930s would have to be characterized as terrorists, as would George Washington and William of Orange. Such an attitude would be at least consistent, even if it were absurd. Contemporary use of the word 'terrorism', however, cannot boast even this strength, for the confusions go deeper than a merely foolish insistence on analytical uniformity. Violent subversive groups have sometimes escaped the terrorist classification altogether and have been rewarded instead with the near-heroic status of 'freedom-fighters'. The Contra opponents of the Nicaraguan government of the 1980s were given this standing, despite their use of terror tactics, and, during the same decade, the Afghanistanian resistance to a Soviet presence in their country was similarly successful in this 'war of labels'.

To make matters even more complicated, certain nations, such as Libya, have come to be regarded as 'terrorist states', while others, some guilty of great extremes of violence, such as Saudi Arabia and Israel, have not. And neither has the United States, despite the bombing of Tripoli in 1986, nor France, despite the deliberate sinking of the Greenpeace ship *Rainbow Warrior* in 1985, an action which caused the death of a photographer who was on board at the time. The status in the West of some nations, such as Syria, Iraq and Iran, depends on considerations of international diplomacy which have nothing whatsoever to do with 'terrorism', however the word is defined. At times, indeed, it has seemed that the words 'terrorist' and 'terrorism' have deteriorated into little more than terms of abuse. Thus President Saddam is a 'terrorist' because of his invasion of Kuwait, just as (in a different context) the defeated secret police were terrorists as far as the new Romanian government was concerned in early 1990. When drug-running began to be considered a serious problem, it was called 'narco-terrorism', while the burning of the rainforests, is now 'eco-terrorism'. The poisoning of supermarket food is immediately declared to be 'consumer terrorism', whatever motives may lie behind such a curious act of malevolence.

It would seem, then, that the words 'terror' and 'terrorism' have come to be regarded as such powerful condemnations that all those looking for a suitable insult have wanted to appropriate them. In its promiscuous desire to please, the idea originally communicated by the words has largely disappeared.

The Literature on Terrorism

Is there any hope for clarification from within academia? Few subjects within the universities have expanded as fast as the study of terrorism over the last twenty years. It dominates many reading lists in political science departments in Europe and North America. So great is the interest that bibliographical volumes are now required merely to keep track of the books on the subject that pour forth in increasing numbers every year. Specialist journals like *Terrorism: An International Journal* and *Terrorism and Political Violence* provide an opportunity for the publication of those articles and monographs which are not of book length. Numerous think-tanks and institutes publish papers, hold seminars and organize conferences to discuss the issues. London at one time had the Research Institute for the Study of Conflict and Terrorism, the Research Foundation for the Study of Terrorism, and the Institute for the Study of Conflict. Despite all this frenetic academic activity, the parameters of the subject remain undetermined.

Broadly speaking, the literature can be grouped into three separate categories. At one end of the spectrum are to be found careful, fully researched accounts of single episodes of subversive violence, such as the bombing of the King David Hotel in Israel in 1946.[1] In a similar vein are well-documented histories of particular groups, such as T. P. Coogan's study of the IRA.[2] Neither type of work has to wrestle with all-embracing definitions of terrorism, since it is concerned with the telling of a particular story. There is no need to link the subject matter with groups elsewhere, and all controversial labelling can therefore be safely avoided, leaving a straightforward narrative from which the reader is left to draw his or her own conclusions.

At the opposite end of the range are books in which the word 'terrorist' is certainly used, but in such a way as to indicate that a moral standpoint has already been taken. The question of definition is, as a result, subsidiary to the consideration of how to deal with it. Titles like *Terrorism: How the West can Win*,[3] *Terror!: The West Fights Back*[4] and *The War Against Terrorism*[5] reveal the style and emphasis of the narrative that they contain. Other works, like *Inside Terrorist Organizations*[6] and *Hydra of Carnage*,[7] focus on the subversive groups rather than on counter-terrorism, but once again the question of definition is largely ignored.

Between these two categories is a third approach, rooted in the traditions of political science, which attempts to ascribe a coherent meaning to terrorism. These works set out definitions which are based on a belief that terrorism is in essence no more than a particular and discernible method of subversion: in other words, that it is a tactical use of violence against an established order, regardless of its moral worth. If it were possible to follow this line consistently, the subject would be relatively straightforward. There would be available a value-free basis for the examination of the actions of groups and individuals, which would allow conclusive determination as to whether their orientation brought them within the sphere of terrorism. Unfortunately, matters are not so simple. The major difficulty is that identifying a terrorist is not simply a matter of ticking off items on a checklist of violent attributes. The label itself is inevitably value-laden. Its meaning is moulded by government, the media and in popular usage, not by academic departments. The word resonates with moral opprobrium and as such is, as far as the authorities and others are concerned, far too useful an insult to be pinned down and controlled. The manipulators of language are no respecters of academic integrity, and, simply to keep up, political scientists who believe a definition is possible have had to broaden their attempts so extensively that the exercise becomes rather pointless.

A Fresh Approach

This book explicitly recognizes the political ingredients in the subject of terror. It charts the rise of the 'terrorist' label, from its definable status twenty years ago to its frustrating vagueness today. Its origins in the violence of the past are examined, after which we trace its development out of both the anti-colonial struggles of the developing world and the urban guerrillas of Latin America. In these sections we consider the influence of Lenin, Mao and others, and examine how their ideas were applied by subversives in many countries and continents.

Pure terror reached its zenith in the Middle East, however, and therefore this troubled region is one we consider at length, having particular regard both to the rival versions of its history and the different perceptions of terror that afflict it. From about 1974, the idea of terrorism there became part of a propaganda battle between rival factions, and this manipulation continued in different guises throughout the 1980s. The decay in the language was such that, by the end of the decade, what meaning the word terrorism may once have had in the region had all but disappeared. Having discussed the Middle East, we turn to examine the history and context of other political conflicts where violence also described as terrorist has been regularly employed, in particular the 'pseudo-colonial' activities of the Tamil Tigers, the Indian Sikh extremists, the Basque nationalists ETA and the IRA, and finally the ideological subversion of European groups such as the Red Brigades and the Red Army Faction. This is followed by discussion of the nature of counter-terrorism, and the threat that state overreaction can pose for the freedom of every citizen.

The theme of the book can be encapsulated in two interrelated questions. Do the words 'terrorist' and 'terrorism' have any coherent meaning today, twenty-three years after they first began to seep into our vocabulary, and if so, what is that meaning? The answers will reveal as much about words and power as they do about life and death, so it is fitting that, as a prelude to the chapters that follow, the next section should attempt to resolve the problems of definition which have been raised.

1 The Trance of Terror

Acts of violence which we consider unambiguously terrorist have certain characteristics in common. They uniformly involve the deliberate infliction or (in the case of hijacking and kidnapping) the threatened infliction of severe physical violence; killing and maiming are the trademark of the true terrorists. Such acts are not in themselves rare in contemporary society. Despotic governments may do the same, but, unlike the practitioner of subversive terror, they have the authority of the state to enforce and legitimate their actions. The genuine political terrorist differs from the criminal because of his or her motive. The purpose is not personal gain, but political advantage. Its perpetrators believe that their actions are part of a long-term struggle. At this level of generality, it is possible to link such disparate episodes as the attacks on airports by Palestinian extremists, the kidnap and death of Quebec's Minister of Labour, Pierre Laporte, at the hands of nationalist separatists in 1970, and the IRA Birmingham pub bombings in 1974. This political dimension is an essential part of true terrorism, and is what separates its exponents from the gangland hoodlum and the drug baron, both of whose terror is but a brutal side effect of what is in each case little more than a selfish and extreme form of criminality. The political message, with its subtext of subversion, is one of the reasons why free societies view the violence of such terrorists with particular dread: the crook merely wants to benefit from society, whereas the rebel wants to destroy it.

The Power of Pure Terror

The means that these core terrorists are prepared to employ to achieve their ends mark them out as special. The violence is inflicted in a place of leisure, travel or tranquillity – a bar, an Olympic village, an airport. It occurs in peaceful, liberal, democratic societies, far away from any front line. The claims of such societies to have matured beyond the violent settlement of political disputes are mocked by such bloody interventions. What is more, the victims are not responsible for the hurt that compels these terrorists to act. Their 'crime' is to belong to, or even merely to live in, a country which the subversives have determined to despise. In the case of the attacks by the Popular Front for the Liberation of Palestine (PFLP) on international airports and the IRA's campaign of pub bombings, it was enough that the victims should have been in the wrong place at the wrong time; it did not matter who they were. A pure terrorist act results in everyone recoiling in horror, with the words 'it could have been me' etched on their mind. It is, therefore, the indiscriminate nature of its victims which gives the act of terror its powerful impact. It disfigures a settled community with abnormalities and uncertainties, in the wake of which follow disruption, fear and anxiety. We are all victims of a successful terrorist attack.

The opportunity for communication with the wider audience that terror violence achieves is, of course, one of the main reasons why it occurs in the first place. Society wonders who will be next and, in its weakened state, is more susceptible to the political message of the moment: why are the British troops in Ireland? why are those Palestinians in Israeli jails? why is Puerto Rica part of the United States? Without this type of terrorism, these questions would not be posed; with each new act of violence, they have to be answered afresh. In this way, such terrorism springboards issues into public debate. It uses horror and fear to jump the queue of ideas waiting for public attention. The South Moluccan separatists knew this when a series of train seizures and the taking over of a school in the mid-1970s dragged their obscure quarrel with Indonesia to the centre of the stage; their tactics involved the simple but callous expedient of threatening the lives of over 100 children. The Ustashi carried their argument for Croatian independence to foreign audiences in a highly efficient way when in 1977 they took over the Yugoslav mission at the United Nations and circulated New York with written calls for a 'free and independent Croatian state'. On a previous occasion, in one of the most famous incidents of its type, five Croatian nationalists hijacked an internal US TWA flight with eighty-eight passengers and crew on board and took the plane on a thirty-hour trip from Canada to Iceland and finally to Paris. Before surrendering, the hijackers' shrewd bargaining with the lives of their hostages had focused unprecedented attention on their cause. Their case for independence from Yugoslavia and for support from the United States was published in full in four leading US newspapers, and leaflets condemning the 'oppression and humiliation of which Croats are victims' were dropped from the air on to the cities of Paris and London. The Croatians may have been infrequent players of this new international game, but their interventions were well timed and highly effective.

The IRA believed for a time that mass killing in Britain would persuade the United Kingdom to disengage from Northern Ireland. George Habash, the leader of the PFLP, a radical organization responsible for many indiscriminate deaths, argued for his group's unqualified practice of terror: 'When we hijack a plane it has more effect than if we killed a hundred Israelis in battle. For decades world opinion has been neither for nor against the Palestinians. It simply ignored us. At least the world is talking about us now.'[1] Similar comments came from a Palestinian spokesman after the attack on Israeli athletes at the Munich Olympics. Despite the loss of five of his colleagues and the failure to secure Israeli concessions, the occasion was one to be celebrated:

A bomb in the White House, a mine in the Vatican, the death of Mao Tse-tung, an earthquake in Paris could not have echoed through the consciousness of every man in the world like the operation at Munich . . . It was like painting the name of Palestine on the top of a mountain that can be seen from the four corners of the earth.[2]

Modern Vulnerabilities

The publicity achieved by terror is fleeting however, and the attention focused on its perpetrators soon wanders. A whole campaign of terror, therefore, is required to reduce the risk of media neglect. But systematic violence is not in itself enough. Terror cannot afford to be repetitive, for the Western public is not much moved by an atrocity which has already distressed them in some earlier incarnation. It becomes just another thing that happens. Thus, as with an old TV soap desperate to keep its ratings, the producers of terror dramas are forced to escalate their actions with each episode. In this regard, they are not as strong as they appear, and the same is true in other respects. Despite its noisy impact, terror is the weapon of the weak.[3] The practitioners of this form of violence lash out because they have no other, more efficient, means of fighting. They have no countries and therefore no access to the authorized and mechanized killing efficiency of armies. They do not even pass the test of the guerrilla leader, who must develop a rapport with the local people in whose communities his forces are expected to operate. The development of alternative structures of government, the mobilization of large numbers of people into irregular armies and the careful politicization of the population are all aspects of guerrilla warfare which involve some degree of political support or at least acceptance. There is, therefore, a constituency of sorts which imposes a form of quasi-democratic accountability. In contrast, the practitioners of terror need answer only their own consciences. In the past, this very isolation would have meant that the terrorists had no political and little military impact, but the technological and infrastructural changes that have transformed Western society since the last world war have given the practitioners of this violence new opportunities.

It is easier now to commit acts of terror. Weapons are more readily available, and are more efficient. The outstanding example of this is the Semtex explosive, which achieves the maximum impact with the minimum of equipment, and is also very difficult for the police and airport guards to detect. The revolution in world transport has led to a vast increase in the movement of people round the globe and this has greatly increased the number of potential targets, in terms of both people and places. Airports, trains and buses have all become prime targets. Once the terror act has been carried out, the world media ensure that the deed, and – if its perpetrator is efficient – the message behind it, can be flashed around the world in seconds. In Western countries at least, this may mean that a whole society becomes embroiled in the human drama of the subversive episode. Classic examples of this approach are the Croatian hijack and the South Moluccan train sieges already mentioned, as well as the better-known air hijacks of the 1980s.

This is another and important change from earlier times. Liberal democracies have a paradoxical attitude to suffering. They make decisions about death and injury where the victims of such policies are numerous and not known, or not yet known. They do so all the time, in relation to foreign policy, the allocation of kidney machines, the closure of hostels for the homeless and the provision of money for research into AIDS, to pick some examples at random. But if a victim has a face, a family and a personality, the same nation will do its utmost to save such a life. No money is spared to rescue the crew member of a boat that has drifted out to sea or a fell walker who has gone missing. The anxiety of a nation over the fate of a hostage or a hijacked jet may well be laudable, but it is also a most desirable bonus for the group responsible for the situation. Since they are usually most anxious to explain themselves to the world, the audience, held by its own scruples, is as important to them as their captives.

The Efficacy of the Terror Method

To say that terror is the weapon of the weak is not to say that terrorism always fails. Publicity may be all that the group wants, in which case the drama itself represents success, as was the case with the assault at the Munich Olympics. And if the motive behind the act was plain revenge or hatred, this can be effectively achieved by the deed of terror itself, independent of the political consequences. Indeed, it is hard to see what else could have been intended by the airport massacres that have occurred in Rome, Athens and Tel Aviv, for example. An assessment of the effectiveness of terror in other ways depends, however, on identifying the goal other than publicity or revenge of those who utilize it.

If we see their ambitions as low-level or short-term, it is evident that deliberate terror does sometimes work. Terror has after all achieved the release of convicted prisoners from European and Israeli jails. It has led to political concessions which have been made as a way of bringing some crisis or another to a successful resolution. It has forced responses from liberal democratic governments which are out of all proportion, in terms of money spent and human resources allocated, to the mischief that it creates; it is only necessary to spend a couple of hours in an international airport to see how a few killers have transformed one whole substructure of the modern world, and in a way which reminds every passenger of the possibility of attack (even though in statistical terms it is too remote to be worthy of notice). The participants in terror acts have often escaped punishment as a result of a bargain struck with local negotiators. This is most clearly the case in many of the jet hostage situations.

All of these are merely small-scale achievements. They do not help the cause which is said to justify the terror. Nor do they tackle the underlying grievances which, it is claimed, compel such terrorists to act. While terror may be effective in terms of securing publicity, this in turn begs an important question: what is all the publicity for? Here we come to the central paradox of terror. The methods terrorists use to get attention mean that the public learns of their aims, but invariably rejects what they stand for. Yet if they had not used terror, their plight might never had been noticed. Having used it, their condition no longer goes unremarked upon, but they are still ignored, this time because their methods make them political untouchables.

The list of rebels who have gone on to become leaders of their countries includes many guerrilla chiefs, among them Michael Collins, Jomo Kenyatta and Robert Mugabe. But no pure terrorist has ever achieved through terror the power that is his or her ultimate aim. The only examples that come close are Yitzhak Shamir and Menachem Begin of Israel, though in both cases it could be argued that their activities in the Stern Gang and Irgun respectively delayed their entry into the political mainstream for twenty years. The path of the genuine terrorist may be littered with minor victories, but the final goal is rarely reached. It is extraordinarlily difficult for a group to break out of this trap of its own making. For if it attempts to eschew terror, it will undoubtedly split its own ranks and see a militant wing spin off to continue the fight. This has been the experience of Fatah, the IRA and ETA. Disavowal of violence is not enough to protect subversive groups from political opponents, who have their own reasons for continuing to accuse them of using it, long after this has ceased to be true; the reformed terrorist must face a long penance of mislabelling. If, on the other hand, the group perseveres with terror, the violence gradually takes on a less political air, becoming little more than a type of existential self-assertion, a childlike demand for attention.

Where once the plea behind the violence was 'listen to me', with long-running terror groups the message eventually becomes the shrill cry, 'I'm still here.'

The Drift from 'Terror' to 'Terrorism'

It is impossible to envisage circumstances in which acts of political terror of the type described above will ever be justified, whether on moral or on utilitarian grounds, since failure to succeed on the big questions is one of the few generalizations that can be confidently made about all terror groups. If the statistics on terrorism were confined to events involving violence, the number of attacks would not be high enough to give rise to the concern that society was on the verge of collapse. Instead, the graph would show a steady but low level of activity, requiring not hysteria but rather careful police action. But the scope of terrorism is not limited in this way. Over the years, there has been a steady increase in the range of activities classified as terrorist, so that we now have a discrepancy between the official, wider perception of what terrorism entails and the popular understanding of the word.

Contemporary definitions illustrate this point. The researchers at the Rand Corporation are among the most intelligent and careful of all the students of terrorism, but even they have shown themselves subject to expansionary temptations:

Terrorism . . . is defined by the nature of the act, not by the identity of the perpetrators or the nature of their cause. All terrorist acts are crimes – murder, kidnapping, arson. Many would also be violations of the rules of war, if a state of war existed. All involve violence or the threat of violence, often coupled with specific demands. The violence is directed mainly against civilian targets. The motives are political. The actions generally are carried out in a way that will achieve maximum publicity. The perpetrators are usually members of an organized group, and unlike other criminals, they often claim credit for the act. And finally the act is intended to produce effects beyond the immediate physical damage.[4]

This definition is essentially accurate, but it is hedged about with numerous caveats and qualifications; 'many', 'often', 'mainly', 'generally' and 'usually' are not the words of writers confident about their comprehensiveness. The definition appears at a glance to cover only specific acts of terror, but it is capable of being expanded indefinitely in various directions. The inclusion of 'threats', for example, adds to the statistics on terrorism a vague and open-ended category of incidents in which no violence has been used.

Professor Paul Wilkinson of St Andrews University may be described as the doyen of British specialists on terrorism. In his important book *Terrorism and the Liberal State*, he suggests the following approach: 'Political terrorism may be briefly defined as coercive intimidation. It is the systematic use of murder and destruction, and the threat of murder and destruction in order to terrorize individuals, groups, communities or governments into conceding to the terrorists' political demands.'[5]

This interpretation would include but take us far beyond the brutality of Munich, Birmingham and Lockerbie. It covers murder but (oddly) not manslaughter or injury to the person, unless these are embraced within the meaning of 'destruction'. That word already covers a multiplicity of misdemeanours, from blowing up an airliner to pricking a balloon; its vagueness greatly expands the definition's scope. Furthermore, the terror need be aimed only at the individual or a group rather than at society as a whole. This takes away the need for the indiscriminate victim, and yet it is precisely the uncertainty engendered by such arbitrariness that helps to create the generalized climate of fear which is an essential part of all classic terror attacks. Like the Rand Corporation, Professor Wilkinson mentions threats. By his definition terrorists would include not only the hijackers and the mass murderers but also the window-breakers, the hoaxers and those who are so careful about their targets that the general public (who know this) feel no fear at all.

Terrorism as Defined by the Authorities

Governments, by definition the upholders of the existing order, will naturally seek to condemn their opponents as terrorists, since the public-relations victory achieved by this linguistic sleight of hand can be crucial in any ensuing struggle for popular support. The pressure for a loose definition will always be strongest when it comes from those who have most to lose from any change. Thus in 1981 the CIA included for the first time threats and hoaxes in its statistics on international terrorism. Their 1979 report identified 3,336 incidents of 'international terrorism' between 1968 and 1979. Applying the new criteria, it was revealed that there had been 6,714 incidents between 1968 and 1980: it looked as though the incidents of 'international' terrorism had doubled overnight.[6] Unsurprisingly in such a context, official definitions of terrorism have occasionally jettisoned the key element in the whole equation, terror, in favour of all-embracing formulas which have come close to designating all insurgency as terrorist subversion. Thus the American Task Force on Combating Terrorism, chaired by the then Vice-President, George Bush, reported in 1986 that terrorism was the 'unlawful use or threat of violence against persons or property to further political or social objectives'. It was 'usually intended to intimidate or coerce a government, individuals, or groups, or to modify their behavior or politics'.[7]

An attempt by Congress to define 'crimes of terrorism' managed to achieve even greater breadth than this. It included:

espionage, sabotage, kidnapping, extortion, skyjacking, robbery, bombing, holding a person prisoner or hostage or any threat or attempt to kidnap, extort, skyjack, bomb, or hold prisoners or hostages, or any threat to do any injury to a human being, animal or personal or real property or any conspiracy to do any of the above in order to compel an act or omission by any person, or any government entity.[8]

It is hard to see how such verbal inflation can do other than render the word terrorist entirely devoid of meaning. The United Kingdom's Prevention of Terrorism (Temporary Provisions) Act 1989 takes a line which is more succint but nevertheless also very wide. It defines terrorism as 'the use of violence for political ends', including 'any use of violence for the purpose of putting the public or any section of the public in fear'. Once again the quality of indiscriminateness has drifted out of the equation. 'Terror' has been replaced by 'fear', a much wider state of anxiety which is far more easily reached: an army officer on patrol, for example, can be afraid without being terrorized. And there is no guidance as to the size the section of the public has to be before putting it in fear will amount to terrorism; it would seem that attacking only police officers or members of the army is enough, even though the general public are not terrified at all. What about the category government ministers or even that one-person section of the public the Secretary of State for Northern Ireland?

Conclusion

Any examination of the historical development of political terrorism needs to keep these ambiguities firmly in mind. The first part of this chapter was concerned with the common elements to be found in all acts of pure political terror. The activities discussed there left no room for argument; it was unequivocally at the centre of all definitions of terrorism. As such, it proved possible to make a number of abstract analytical points about the nature of the tactic, its efficacy and the overall prospects for those who use it. But these remarks were specifically concerned with what we have been calling and what we shall continue to call 'core', or 'pure' or 'genuine' political terrorism. This is to distinguish it from the much wider category of behaviour that can count as 'terrorist' when the word is given various expanded meanings. For the further we move away from this central definition, the less easy it is to make generalizations, and the more important it becomes to put the stigmatized behaviour in its historical and political context. Indeed, this is crucial if we are to avoid being trapped by manipulative uses of the term. In the penumbra of meaning that surrounds terror, as the word broadens to the point where it includes all subversion and finally all opponents, local circumstances and background assume a crucial role and the pursuit of a valid definition becomes correspondingly unimportant and irrelevant.

2 Sparks

Subversive violence has existed for as long as there have been governments to subvert. Indeed history can be seen as a series of violent struggles for power; and the very least that can be said is that those who practise unofficial political violence follow in a long (and where the insurgents have been successful, honourable) tradition. Pre-modern times may be awash with examples of rebellious activity but the options were varied, and terrorism, whether broadly or narrowly defined, was chosen only erratically. But even though terrorism as we understand it today is a late arrival on the spectrum of political violence, its emergence owes something to older forms of subversion.

Traditional Forms of Combat

Until relatively recently the commonest way of practising political violence was through a conventional war. There were medieval insurrections, such as those by the peasants in Flanders in 1323–7 and in England in 1381, but these were the exception rather than the rule and, furthermore, they involved a type of popular or mob uprising far removed from what we understand terrorism to encompass today. It is stating the obvious to remark that conditions in pre-Enlightenment Europe were harsh, but this meant that, in circumstances where great brutality was being shown by all sides, revolts could expect no more than to be ruthlessly suppressed by the authorities. As Richard Clutterbuck has pithily put it, the 'only variation in punishment would be whether death was or was not preceded by torture. Might was right.'[1] In such a context it is easy to see why a medieval version of modern-day pure terrorism would have been ineffective. It would not have been damaging enough to have had an impact, and even if it had, the mêlée of contemporary brutality would have ensured that it was soon forgotten. The weaponry essential to a potential terrorist of this sort would have been ineffective in comparison with the opportunities of today, and would have been extremely hard to obtain since the state enjoyed a virtual monopoly of technology. In short, these putative insurgents would have been starved of equipment and of attention, two essentials without which no genuine terrorist could have come to the fore. None contrived to operate against such towering odds.

Nor was substate subversion or any of the contemporary terrorist varieties behind the initial success of the French Revolution, the starting point of modern history. The tactics of 1789 involved popular agitation on an unprecedented scale, and the mobs that made it possible were the antithesis of today's isolated terrorist cells. Their achievements were to bewitch subsequent generations of subversives. Thus when an outburst of nationalist fervour followed the post-Napoleonic stitching-up of Europe by the five old powers at the Congress of Vienna in 1815, the French model was widely regarded as the one to emulate. The fashion was for the erection of a barricade in the city as a prelude to an urban insurrection which would then win the support of the army and achieve freedom for a newborn republic. It never happened that way. National feeling may have been bottled up after Vienna, but the forces of reaction that the old powers had become were quick to stamp out rebellion.

Terrorism, whether in its pure or expanded version, was not part of the equation of revolt. It had not even figured in the resistance to Napoleon, though opposition to the French occupation of other European nations had found military expression in the revival of a form of political violence that was truly ancient: guerrilla warfare. The main theatres for the practice of this unconventional method were Spain (1808–13), the Tyrol (1809) and Russia (1812).[2] The opportunity arose because, although the French military were typically far stronger than their local opposition, they were also usually both unfamiliar with the terrain in which they were operating and widely despised as an occupying army. The essence of the guerrilla tactic was for small bands of local fighters to exploit these weaknesses by skirmishing with the larger force and attacking its supply lines, without ever confronting it in open combat. The usual rules of war could not apply, and the occupying troops were compelled to exhaust both their resources and their nerves in trying to swat an army of invisible flies. Sometimes such guerrilla activity developed quickly into full-scale combat; on other occasions it remained at the nuisance level. To be successful, it needed both a rural base and plentiful local support. This makes it quite different from terrorism as we understand that word today, but many whom we so label desire to be thought of as 'guerrillas' instead, because they rightly perceive that the name carries with it a positive image.

This glance at history does not reveal a consistent thread of activity which could in any sense of the word be deemed terrorist. Those who seek to establish such a tradition usually point to five historical movements: the Sicarii from ancient times, the Assassins from the medieval period, the protagonists of the French Terror of 1793–4, and the Irish nationalists and Russian anarchists of the late nineteenth century. Though none of these could be thought of as anything other than peripheral to world affairs, a brief examination of each is useful, because of their importance to the development of our subject.

The Sicarii and the Assassins

The Sicarii were an offshoot of the Zealots and continued their struggle against Roman rule in Palestine in the first century after the birth of Christ. Their ambition was to free the people from Roman control, but their quarrel was not only with the foreigners but also with those local Jews who were willing to accommodate the imperial presence. The historian Josephus described them as 'brigands who took their name from a dagger carried in their bosoms'. He tells how on one occasion, after they had burnt down the palace of Agrippa, 'they took their fire to the Record Office, eager to destroy the money-lenders' bonds and so make impossible the recovery of debts, in order to secure the support of an army of debtors and enable the poor to rise with impunity against the rich'. Their methods certainly caused terror in those against whom they moved:

Their favourite trick was to mingle with festival crowds, concealing under their garments small daggers with which they stabbed their opponents. When their victims fell the assassins melted into the indignant crowd, and through their plausibility entirely defied detection. First to have his throat cut by them was Jonathan the high priest, and after him many were murdered every day. More terrible than the crimes themselves was the fear they aroused, every man as in war hourly expecting death. They watched at a distance for their enemies, and not even when their friends came near did they trust them; yet in spite of their suspicions and precautions they were done to death; such was the suddenness of the conspirators' attack and their skill in avoiding detection.[3]

The targets of the Sicarii were not chosen at random but because their lists of enemies were so large the killings often appeared indiscriminate. The message was that Jews who assisted the Romans did so at great risk to their lives. The strategy of using terror to provoke conflict was to find echoes in the theories of South American urban guerrillas two millennia

19

later, though the latter would have been well advised to have pondered the fate of this early role model, for the Zealots' activities were one of the factors that led the Romans to besiege and eventually destroy Jerusalem.

Selectivity was a characteristic of that other famous 'proto-terrorist' group, the Assassins. They belonged to the Ismaeli sect of the Shia branch of the Islamic faith and lived in the Middle East during the twelfth and thirteenth centuries. They became known in western Europe for their occasional use of assassination against the Crusaders, most notably when one of their members killed Conrad of Montferrat in 1192. The group reserved its main anger, however, for fellow Muslims. Its campaign of murder against specific Islamic leaders was certainly designed to terrorize; the killings were always carried out with a dagger, thereby ensuring close personal contact between assailant and victim, and the willingness of the Assassins to die for their cause meant that an indication from them of an intention to kill was tantamount to death. This had the desired effect of influencing the policy of those vulnerable to such threats.

But it is going rather far to conclude from this that the Assassins were terrorists, at least in the pure sense of the word. As their leading historian in the West, Bernard Lewis, has pointed out, they 'assassinated only rulers, ministers and generals. And while from the point of view of rulers, ministers and generals this is deplorable, it does not qualify for comparison with the kind of terrorism prevalent today.'[4] Unsurprisingly, those who were more vulnerable than anyone else precisely because of this selectivity did not draw comfort from the discipline of their opponents. Rather the reverse; like Josephus, with his remark about every man 'hourly expecting death', they tended to treat their own position of acute insecurity as a reflection of a generalized state of terror affecting all and sundry, a perception which might have been psychologically understandable but which was hardly borne out by the facts.

The French Terror

The Sicarii and the Assassins were exceptional not because they were 'terrorists' but rather because they employed methods which were highly unorthodox for their day. The first use of the word 'terror' in its modern sense came during the latter part of the French Revolution. The regime of terror in France in 1793 and 1794 contained many of the themes that, for succeeding generations, were to become painfully familiar emblems of the practitioners of the politics of fear. At its root, the Terror was simply the logical application of a particular philosophy: the people had to be regenerated in new and truthful forms, and if some of them got in the way, then they were 'enemies of the Revolution' and had to be removed. One architect of the Terror, Saint-Just, was quite specific about this: 'We want to estabish an order of things such that a universal tendency towards the good is established and the factions find themselves suddenly hurled on to the scaffold.'[5] The problem here was the definition of 'we'. It began as the people but, as one writer has remarked, was 'progressively restricted to the republicans, the Convention, the Montagnards, the Committee of Public Safety and eventually a minority within the Committee itself'.[6]

The narrowing of the category of those entitled to act on behalf of the people was matched by a continued widening in the range of their victims. Initially, the Terror was aimed at the aristocrats, but the Law of Suspects of 17 September 1793 allowed action against a far broader and more ill-defined group. The chief advocate of terror, Robespierre, proceeded to turn this law on those of his fellow revolutionaries, the Girondins and the Cordeliers among them, whom he judged to be too moderate for the people's good. Eventually, such enthusiasm proved to be his downfall, and he and his cohorts were executed by former zealots of the Revolution, just before he had the chance to kill them. The total number of executions during the Terror has been estimated at 40,000, and one study has concluded that of the 12,000 persons guillotined during the Terror, only 37 per cent were aristocrats.[7] While it is true to say that the ideology and brutality of at least some of today's terrorism unconsciously echoes the seminal events of 1793–4, particularly in the sense of the killers' being the guardians of the people's will, the level of harm caused by modern emulators of Robespierre is infinitely *less* great: while Robespierre could call on the power of the state, the Red Brigades, the Red Army Faction, the IRA and so on have always been fighting authority. The lesson of the French Revolution is that state terror can do more damage in a year than insurgents can do in a lifetime.

Irish Nationalists and Russian Anarchists

The failure of many popular revolts across Europe in 1848 led to renewed debate about the methodology of subversion. The new generation of subversives looked to different tactics and a type of violence described as terrorist gradually emerged. In the second half of the century, two places came to be particularly associated with its use: Ireland and Russia. In Ireland the motivating force was nationalism: a large section of the Irish population wanted to free the country from British control. This sentiment expressed itself mainly in support for the Home Rule policies of the Irish Parliamentary Party at Westminster, but there was also a more militant group, committed to the 'physical force tradition' in Irish affairs.

The Irish Republican Brotherhood (IRB) was a secret society dedicated to the achievement of an independent Ireland by force of arms. Like the Jacobins before them, they claimed an exclusive right to decide what was best for their country's people. But this did not make them a terrorist group in the pure sense of the word. On the contrary, the IRB eschewed terror tactics and preferred the old-fashioned approach of open insurrection, a choice which reflected not so much the acumen of the organization as the extent to which its leaders had deceived themselves into believing their own propaganda. Their one effort at open revolt, in 1867, was an unmitigated disaster, floundering on a variety of rocks including a less than enthusiastic Irish public. Indeed, it can be argued that the IRB would have got much further if they had been genuinely terrorist, in the sense of being prepared to sacrifice the lives of uninvolved innocent civilians to their cause. In 1867, an attempt by them to secure the release of Irish prisoners in London's Clerkenwell jail by bombing the exterior wall of the prison went horribly wrong and caused the death of passers-by. The mistake made their attempt look like a classic act of terror, and the English public reacted by showing a far greater interest in Irish affairs than the puny rebellion of the same year had managed to stimulate. The British Prime Minister, W. E. Gladstone, later reported to parliament that the IRB 'conspiracy [had] had an important influence with respect to Irish policy'.

If Clerkenwell gave the false impression that the IRB was a terrorist gang, the activities of maverick groups on its fringes tended to reinforce this idea. The leading historian of the period, Charles Townshend, has examined in detail the bombing campaign conducted in England in the early 1880s by Clan na Gael and the Skirmishers and concluded that, though they were 'an early example of modern political terrorism', their 'effect in inducing terror . . . was problematical. As with subsequent campaigns, the impact lessened with time.'[8] The anxiety shown by the bombers to avoid causing any loss of human life was their Achilles' heel, for without deaths their violence remained inconvenient rather than revolutionary.

The most important act of the period to be designated terrorist was carried out by a mysterious group connected with the agrarian movement called The Invincibles. This was the assassination in Phoenix Park, Dublin, in 1882 of two leading representatives of British rule, Lord Frederick Cavendish and Mr T. H. Burke, an event which belonged to that long tradition of precise action against particular leaders which can be traced back to the Sicarii and the Assassins.[9]

If Irish separatists have a reputation as nineteenth-century terrorists, this has less to do with what actually happened and more to do with the willingness of voluble revolutionaries on the fringes to talk tough and to call for extraordinary extremes of aggression. Those who extrapolate historical truth from such records do so at their peril. One maverick figure, O'Donovan Rossa, for example, was said to have produced an hilarious scheme for spraying the House of Commons with lethal gas, and this duly makes its appearance in the literature on terrorism[10] – without the caveat that the same man was so squeamish about the use of explosives that his own bombing campaign never got off the ground.[11]

The same overemphasis on the written word rather than action has afflicted analysis of the role of terrorism in Russia, the second country in which the method rose to the surface in the late nineteenth and early twentieth centuries. The facts point to two periods of subversive activity. The Narodnaya Volya were responsible for the first, which began in 1878 and ended with the clampdown by the authorities which followed the assassination of the Tsar, Alexander II, in 1881. The second was the work of the Social Revolutionary Party, through its surrogate, the Fighting Organization, whose campaign opened with the murder of the Interior Minister, Dmitrii Sipiagin, in 1902 and ended with a whimper in the midst of the far greater violence of the revolutionary action of 1905.

The literature of the time is replete with revolutionary rhetoric and it is possible to draw from this some sort of picture of the rebels, at least with regards to the first phase of violence. Their underlying philosophy was a type of idealistic anarchism, which required the destruction of the existing order as a prelude to a new and better (though rarely described) society. They believed that a single act of destruction would do more than could ever be achieved by publications and political debate. This idea was encapsulated in the memorable phrase 'propaganda of the deed', although what was to be communicated was never as clearly defined as these words would suggest. Into this was mixed a celebration of the criminal as the 'only true revolutionary', a point formulated by Wilhelm Weitling and developed by one of the most influential writers on the subject, Mikhail Bakunin:

Banditry is one of the most honorable ways of life within the Russian state. Since the establishment of the Muscovite state, it has represented a desperate protest by the people against the infamous social order, perfected on the Western pattern and still further consolidated by Peter's reforms and the benign Alexander's grants of freedom. The bandit is the people's hero, defender, savior. He is the implacable enemy of the state and the whole social and civil order set up by the state; he is a fighter to the death against the entire civilization of the aristocratic *Chinovniks* and governmental priesthood.[12]

Whatever the basis of their philosophy, the writings of these revolutionaries suggested that they were extremely bloodthirsty. Bakunin declared that the

present generation must in its turn produce an inexorable brute force and relentlessly tread the path of destruction. The healthy, uncorrupted mind of youth must grasp the fact that it is considerably more humane to stab and strangle dozens, nay hundreds, of hated beings than to join with them to share in systematic *legal* acts of murder, in the torture and martyrdom of millions of peasants.

Sergei Nechaev's renowned *Catechism of the Revolutionist*, published in 1869, described the revolutionary as 'a doomed man' who 'knows of only one science, the science of destruction'; he 'is an implacable enemy of this world, and if he continues to live in it, that is only to destroy it more effectively'. During both '[n]ight and day he must have but one thought, one aim – merciless destruction'.[13] Nikolai Morozov looked forward to the day when 'the despots will feel that the earth is collapsing under their feet among the sounds of music, the frightened screams of innumerable crowds, during the dessert at a refined dinner'.[14]

Much of the subversive literature of the time is written in this melodramatic, overblown way. Despite this, a great deal of care was taken in the execution of revolutionary criminal acts. The essence of the tactic of terrorism, as it was understood in Tsarist Russia, lay in the precision of its targeting. Underground activists believed that the assassination of one or a small number of key officials within the government would ignite revolution across the land. This was not a special Russian phenomenon. One commentator has remarked that nothing was 'more indicative of the special quality of nineteenth- and twentieth-century European notions of insurgency than the hope of achieving revolutionary ends by translating a specific attack on an individual target into the signal for mass action'.[15] This 'spark-on-tinder' theory required the rebel to make a number of extremely optimistic assumptions about the general public's preparedness for action.

Government was divided into good and bad men, a distinction which shows the degree to which the insurgents were untouched by Marx's far deeper criticisms of social structures; there is something naïve, almost childlike, about Morozov's remark, written in 1880, that '[b]rutal force and despotism are always concentrated either in a few or more often in one ruling person (Bismarck, Napoleon) and stop with his failure or death'.

This approach, however, meant that the range of victims available for terrorist action was greatly reduced. Thus on one occasion a bomber felt unable to act against the Grand Duke Sergei Alexanderovich because the intended victim was accompanied by his family and it would be wrong to act in a way which would endanger the life of children. Partly because of this fine discrimination and partly because their criticisms of the regime were widely shared, the revolutionaries enjoyed a degree of popular support during each phase of their activity.

The atmosphere of the time was not that of a nation terrorized by arbitrary murder, at least as far as the anti-government factions were concerned. Of course, top officials were afraid. As the head of the political police remarked at the time: 'All ministers are human and they want to live.'[16] But even in this area of allegedly maximum revolutionary activity, the statistics are surprising. During the supposed peak of terrorism, from 1878 to 1882, there were no more than six serious attacks on senior officials other than the Tsar. During the same period there were no less than seventy-two trials involving 397 defendants; the sentences meted out included nineteen of imprisonment, 159 of forced labour (usually in Siberia) and fifty-seven of exile. Thirty-one prisoners were sentenced to death and executed.[17] Insofar as there was any 'propaganda of the deed', the message from the authorities was much the clearest.

Conclusion

What lessons are to be drawn from this brief survey? There can be no doubt that these groups provided an intellectual and historical base for the evolution of modern terrorism. However, it is also clear that terrorism, even when loosely defined to include a whole range of subversive activity, played a very small role in any important conflict. And if the word is limited to the use by substate factions of indiscriminate and petrifying violence in order to communicate a political message, it is clear that such terror is hardly ever to be found in any century up to and including the nineteenth. Supposedly quintessential terrorist organizations of the past reveal themselves on closer examination to have been selective and careful in their use of force. The most we can say is that they used a form of political violence which was not easily classifiable under any of the traditional heads of combat. The subversives of the last century in particular were often fighting for rights that we take for granted today, and their methods revealed a strong sense of moral responsibility which was not always reciprocated by the all-powerful authorities which they opposed. If the IRB and the anarchists had a fatal weakness, it lay in their tendency to arrogate to themselves the right to decide what was good for their people. Their failure was due at least in part to the fact that the elitist self-confidence that flowed from this prevented any clear realization of their isolation or the strength of the forces of authority marshalled against them.

3   The Spiral of Brutality

The violence of the first half of the twentieth century was on a unique scale, but this was not a fact for which terrorist factions had any responsibility. Nor was the upsurge in the statistics of politically inspired casualties entirely accounted for by improvements in the technology of killing, though clearly this played a part. The main reason for the increase in violence of this sort lay in the fact that the task of causing death was taken up by the nation states themselves.

War and Official Terror

The involvement of governments in officially sponsored violence distinguished this period from the preceding 100 years. States regularly mobilized their might so as to kill people from other countries in pursuit of some patriotic or ideological goal. The First World War may have been ignited by a political assassination reminiscent of earlier times, the killing of Archduke Franz Ferdinand, but it is ludicrous to draw portentous lessons about terrorism from this. The ensuing bloody bonfire would not have been possible without the commitment and selfish, blinkered pride of national leaders. Similarly, the Second World War was a battle fought by many countries against the tendency of Germany and Japan to strive for near-total domination. The multiplicity of disasters that afflicted the world during these conflagrations included many whose effects were as severe as any pure act of terror: the London blitz, the siege of Leningrad, the bombing of Dresden and – most horrifically of all – the nuclear attacks on Hiroshima and Nagasaki. In each case, the motives of the killers were broadly political, the victims were indiscriminate and the message in the death was aimed at a wider audience, whether the general public, the armed forces or the government (or Emperor) of the country concerned.

But the state terror of the first half of the twentieth century did not stop at wars with other nations. The violence shown by Stalin and Hitler towards

27

certain of their own people was just as brutal and just as terroristic. The calculated destruction of peasant communities in the Soviet Union, the 'show trials' of the 1930s, and, above all, the mass killing by the Nazis of homosexuals, political subversives and the gypsy and Jewish peoples – all added a new dimension to the litany of horror. In many respects this violence was worse than war, in that it was more terrifying, both because of the defencelessness of the victims and because the only guardian they could claim – their own government – had chosen to become their tormentor. The genocide practised by the two leaders made even the fervour of Robespierre appear restrained. These years were unprecedentedly brutal precisely because the terror that was practised between and within nations was authorized; subversive violence then and now appears trivial in comparison.

The Intellectual Origins of Modern Terror: Lenin and Mao

The contemporary violence that we have called pure terrorism cannot be placed within an historical tradition which embraces any of the bloody events of the first fifty years of this century. Its practitioners can point to no past tyrant from that time as the unequivocal 'father' of their brand of violence, for it is not even true to say that any of the leaders responsible for these multifarious holocausts achieved power through any form of political terrorism. The British, with their parliamentary system, were at least partly responsible for the tragedy of the First World War. Hitler may have made pragmatic use of terror on his way to the top, but his attainment of power was achieved through the ballot box. Even Stalin inherited a position of dominance which had been won by Lenin through the Bolshevik's seizure of power in 1917, an event which more resembled a traditional coup d'état than an act of political terror. None of these men structured their military plans solely around such acts; indeed none of them was a terrorist, even under extended definitions of the word. Nevertheless, some of the tactics they adopted have been followed by subsequent groups, for the strategy of militant subversion loosely known today as terrorism has no victories to its name, and this has made its proponents necessarily promiscuous in their search for heroes. In particular, those who practise pure terror have constructed their ideology of violence from a pantheon of borrowed paradigms.

Lenin has been especially influential in the development of modern subversive methods in general and in the emergence of the tactic of political terror in particular. This is in spite of the fact that he was critical of the activities of the anarchists in nineteenth-century Russia. He considered the Narodnaya Volya and the Social Revolutionaries to be misguided zealots whose few successes were far outweighed by the damage they were doing to the true cause of revolution. (His own brother had been hanged in 1887 for plotting to take the life of the Tsar). His opposition was pragmatic rather than moral; their answer was wrong not because it was evil but because he believed he had a better one. Lenin's solution to the problems posed by the needs of the backward and pre-industrial society of turn-of-the-century Russia was not to throw bombs at ministers but rather to create a revolutionary elite dedicated to one simple aim: the seizure of power. His cadre of revolutionaries exploited the popular grievances of the day as a way of extending and consolidating their support. In Russia these were the issues of land, food and war. It did not matter that the complaints might be from nationalists, aspirants to land ownership or other persons of whom the Bolsheviks disapproved; what counted was that their ill will towards the authorities made them potentially sympathetic to the subversives, whose state of political powerlessness enabled them to promise all things to all men.

Modern subversive groups have drawn three lessons from Lenin. The first is that the city rather than the country is the key to revolution, and that an urban elite is essential both to its success and to its survival. This principle was downgraded somewhat during the guerrilla phase of colonial struggle, but with the ascendancy of terrorism it has returned to its pre-eminent position. The second lesson draws on Lenin's attacks on the affluent West on account of its exploitation of the colonies. Lenin saw such 'imperialism' as a key element in late capitalism and he called for the liberation of these subjugated territories. This Marxist–Leninist language of anti-imperialism has entered the vernacular of revolution and has functioned as the basis for rebellions that use terror as a method of revolt. Finally, astute revolutionaries follow Lenin in exploiting every fragment of local alienation to their own end. It was war and bread in his day, but in contemporary social democracies it could be the problems of inequality, bad housing and local taxation. It was clear that Lenin viewed terror as a perfectly appropriate weapon if it could be depended upon to yield results. In this respect, his lack of scruples in relation to the choice of tactics is probably his most lasting contribution to the development of contemporary terror.

Another key figure in modern terrorism, and another who, ironically, was not a true terrorist, is Mao Tse-tung. Mao was born to a peasant family in Hunan province, China, in 1893. He was educated at Changsha and worked first as an assistant librarian and then as a schoolmaster. The times in which he grew up were unsettled. The ancient Manchu dynasty had finally collapsed in 1911, after which China was in the hands of various factions jostling for power. In 1921 Mao became a founder member of the Chinese Communist Party. Inevitably, the early ambition of the Party was to emulate the success of Lenin, but the urban revolution that they sought to bring about stubbornly refused to happen. Mao saw the futility of such tactics earlier than most. From about 1927 he began to develop new ideas about the power of the rural peasantry. A prototype guerrilla organization did emerge in the Party's base in the country, but the leadership mistrusted it, favouring conventional methods of warfare. Eventually, however, massive defeats in 1934 made inevitable a strategic reassessment and Mao's ideas finally gained intellectual ascendancy.

The change in tactics was both symbolized and achieved by the Long March that then occurred. The mythology that has grown up around this event should not be allowed to diminish its epic qualities. Mao took tens of thousands of his communist followers on an extravagant one-year-long journey to new bases in northern China, from where guerrilla warfare could be more effectively practised. The Japanese invasion of China in 1937 confirmed the predominance of this new military tactic. But Mao was not so much fighting the foreign invader as the local Chinese forces, the Kuomintang. He reasoned that Japanese influence over the country could be only temporary and that therefore the Kuomintang were his real rivals for power. So it proved. Mao's success over all domestic opposition came after the withdrawal of the Japanese, and after a successful guerrilla campaign. Why did he succeed? The Kuomintang leaders had a reputation for corruption and incompetence, but this would not have been enough in itself – many Chinese forces were so regarded. The instability and insecurity caused by the war played an important part, as did the fact that a power vacuum was left when the retreating Japanese departed. But these were opportunities that could have been seized by other factions. The key to Mao's success, and the reason for his importance in any discussion of the development of subversive terror, lay in his grasp of tactics and ideology.

Traditional Marxism was preoccupied with the urban proletariat. It saw military action as very much the last stage after political agitation had done the bulk of the work. Mao's sensitivity to local conditions made him reject both of these approaches in favour of an old-style guerrilla operation, but one with important innovations. He realized that, viewed solely in conventional terms, his forces were technologically and militarily much weaker than those of his opponents. Turning this weakness into a strength, Mao evolved the concept of the People's War. In the 1930s he planned a long campaign, to be fought with great patience over many years if necessary. The enemy was not to be engaged in full open combat but was to be subjected to consistent attack on Mao's own terms. The guerrilla was not to hold territory but was rather to absorb enemy action, withdrawing where necessary but attacking when the opportunity arose. Mao's thinking was that the guerrillas would gradually build up their forces and eventually move from the countryside to encircle the cities. This was to herald the final stage in the struggle, when the communists would forsake their guerrilla habits for the conventional war that was to be the prelude to total victory.

This strategy was successful in China because of the links that Mao forged between the guerrillas and the peasant communities living in the regions in which they operated. He saw that without local approval, the long war he regarded as essential would have been impossible. Mao grasped that in order to achieve such support, military action had to be directed towards and subjugated to clear and popular political goals. In developing this insight Mao made his two key contributions to the theory of subversive violence. First, the Party had not only to fight but also to have something to say. Mao's message was one of incorruptibility and solidarity with the poor. The point was demonstrated by the contrast between the guerrillas' harshness towards their enemies and the solicitousness shown towards those whom they claimed to represent. It was fortified by the insensitive brutality of their opponents. This careful marriage between force and friendship slowly turned propaganda rhetoric about support into reality, and made possible Mao's eventual triumph.

Terror and terrorism rarely achieve the level of approval attained by Mao's guerrillas. Indeed, such methods tend to have the reverse effect of alienating the local people, a point realized by Mao when he emphasized the need for selectivity in the administration of force. But practitioners of terror and of terrorist violence have gained from the second lesson that flows from Mao's recognition that every military action has political consequences. This is that every act of violence affects more than the few combatants who are engaged in it. There is a wider range of participants, an audience. Mao's breakthrough was to think of his violence in terms not only of those against whom it was physically directed but also of this broader, and ultimately more important, group. One writer describes the consequences of Mao's novel perception thus:

This added a new dimension to armed conflict: Instead of gauging success primarily in terms of the physical effect that military action had on the enemy, strategists could now say that the effect a violent action has on the people watching may be independent of, and may equal or even exceed in importance the actual physical damage inflicted on the foe. Terrorism is that proposition pursued to its most violent extreme, though terrorists have not been very good at explaining it.[1]

The Ascendancy of the Guerrilla: Giap, Colonial Struggle and Che Guevara

General Giap carried Mao's strategy several stages further in the course of Vietnam's long-running wars in south-east Asia. His classic Maoist techniques had succeeded in winning the north of the country from France in the 1950s, but in the following decade successive governments in the southern part of the country had been able to call upon the support of the United States. Faced with an opposition of seeming military and technological impregnability, Giap conducted a campaign that would gradually swing the balance his way. The United States wanted a quick war leading to an advantageous peace, so it was vital to deny them both. The Vietnamese could wait. They were fighting for their survival; while the longer the Americans fought, the less sure they were of what they were fighting for; theories about the domino effect looked less and less convincing with each returning corpse. The sophistication and power of the modern media, particularly television, meant that often in Vietnam there was quite literally that wider audience for military actions about which Mao had theorized. Giap kept this fact firmly in mind throughout his long campaigns; the United States' liberal sensibilities did the rest.

At the time, political and military leaders in the United States criticized the Vietcong for conducting a war of treachery and terror. There were certainly acts of terror, but one has only to recall napalm bombing to be reminded that it was on both sides. The Vietcong were simply turning their manifest weakness to good advantage, something which they managed owing to the brilliance of Giap's planning. Had they chosen a 'fair' means of attack, for example, had they mounted aerial assaults on US positions, they would not have lasted long.

Vietnam was a colonial-type war, and it was in the context of such liberation struggles that Maoist theory found full expression. The period after the Second World War witnessed a great flowering of national sentiment and self-confidence, all the more powerful for the fact that it followed an earlier false start when the Treaty of Versailles and the League of Nations had promised far more than they ever delivered. Europe, however, was not at centre stage this time. Half of the continent was fast being put under Stalinist lock and key, and the rest was expiating its war guilt or tempering its triumph by constructing new supranational political and economic organizations. The nationalist renaissance spread itself across Europe's old empire, leaving few of its territories untouched. The list of countries in which ultimately successful guerrilla campaigns were waged is a long one: it includes Kenya, Oman, Cyprus, Aden, Guinea-Bissau, Angola, Mozambique and Algeria. By the end of the 1980s, the 'winds of change' had left no more than a smattering of anachronistic European dependencies scattered across the world. In many ways, these campaigns were easier than the long war that Mao had fought. Whereas he had had to direct his followers primarily against domestic opposition in the form of the Kuomintang, the 'national liberation armies' that followed him had the luxury of fighting against wholly foreign forces. The combination of ideologically correct Marxist–Leninist formulas about imperial oppression with nationalist rhetoric was a powerful one.

Such anti-imperialist guerrillas enjoyed the additional advantage that their opponents had another home to go to, as a result of which, and despite claims to the contrary, they were never indefinitely committed to the retention of their colonial power. Successive campaigns from the 1950s on proved that there was always a price above which even the most determined of European powers was unwilling to go. The situation was different where the subversive action was against indigenous authorities. One of the few defeats for guerrilla activists in the post-war period occurred in Malaya, where for the last years of the struggle (1957–60) the country was independent of the United Kingdom, although it continued to rely upon British army advice and assistance – a fact which was crucial to the government's victory over the communist subversives.[2] The most intractable of colonial-type problems have been in those areas, such as Northern Ireland, Rhodesia and South Africa, where the settlers have felt themselves to be backed into a cul-de-sac which is their only home.

Similar considerations may explain why so few local local regimes have been brought down by subversion. Mao's triumph over domestic authority was not repeated until Castro's success over Fulgencio Batista in Cuba in 1959. His campaign will be for ever associated with another theorist of revolution, Ernesto 'Che' Guevara, whose influence on the development of modern subversion matches that of Lenin and Mao. Guevara and his intellectual disciple Regis Debray were too impatient for Mao's 'long war'. The alternative revolutionary methodology that they recommended would prove highly attractive to those who did not feel inclined to spend twenty tough years establishing their political credibility in the countryside. It is difficult now to re-create the political and cultural atmosphere in which the naïve idealism of Guevara and Debray could have been taken seriously. Their starting-point was the successful revolution in Cuba, from which Guevara – who was intimately involved – drew the following three fundamental lessons:

1 It is possible for the forces of the people to triumph against the established army.
2 It is not necessary to wait until the conditions for revolution are right; an insurrection can create them.
3 The countryside is where the guerrillas should fight the regular army.[3]

Guevara's thinking differed from both Marxist–Leninism and Maoism. He played down the political dimension to the armed struggle in favour of an emphasis on military action. The Party was not an important part of this strategy. The key to radical change lay with a small number of professional guerrillas who could provoke the revolution by initiating and sustaining the military campaign. The *foco* was to be their centre of insurrection. Organized as mobile guerrilla camps moving across the countryside and engaging the regular army on their own terms, the *foci* would not by themselves overthrow the system, but they were to be like 'a detonator planted in the most exposed enemy position, timed to produce an explosion at the moment of choice'.[4]

This raised obvious questions about how such a detonator was to work. Guevara saw three stages in the process. The *foci* would first defend themselves against the superior might of government forces. This would be a difficult, high-risk phase. Then, when the point of equilibrium had been reached, with the opposing forces more or less equal, the revolutionaries would expand their operations to conduct guerrilla warfare on a large scale. Finally, out of this campaign would emerge a popular army which would overrun the government and place the guerrillas in power. In this way it was possible to describe the guerrilla force as the 'Party in embryo'. The terror tactic played little part in any of these phases; it was held to be 'generally ineffective and indiscriminate in its results, since it often [made] victims of innocent people and destroy[ed] a large number of lives that would be valuable to the revolution'.[5] The 'killing of persons of small importance [was] never advisable' because it brought on 'an increase of reprisals, including deaths'.[6]

Guevara never seriously addressed the question of how his third stage was to be reached. In place of analysis there was a simple conviction, based on the appreciation of the plight of the poor, that the people would be on the side of the revolution. Similar enthusiasm infected Che's view of the whole South American scene. His life after the victory in Cuba was a struggle to galvanize the countries of Latin America into a continent-wide revolution. But even this victory, from which he was so quick to draw general lessons, was a misleading precedent. Fulgencio Batista had been a weak and corrupt local ruler who ran before he had no other choice. The United States had initially not been too opposed to Castro. Not even the guerrilla methodology espoused by Guevara was entirely relevant in Cuba, where urban fighting had been essential to Castro's successful seizure of power.

The South American unity sought by Che after Cuba never occurred and no generalized or even local revolution ever took place. The 1960s saw little more than a long litany of failure: Douglas Bravo in Venezuela, Hugo Blanco in Peru and Camilo Torres in Colombia are only the most memorable among the many unsuccessful emulators of Castro's triumph.[7] By the time of Che's death at the hands of government troops in the Bolivian outback in 1967, the phase of guerrilla revolutions which he pioneered had drawn to a close. He died using a method of insurgency which had by then become an heroic anachronism.

The Emergence of the Urban Guerrilla

The ideals for which Che stood, and the conditions which had made his and Castro's message so powerful, survived his early death. The countries of South America remained deformed by inequality and injustice. During the 1960s the extremes of wealth which existed in most countries of the region were exacerbated by economic recession. The lower middle classes suffered most from the squeeze on incomes which accompanied this decline. The need for land reform to counter the poverty of the peasants tended to go unheeded by the ruling factions. Instead, most of the countries embarked upon policies of increased repression.

Countries as diverse as Uruguay (after 1965), Brazil (following the army coup in 1964) and Argentina (after General Ongania deposed President Illia in 1966) all experienced a sharp decline in political freedom during this period. The universities, which had in any event become little more than centres of learning for the future unemployed, were regularly invaded by the police and purged of liberal academics. The aggrandizement of the armies of the region led to increased militarization everywhere. Over the whole continent lay the spectre of 'Yankee imperialism'. The new economic policies which were further impoverishing the poor and under-mining the middle classes were perceived to be the result of the intervention of foreign (for which read US) capitalists. This combination of economic failure, national thralldom and political constriction was more than many activists could bear.

The problem was what to do about it. The Guevara method of hanging around the jungle until you inspired a popular revolution was clearly no longer an option. If it had not been irredeemably flawed in theory, it would have been rendered useless by the improved equipment of the armed forces, which now enabled *foci* to be located by helicopter and bombed into oblivion. At the same time, the traditional left, with their interminable meetings and obsession with adopting the correct Marxist approach, appeared to be no more than talking-shops for the self-righteous. The idea of the 'urban guerrilla' emerged out of a marriage between these two subversive styles. Taking the guerrilla into the town seemed to make tremendous sense in the South American context, in three ways in particular.

First, many Latin American countries were urban in character: in Brazil 54 per cent of the population lived in towns and in Argentina and Uruguay the total was as high as 80 per cent. Cities like Buenos Aires and Montevideo accounted for nearly half the population of their respective nations. Many of these metropolitan giants had spawned vast areas of suburban deprivation, and the resultant shanty towns of the dispossessed stood in marked contrast to the islands of guarded affluence inhabited by the rich. Such obvious unfairness seemed to open the way for the dedicated revolutionary, making it probable that he or she would find in the slums both a receptive audience and eventual popular support. It was certainly more likely than coming across sympathizers in the jungle. Second, the city, the heart of state infrastructure, was where the despised authorities were at their most vulnerable. Troops in the field were the hard edge of the 'forces of reaction' but here was their soft underbelly. An attack in such a sensitive spot would count for more than many a successful ambush in the field. Third, the city was the centre of communication. This was where the new and burgeoning media industry, with instant connections across the continent, was to be found. Mao and Giap had demonstrated the importance of directing political violence to the wider audience. This had been hard to achieve in the jungle, where each death was rarely more than a private act. Urban subversion, in contrast, was necessarily public. An audience was guaranteed, both 'live' on the streets and watching on television in a million homes. Never before had the revolutionary had such a potential platform or so potent an opportunity to use force directly to spark the uprising to which any rebel's life was dedicated.

It was one thing, however, to know that this scope for subversion existed and quite another to decide exactly how to subvert. It was after all much more straightforward in the jungle, where there were regular armies on the move with which the guerrillas could skirmish in a quasi-military way. To engage an army on any terms in the city would have been at best absurd and ineffectual, at worst disastrous. Inevitably, the focus turned to symbolic acts of violence. The desirable targets were immobile and in this sense vulnerable, but the choicest of them – the presidential palaces, the headquarters of the generals, the parliament buildings, for example – tended to be very well guarded and extremely hard to penetrate. This made the selective assassination of high officials of the type that took place in nineteenth-century Russia difficult to emulate. In the absence of conventional military or political targets, what were the urban guerrillas to do?

Guillen and Marighela

The first and most influential of the theoreticians of urban subversion, the Spanish exile and 'anarcho-Marxist' Abraham Guillen,[8] thought that 'under conditions of a pretorian dictatorship it [was] necessary to resort to an urban strategy that upsets the political apparatus, replying to violence with violence'.[9] The tactics of the guerrilla were straightforward:

The basic strategical principle of the guerrilla has to be: Live separately and fight together in order to elude police repression. Under no circumstances should the urban guerrilla ever leave a suburb densely populated with houses and reside several months in a house outside the city where he is easily identifiable. If he does not wish to expose himself to detention early or late, the urban guerrilla will have to remain, like a fish in water, within a favorable urban milieu. And in order to endure he will have to change his domicile constantly, never settling in a given place.

In a large city where there are a hundred guerrilla cells of five persons living separately and fighting together, the police will be unable to control matters; they will have to cede terrain, especially at night, in unfavorable population zones where no police dare appear separately or in small groups. If at night the city belongs to the guerrilla and, in part, to the police by day, then in the end the war will be won by whoever endures longest.[10]

Significantly, Guillen tells us nothing about the type of violence in which his prototype urban guerrillas would become involved. We learn only about the conduct of which he disapproved: 'In revolutionary war any guerrilla action that needs explaining to the people is politically useless: it should be meaningful and convincing by itself. To kill an ordinary soldier in reprisal for the assassination of a guerrilla is to descend to the same political level as a reactionary army.'[11]

Furthermore, in a 'country where the bourgeoisie has abolished the death penalty, it is self-defeating to condemn to death even the most hated enemies of the people . . . A popular army that resorts to unnecessary violence, that is not a symbol of justice, equity, liberty and security, cannot win popular support in the struggle against a dehumanized tyranny.'[12] Not even kidnapping met with the approval of this highly principled subversive. It was 'intolerable to keep anyone hostage for a long time'[13] and demanding huge sums of ransom for such victims made the guerrillas come 'perilously close to resembling a political mafia'.[14]

The theatres of combat left were slight indeed. Guillen's approach evoked memories of the nineteenth-century advocates of 'propaganda of the deed', but, just as with his Russian predecessors, he appears to have been all propaganda and no deed. The other old-fashioned notion to which he adhered was that the urban guerrilla could, by his or her acts, spark the popular revolution that was just under the surface. To this end he emphasized political work and depended in a touchingly desperate way on eventual support from the masses, whose 'revolutionary spirit' would eventually be 'draw[n] out . . . with small and repeated military actions until they willingly enter[ed] into battle'.[15] But the main indictment of Guillen is that he provided an intellectual framework for violent subversion in the cities without thinking through the nature of the violence for which he called, or analysing its relationship to the political work to which he gave such a high priority. This left a vacuum at the centre of urban guerrilla theory which was soon filled by a man whose approach to violence was more coherent, but also far less squeamish, than that of his ethical but uncertain predecessor.

Carlos Marighela was a Brazilian who broke with orthodox communism and founded his own Revolutionary Communist Party of Brazil in 1968. His solution to the problem of what to do in the cities was to engage in a strategy of provocation in order to win the people over to the guerrillas' side:

From the moment a large proportion of the people begin to take his activities seriously, his success is assured. The government can only intensify its repression, thus making the life of its citizens harder than ever: homes will be broken into, police searches organized, innocent people arrested, and communications broken; police terror will become the order of the day, and there will be more and more political murders – in short a massive political persecution . . . the political situation of the country will become a military situation.[16]

To stimulate this reaction from government successfully, the subversive had to be dedicated to violence:

It is necessary for every urban guerrilla to keep in mind always that he can only maintain his existence if he is disposed to kill the police and those dedicated to repression, and if he is determined – truly determined – to expropriate the wealth of the big capitalists, the latifundists, and the imperialists . . . Men of the government, agents of the dictatorship and of North American imperialism principally, must pay with their lives for the crimes committed against the Brazilian people.[17]

This language is reminiscent of the calls of Weitling and Bakunin for an alliance between the anarchists and the criminal underworld. The callousness may be shocking, but it is the inevitable consequence of the arrival of the urban guerrilla. Marighela is answering the question that Guillen glossed over. Because conventional targets are impregnable and armies not available to be attacked in the ordinary 'warlike' way, the soft target is all that is left. If the urban guerrilla is to act at all, that is where they must strike. Thus we see a narrowing of the category of the innocent bystander and a broadening in the range of legitimate targets (by which we mean those whom the guerrillas determine they can execute as 'enemies of the people'). This has to happen if the urban guerrilla is to make an impact; such deaths not only form part of a campaign, they are also an assertion of continued existence. This double pressure on an urban guerrilla group – to increase both the range and number of its victims – is bad enough, but in addition comes the constant fear of detection and betrayal, as the forces of the state respond. Inevitably in such harassed circumstances, political considerations are downgraded, and the military element develops a life of its own. The aim of igniting a popular revolution is gradually forgotten, but the

39

impossibility of a military defeat of the government's forces remains. Eventually, the point may be reached when what seems discriminate violence to the subversive is indiscriminate to all sections of the community in which the group is operating, including those on whose behalf they purport to act. This is when the urban guerrilla gang completes its grizzly transition into a truly terrorist organization.

The Urban Guerrillas in Action

The story of the urban guerrillas in Latin America in the late 1960s and early 1970s confirms the impression that they entered into a doomed spiral of brutality when they forsook the countryside for the towns. A plethora of groups surfaced in Brazil, of which the most prominent were the VPR, MR–8 and Marighela's organization, the ALN. Their preferred method of subversion was kidnapping. In September 1969 MR–8 secured the release of fifteen political prisoners and the publication of a revolutionary manifesto in return for the safe return of the then US Ambassador, C. Burke Elbrick. He later described his captors as 'all young, very determined, intelligent fanatics' who 'seemed to ascribe all the troubles and difficulties they saw in Brazil to what they called North American imperialism'. Subsequent seizures of diplomats from Japan, Germany and Switzerland were equally successful. All the men were released unharmed in return for numbers of prisoners that began to escalate sharply; the peak was reached when seventy political detainees were flown to Chile in return for the Swiss Ambassador in January 1971.

Where all this was designed to lead was not obvious. Certainly it made headlines, but it did little to forge alliances with labour groups or other elements of substantial opposition within Brazil. The urban guerrillas were regarded as too elitist and militaristic for many people's tastes. Without such wide support, however, they were vulnerable to governmental counter-attack and when it came, it far exceeded in ferocity anything that the guerrillas themselves had been able or willing to perpetrate. The authorities had long had a programme of mass arrests and detention for suspected subversives; this was what had inspired the kidnapping campaign in the first place. This policy was now stepped up and torture was routinely employed as an instrument of interrogation. Two days after the US ambassador's release, the military junta reintroduced capital punishment for the first time outside war since 1891. Police action on the ground often made recourse to this official form of execution unnecessary. Marighela was ambushed and shot dead by the police in autumn 1969. His successor was killed the following year, as were numerous other victims identified as leaders of one faction or another. By the end of 1972, the urban guerrillas' campaign had effectively been strangled by state power.

The Uruguayan Tupamaros opposed a democratic rather than a military government and were initially much more successful at developing a broad base of support than any of the Brazilian groups had been. From their inception in the early 1960s, they were far more aware of the political consequences of their actions. Their leader, Raul Sendic, had been involved in the organization of sugar cane workers in northern Uruguay and this gave the group a knowledge of the labour audience which had been absent in Brazil. In its early years, the Tupamaros seized public imagination with a series of daring and at times philanthropic raids. A leading banker and publisher, Caetano Pellegrini Giampietro, was kidnapped in 1969 and held for seventy-three days. The price of his release was the payment of about $60,000 in ransom – not to the Tupamaros themselves but rather to the medical clinic of a specified meat workers' union. The same year the Tupamaros raided a casino at Punta del Este, stole $220,000 and then offered to return that part of the sum which was made up of tips earned by the workers. A series of mass break-outs from jail added to their appeal. In the most famous incident, 106 prisoners escaped through a 40-foot tunnel dug from a house across the street right into a prison cell.

Their romantic image was helped by their daring celebration of the second anniversary of Che Guevara's death. About forty of the Tupamaros seized the town of Pando, having entered unnoticed by posing as a funeral cortège (with hearse, coffin and black clothes to add to the authenticity). Once established in control, they robbed three banks and took over the police station, only departing after a cowboy-style shoot-out with the authorities. Meanwhile, a succession of kidnappings raised the inter-national profile of the group. Among those taken were a number of local businessmen, the Brazilian Vice-Consul, an American adviser to the government, the British Ambassador, a criminal court judge and the attorney-general. One Argentinian-born industrialist was returned to his family only after they had acceded to a demand that they pay $300,000 to textile workers in compensation for the fact that the family had recently closed down their factories. The fact that all these hostages were released unharmed added greatly to the already high prestige of the Tupamaros.

This largely non-violent strategy was designed to avoid the sort of narcissistic criminality which had alienated similar groups from their natural constituencies in other South American countries. But the problem remained of how to translate symbolic actions into political gains. The government's power was infinitely greater than that of the guerrillas, and no end of public-relations victories would ever change that fact.

In November 1969 the authorities introduced extensive censorship of the media. The words 'Tupamaros', 'commandos', 'cells' and (surprisingly perhaps) 'subversives' and 'extremists' were banned from the newspapers; permissible replacements included 'delinquents' and (oddly) 'rapists'. All reporting on guerrilla activity which was not from official sources was prohibited, and in June 1970 two newspapers were temporarily suspended for 'violation of security measures'. Radio and television were similarly affected. A year later, in an ominous move for a democratic state, the army was put in charge of all counter-terrorist operations. In November 1971 a general election was held and the Tupamaros declared a truce and sought to establish a legitimate political personality through their support for the Broad Front coalition. This was difficult to achieve in view of the wholesale censorship which still inhibited the group's public profile and it came a poor third. Victory was claimed by the ruling Colorado Party, but the narrowly defeated leftist National Party made allegations of serious electoral fraud and vote-rigging. The Tupamaros had been broadly sympathetic to the National Party presidential candidate, Wilson Ferreira Aldunate, and his controversial defeat was an additional blow.

The Tupamaros experiment with democratic legitimacy failed in these bitterly disputed circumstances. Their ten-year-long, carefully controlled campaign, orchestrated with great discipline by the group's leaders, had climaxed in disillusionment. Unsurprisingly, Marighela's strategy of provocation gained support from those desirous of a quick collapse in the old structure. There had always been a violent side to the Tupamaros. The American adviser Dan Mitrione had been killed in 1970 and a couple of police officers were similarly dealt with the same year. But after the elections such military activity was increased. Four policemen were killed in attacks on two police stations in the first months of 1972, and in April that year the death of four officials in the governments' anti-guerrilla campaign sparked off a series of battles with the police which left nineteen dead in just four days. Unsympathetic journalists were abducted and a doctor resisting a Tupamaros kidnap attempt was killed. A number of senior officials died in guerrilla ambushes.

The President asked for and was given state of war powers. Thereafter the story is one of random violence, military clamp-down and a fast-eroding democracy. In the two months after the declaration of internal war, the authorities conducted 1,093 raids, arrested 846 suspects, killed sixteen people, confiscated 317 firearms and discovered thirty-eight guerrilla hideouts. The Tupamaros were crushed by the armed forces but, despite this, the state of war was replaced by a new and more permanent apparatus of repression. The drift to military rule which had been evident as early as the summer of 1971 was fully in place by mid-1973. The guerrillas were said to be regrouping in exile and subversives were said to represent a threat that was 'always latent'; the Tupamaros remained useful alibis even after their obliteration.

The Argentinian Montoneros provide us with a final example of the failure of this brand of violent subversion. Great disaster eventually befell the Montoneros, though their beginnings were promising. In the period from 1970 to 1973 their violence was well controlled. The targets they selected were carefully chosen so as not to cause alienation among their supporters, and the group expended great energy in the promotion of the Peronist youth movement. Most importantly, there was a clear subordination of guerrilla warfare to political work. This was particularly the case in 1972 and early the following year, when the Montoneros campaigned for the return of Perón and the election of Campora as president. In the sixteen months of mass activity from May 1973 to September 1974, during which they suspended regular armed action, the Montoneros achieved a popular following of over 100,000 people. Their fatal mistake was the resumption of warfare in September 1974, after the death of Perón and his replacement as president by his wife Isabel. The group had incurred heavy losses from attacks by government death squads while acting lawfully, but the return to militancy was a turning-point. Their subsequent fall has been well described by a leading expert on Argentinian politics:

[T]heir resort to arms denied them the chance to capitalize upon growing labour opposition to the government, seen especially in the general strike of mid-1975. In military and financial terms, they became the strongest urban guerrilla force yet seen in Latin America: their peak military action in the northern city of Formosa involved the mobilization of some 500 members, and their famous kidnapping of business magnates Juan and Jorge Born earned them a record ransom of over 60 million dollars. However, while their operations represented a spectacular military advance, all lacked popular participation and the political constituency of the Montoneros ceased to expand. They . . . were weakened severely by the repressive measures introduced after the military takeover of March 1976. Though dozens of security policemen were killed by powerful Montonero bombs in that year, the conflict became increasingly one between unevenly matched military apparata. Between March 1976 and July 1978 some 4,500 Montoneros perished and by the end of the decade the urban guerrillas had been obliterated.[18]

Conclusion

The urban guerrillas believed themselves to be involved in a battle against repressive government on behalf of the poor and the marginalized in Latin American society. Their tactics, however, and in particular their occasional use of provocation, allowed repressive tendencies in the state apparatus to be reinforced and justified. This was the case regardless of whether the challenge was to a military regime, as in Brazil, or to a weak democracy, as in Uruguay. The power of government to inflict violence was epitomized by the way in which the Brazilian groups, the Tupamaros and the Montoneros were destroyed by army and police action. The Triple A death squads of Argentina were only part of a whole series of authoritarian vendettas that were officially sanctioned by the military governments of South America in the 1970s. The thousands who 'disappeared' and the countless cases of death and torture during that bloody decade demonstrate that, in terms of victims and impact, by far the worst perpetrators of terror on the continent – and therefore, if the word has to be used at all, the most brutal terrorists – were the governments themselves. In the light of this, discussion of the violence inflicted by substate subversive groups seems curiously peripheral, and moral condemnation of such 'terrorism' is absurdly selective.

Indeed, we may well ask whether groups like the Tupamaros and the Montoneros were terrorist in the strict sense of the word. They emerged from an intellectual tradition that borrowed from Lenin, the rural guerrilla theories of Mao and the *foco* ideas of Debray and Guevara, none of whom could properly be called terrorist. In the later phases, when the spiral of their violence had reached its bloodiest point, the urban guerrillas could perhaps be said to have so expanded the range of their potential targets that they had come close to that arbitrariness in the application of force which we recognize as terror. But they never deliberately embraced indiscriminateness as a tactic in itself. However misguided their self-perception and however unequal the terms on which they fought, these South American groups understood themselves to be involved in a battle against the forces of the state, manifested not in the population as a whole but in certain defined categories of person. Terrorism in the pure sense of acts of violence which through random killing and kidnapping terrorize the whole population emerged not in Latin America, but in the Middle-East.

4   The Dispossessed

The development of political terror into a deliberate strategy of violence took place in the Middle East. Its heyday was during the years 1968–74, when it seemed as though the whole democratic world had become infected with a contagion of mindless Palestinian brutality. Hijacks, indiscriminate gun attacks and widespread bombings horrified and terrified the people of the West. At the centre of the mayhem, and its chief victims, were the people of Israel. The state had been created after the momentous tragedy of the Holocaust and it seemed to many of its citizens that a new variety of evil was now about to engulf it. The political outlook of the Jewish people had been transformed by their partial genocide during the Second World War and this now found expression in a determined commitment to the survival of their nation, whatever the costs that this might entail. The Holocaust has had a profound effect on the psychology of those whose job it has been to rule and to protect the new Jewish state. The origins of terror in the region lie in the seemingly intractable conflict between Israel and the Palestinians. In order to understand its sudden upsurge in 1968, we need to examine the context and history of the region's multifarious hostilities. Nowhere are the words 'terrorism' and 'terrorist' more fraught with confusion or more prone to deliberate manipulation. The region is simultaneously the most important focus of study for any attempt to grapple with the true meaning of terrorism, and also, on account of this obfuscation, the most difficult to penetrate. Under any definition of terrorism discussed so far, it is unarguable that the PLO and many of its supporting factions were (and possibly still are) terrorist. For over twenty years they have attacked Israeli targets and inflicted heavy casualties on Jewish civilians. This point has been emphasized time and again by Israeli governments and by those in the West sympathetic to their interests.

But the 'terrorist' label does not end the matter. All our definitions have concentrated attention, and therefore (since terrorism is a value-laden subject) criticism exclusively on a single type of violence: terrorism by substate groups aimed against an established order. In the context of the

Middle East Israel is an 'established order' and the violence in which it chooses to engage is invariably both authorized and executed by an official arm of the state, namely its police or military. Because of this, violence by Israel never falls within any category of 'terrorism', but all forms of Palestinian action invariably do, not least because they have no land and therefore no authorized army to function on their behalf. Thus what looks initially like a neutral definition of terrorism becomes a propaganda stick with which to beat the Palestinians on the international stage. Of course, this is not to say that such terrorism does not occur or that it is morally justified. However, it helps explain why those sympathetic to the Palestinians quickly become cynical during discussions about the problem of terror. As far as they are concerned, such violence, serious and awful though it sometimes is, features as no more than a detail in a much broader and infinitely bloodier picture.

The Palestinian Perception of Terror

As far as the Palestinians are concerned, the story of their country is one of unrelieved suffering, oppression, betrayal and double standards which began before the war, when Britain controlled the territory under mandate from the League of Nations. This period saw increased Jewish immigration and the pressures which this caused for the indigenous population were already beginning to make themselves felt by the middle of the 1930s. Arabs found that more and more of their land was being bought by recently settled Jews. In addition to this, the relative affluence of some of these new arrivals changed the economic life of the place in a way which was detrimental to Arab interests. The tensions in the region spilled over into conflict in the Arab Revolt, which started in 1936 with a general strike and the shooting of two Jewish travellers and the robbing of a number of Europeans. The insurrection quickly escalated and, at its high point, the Arabs had managed to seize control of substantial parts of Palestine, including Galilee, Hebron, Beersheba and Gaza. It was finally crushed in 1939 when a force of some 20,000 British troops was mobilized in the region. The cost in terms of Arab casualties has never been finally confirmed, but one scholar has reckoned it to be in the region of 5,000 dead and 14,000 wounded. In contrast, the British and Jewish death tolls were estimated to be 101 and 463 respectively.[1]

The harshness of the British response to the Arab rebellion in 1936–9 appeared to the Palestinians to be in marked contrast to their handling of the Jewish revolt which came to a head in the three years after the end of the Second World War. The Haganah were the official Jewish resistance and the main proponents of an independent Jewish homeland, a plan which shot up the international agenda in the aftermath of the horrors of the Holocaust. But the most strident Zionist militancy came from two fringe groups, the Stern Gang and Irgun Zvai Leumi, loosely associated with the Haganah. In their lack of a guerrilla base, their tightly knit organizational structure and above all in their calculated disregard of civilian lives, these two groups were close historical forerunners of the Palestinian terrorists of a later generation.

Two leading figures were Menachem Begin and Yitzhak Shamir, who both went on to become prime ministers. Each of their organizations engaged in the routine terror of subversive groups but both were capable of grander actions. Shamir belonged to the Stern Gang, whose most dramatic strike was the assassination of Lord Moyne, the British Minister of State in the Middle East, in 1944. Begin ran the Irgun Zvai Leumi, which was responsible for one of the most calamitous acts of terror this century. This was the bombing of the King David Hotel in Jerusalem on 22 July 1946. The British administration was based in one of the hotel's wings, so to this extent it could be argued that, in the language of subversive warfare, the target was a 'legitimate' one. Nevertheless, out of a total of ninety-one people killed, only twenty-one were senior government officials, thirteen were soldiers and three were policemen. The remaining fifty-four were a hotch-potch of ordinary, innocent people: members of the public, typists, clerks, messengers, employees of the hotel and canteen workers. The nationality breakdown revealed that twenty-eight of the dead were British, but seventeen were Jewish and forty-one were Arab.[2]

Despite – or possibly because of – such provocation, the British withdrew from Palestine without a fight and the United Nations decided that, with effect from 15 May 1948, a new State of Israel should come into existence, occupying a part of ancient Palestine. To the Arabs, it looked as though Jewish terror had worked; in fact, they were to grow to believe that it had only just begun. The United Nations appointed a special mediator, Count Folke Bernadotte, to oversee Israel's transition to independence. When he expressed public concern about the way Arabs were being treated in the new nation, the Stern Gang shot him dead. The Count had stumbled upon the grievance which has over time become etched on the heart of every Palestinian. This was the forced flight of tens of thousands of Arabs from Israel around the time of its birth. Surrounded by enemies dedicated to its extinction, and with a hostile indigenous population, the rulers of the new nation may have felt that they had no option but to take strong action. But the message that they communicated, sometimes brutally, was that Israel had no room for many local people.

The most evocative name of all in the roll call of Palestinian tragedy is Deir Yassin, a small Arab settlement which had the misfortune to be awkwardly placed between the two strategic cities of Tel Aviv and Jerusalem. On the night of 9 April 1948 the Irgun and the Stern Gang attacked the village and indiscriminately killed two-thirds of its inhabitants. This assault was particularly savage, but it was only an extreme example of the tactics employed by the victorious Zionists to coerce inhabitants within their official borders and also to expand the territory which the UN had allocated to them, a policy which would lead eventually to war with neighbouring Arab states. David Hirst describes the effect of the upheavals of 1948–9 in the following terms:

When the war ended, in early 1949, the Zionists, allotted 57 per cent of Palestine under the Partition Plan, had occupied 77 per cent of the country. Of the 1,300,000 Arab inhabitants, they had displaced nearly 900,000. They came into possession of entire cities, or entire quarters of them, and hundreds of villages. All that was in them – farms and factories, animals and machinery, fine houses and furniture, carpets, clothes and works of art, all the goods and chattels, all the treasured family heirlooms of an ancient people – was theirs for the taking. Ten thousand shops, businesses and stores and most of the rich Arab citrus holdings – half the country's total – fell into their hands.[3]

From the Palestinian perspective, the period from 1949 to the 1967 war was one of grinding poverty and continuing Israeli coercion. Two particular incidents stand out as highlights in this litany of violence. The first was Qibya. In 1953 the killing of a Jewish mother and two children in a grenade attack led to the destruction of this Arab village. Sixty-six people died in the action, the scene of which was described in the following terms by United Nations military observers who arrived two hours after the village had been sacked:

Bullet-riddled bodies near the doorways and multiple bullet hits on the doors of the demolished houses indicated that the inhabitants had been forced to remain inside until their homes were blown-up over them . . . Witnesses were uniform in describing their experience as a night of horror, during which Israeli soldiers moved about in their village blowing up buildings, firing into doorways and windows with automatic weapons and throwing hand grenades.[4]

The Israeli government denied that its troops had been involved at Qibya and, in particular, rejected the allegation that a special unit, commanded by Ariel Sharon (subsequently a minister in the Israeli government), had done the killing. The responsibility of the army for the second incident, at Kafr Qasem in 1956, was more clear-cut. A curfew was imposed on this Arab village half an hour before it was due to go into effect. As a result of such short notice, it proved impossible to inform all the Arab villagers that they should not have been out and about. In the first hour of the curfew the authorities shot dead forty-seven Arabs, many of whom were on their way home from work. The killing was halted after a group of fourteen women, a boy and four men had been rounded up and executed. A criminal trial followed this incident. However, the soldiers held to have been responsible were released from detention within a year of having been given seventeen- and fifteen-year jail sentences.

Fatah

Even as early as 1960 there was, from the Palestinian point of view, a clear basis for feeling aggrieved about Israel's policies. Harakah al-Tahrir al-Falastini, better known as Fatah, emerged in the region in the early 1960s, its thoughts and ideals first appearing in *Our Palestine*, a monthly journal published in Beirut. In its early days Fatah was concerned as much with pride as with power. The small group of fedayeen ('the men who sacrificed themselves') who gathered around Yasser Arafat preached the violent destruction of Israel and the return of the Palestinians to their homeland. Beginning in 1965, these fighters occasionally sabotaged Israeli instal- lations and engaged in hit-and-run tactics within hostile territory. The subversion to which they aspired, however, was circumvented by their lack of a popular home base; the fedayeen were operating from Beirut or Cairo, not fighting on enemy ground.

This point was emphasized by Israel's stunning success in the Six Day War, which followed an Arab attack in 1967, during which it inflicted a series of defeats on its Arab neighbours and seized a vast amount of land, thereby greatly increasing its own size. In the aftermath many thousands more Palestinians found themselves being uprooted from their homes, and for some families this was a repetition of the upheavals of 1948. Arafat, who had by this time extended his power so that he was now also in effective control of the PLO, turned his attention to the newly occupied territories, principally the large area west of the River Jordan, which the Israelis had seized from

King Hussein. Surely this was a classic opportunity for the successful promulgation of an anti-colonial guerrilla struggle? Here was a population of Palestinians newly subjugated by an alien force which was both unversed in the geography of the area and despised by the locals. There were analogies with not only Giap and the liberation struggles in Africa but also the opponents of Napoleon in Spain and in Russia generations before.

Arafat had read his Mao, and possibly also his Guevara, and he lost no time in personally entering the West Bank so as to organize the supposedly incipient revolt. But the guerrilla war never came and the opportunity for revolution soon frittered away. Only a short while after his arrival, Arafat was compelled to escape back across the River Jordan, barely ahead of the Israeli security forces hunting for him. The West Bank did not ignite and Fatah were soon reduced to sniping from the relative safety of land outside Israeli control, much as they had done before 1967.

In retrospect, it is possible to isolate a number of reasons for the failure of Fatah's guerrilla tactic. First, they were, even after 1967, a weak group, isolated within the Arab world and composed of fedayeen whose backgrounds were not identical to those of the communities which they were expected to infiltrate and influence. The inhabitants of the West Bank were always likely to be conservative rather than militant; they at least still had something to lose – their land – whereas the Palestinians, displaced by the Israel of 1948, had lost everything. In addition, there was the technological and military superiority of Israel, which had invested heavily in the equipment necessary to make crossing into the occupied territories a deeply hazardous operation for the Palestinians. Traditional guerrilla activity behind enemy lines became very difficult. As early as March 1968 the Israeli authorities were boasting of having captured or killed thirty-five out of fifty fedayeen who had crossed the River Jordan in the previous ten days.[5] Finally, however, and despite all these drawbacks and disadvantages, it may be that Fatah lacked the one attribute essential to the successful guerrilla: patience. Mao had warned of the need for the 'long war', but Arafat and his followers had gone looking for the short fuse. A successful guerrilla strategy rarely comes to the fighter in a hurry.

The Rise of Fatah Terror

The PLO did indeed believe that their mission was an urgent one. Their people had no home, and Israel – triumphant, apparently impregnable and adored by the West – looked set to deny them one permanently. By 1968 they stood alone in the Arab world, cut adrift by Egypt and increasingly disliked by King Hussein of Jordan, into whose country the PLO evacuees had poured after their guerrilla tactics within the occupied territories ended in failure. This was the context in which Palestinian nationalism drifted inexorably during the last few years of the 1960s towards the tactic of terror. The fedayeen had not forgotten the disasters of 1948 and 1967 and such individual atrocities as Deir Yassin, Qibya and Kafr Qasem. The tragedies of their own people now inoculated them against the hurt they began to impose on others. In November 1968 a bomb exploded in a crowded marketplace in Jerusalem, killing twelve people (ten of whom were Jewish) and injuring fifty-five. The explosive was concealed in a parked car. Three months later another device exploded in a Jerusalem supermarket packed with shoppers buying provisions for the approaching Sabbath. Two youths were killed. In March 1969, a bomb in the cafetaria of the Hebrew University of Jerusalem wounded twenty-nine Israelis, and later explosions at the central bus station in Tel Aviv caused a fatality and a large number of injuries. Attacks in the occupied territories were more frequent and often just as bloody. Hundreds of Arabs in the West Bank were injured by Palestinian explosions. In October 1969 five apartment buildings in Haifa were blown up, killing two Israelis and injuring twenty people.

Even at this early stage in its campaign, Fatah seemed to have come a long way from its founding declaration that 'Zionist institutions' were its target, not civilians, 'particularly women and children'.[6] This increased range of victims did not have an inhibiting effect on the Israelis, whose policy appeared to be one of immediate and disproportionate retaliation. As early as the end of 1969, for example, Palestinian leaders in the occupied territories were claiming that the authorities had destroyed 7,500 of their homes in reply to some alleged terrorist or guerrilla activity (the Defence Ministry admitted to 516 such actions). And after one incident in March 1968, in which a doctor was killed and a number of children were injured when an Israeli school bus hit a mine, the government retaliated by sending a force of 15,000 men on a huge assault into Jordan. The ensuing bloody battle between the Israeli defence forces and the fedayeen has entered Palestinian folklore as the 'Battle of Karameh'.

Above all, with Israel's effortless aerial supremacy, it was possible to bombard alleged PLO bases in Lebanon and Jordan by way of revenge for domestic subversion or for successful guerrilla incursions into their self-declared occupied territories. The problem of how to distinguish ordinary Palestinians from PLO terrorists was not one which greatly preoccupied the pilots or their military chiefs. Despite frequent condemnations of such raids in the United Nations, Western – and in particular US – opinion remained unmoved. When Israeli air strikes killed eighteen civilians in a town north of Amman in March 1969, the United States and Britain abstained on a United Nations Security Council vote to censure Israel, the US Ambassador saying that 'death is just as final and as shocking if it comes from a bomb in a supermarket or from a bomb from the air'. The United States abstained again in two later votes by the Council condemning sustained incursions by Israel into southern Lebanon.

Possibly PLO leaders hoped that their campaign of guerrilla action and terrorism within Israel and the occupied territories would educate Western public opinion. In fact, the opposite seemed to be true. PLO violence became the best argument for continuing to give the Israelis the support they demanded. Faced with such a response, Palestinian violence moved towards even greater brutality. The organization most involved in the escalation that now occurred was the PFLP, whose leader, Dr George Habash, had always adopted a more uncompromising and radical stance than had the mainstream of the PLO. From the start the PFLP took the fight with Israel outside the Middle East. Notice of their intent was served as early as July 1968, when they hijacked an Israeli commercial airliner en route from Rome to Tel Aviv. All the passengers and crew were eventually released, after negotiations involving the Red Cross and the Italian and Algerian governments had resulted in a promise from Israel to release sixteen convicted Arab infiltrators captured prior to the Six Day War.

On the day after Christmas the same year two PFLP members attacked an Israeli jet which had stopped at Athens airport on its way to New York. The men fired a sub-machine-gun at the plane and its passengers and threw grenades at its engines. One passenger died. The PFLP issued a statement declaring that El Al, the Israeli carrier, was no longer 'an airline undertaking innocent civilian transport' since some of its planes had made 'secret flights under supervision of the Israeli Defence Ministry' and had transferred 'air force pilots trained in flying Phantom jets in preparation for a surprise attack and new aggression against the Arab states'. Within two months yet another El Al flight was attacked, this time in Zurich, where four Palestinian rebels again used guns and grenades. This assault was foiled, but not before one of the assailants had been killed by an Israeli security guard and three passengers and three crew members had been injured in the struggle. During the summer and autumn of 1968 the battleground remained international, but the emphasis shifted away from airports. In August an explosion at the London offices of an Israeli shipping company injured two people. In the following month bombs went off at El Al offices in Brussels and grenades were thrown at Israeli embassies in The Hague and Bonn. In November a grenade attack on El Al's office in Athens wounded fourteen and killed a two-year-old boy. (A new group, the Palestine Popular Struggle Front, claimed responsibility for this attack.) The old policy reasserted itself in Munich early in 1970, when three Arabs threw grenades into an airport bus crowded with passengers being ferried to an El Al flight. They also attacked the departure lounge in the same way. One person was killed and eleven were injured.

Spreading the Blame

The PFLP decided early in its campaign to extend its international reach beyond Israel and El Al, and this change in policy quickly produced success. In August 1969 a passenger jet belonging to the US-based company TWA was hijacked over southern Italy. The plane was flown to Damascus, Syria, where all the passengers and crew were eventually released unharmed, but not before the Syrians had successfully brokered the release of thirteen of their own nationals from jails in Israel. Unsurprisingly in view of this outcome, the two hijackers escaped unpunished.

The most dramatic hijack of all, however, and the event that signalled the arrival of international terrorism as a force in world opinion, occurred in September 1970. On the same day that month members of the PFLP managed to take control of three jet airliners bound for New York from Europe. The total number of hostages obtained was 475. A fourth seizure was unsuccessful, with one of the hijackers, Leila Khaled (who had also been involved in the TWA action), being taken into custody. One of the planes was flown to Cairo, emptied of its personnel and blown up. The other two were ordered to land at Dawson's Field, a deserted airstrip in Jordan, where they were soon joined by yet another reluctant arrival, this time a British VC-10 containing over 100 passengers and crew. There then followed several days of tense negotiation, during which Red Cross officials acted as intermediaries and the Western world looked on aghast. A price for the safe return of the passengers emerged: the freeing of certain Palestinian fighters held in European jails. A deal was eventually made under which seven detainees were released from prisons in Switzerland, Britain and West Germany. All the hostages emerged alive from the incident. The abiding image left by the affair was that of the three jets stranded at the desert airfield, stricken symbols of Western technology, being methodically blown up by PFLP operatives.

This wave of hijackings had its romantic dimension, especially where the message was passed on by bluff rather than with blood. The female member of the group, Leila Khaled, enjoyed a brief Western vogue as a charismatic revolutionary and the already rebellious youth of the period were quick to see in the Palestinians another oppressed group with which they could show solidarity.

King Hussein of Jordan might have been prepared to tolerate international subversion against Israel emanating from the Palestinian 'state-within-a-state' notionally under his sovereign control. However, he was not prepared to have the impotence of his government displayed on television screens across the world, and this was precisely the effect created by the PFLP's theatricals at Dawson's Field. On 17 September 1970, even before the hijack crisis had been finally resolved, the Jordanian army launched a concerted military attack on the PLO. After ten days of ferocious fighting, Palestinian resistance to the King's rule was severely weakened. The following summer, further bitter hostilities were sparked off by King Hussein's call on 2 June for a 'final crackdown' against those attempting 'to establish a separate Palestinian state and destroy the unity of the Jordanian and Palestinian people'. Hirst comments that the drive was so 'ruthless that scores of fedayeen, in the last extremities of exhaustion and despair, crossed the River Jordan rather than fall into the hands of the King's vengeful troops'.[7]

By the autumn of 1971, therefore, the Palestinians found themselves more isolated than ever, friendless in the international corridors of power, shunned by Arab states and actively despised and hunted by the two countries, Israel and Jordan, whose land they laid claim to. New and loosely organized militant strands of the PLO rose to the surface, the fiercest of which, Black September, took it name from the humiliations of the year before. It began its operations by assassinating one of the architects of the Palestinian defeat, Wasfi al-Tal, the Prime Minister of Jordan. Having nowhere to turn, Palestinian nationalists had chosen to console themselves with death.

A Crescendo of Terror

The violence that followed in 1972–3 was gruesome rather than glamorous. It amply demonstrated that the spiral of brutality which was contaminating

South American subversion at around this time had an international logic. Attacks on Israeli personnel and targets abroad were stepped up. In May 1972 the hijack of a Belgian airliner led to a gun battle between Israeli paratroopers and Black Septembrists in which two hijackers were killed and one passenger later died from the injuries she sustained when caught in crossfire. The death of the Palestinians led to a reprisal two weeks later which resulted in a massacre at Lod International Airport near Tel Aviv.

On the night of 30 May three young Japanese men were among the 119 passengers who had travelled on an Air France flight from Rome. In the baggage hall they waited with the others for their luggage and, when it arrived, they produced from it machine-guns, opening fire indiscriminately on the crowd of over 300 people milling around them. They also lobbed grenades at the panic-striken throng and fired at stationary aircraft. The final casualty list was twenty-eight dead and seventy wounded, many of them grievously. Among the fatalities were a renowed Israeli scientist and sixteen Puerto Rican pilgrims on their way to visit Christian shrines in the Holy Land. It emerged afterwards that the gunmen were members of a group calling itself the Japanese Red Army and that they had been acting on behalf of the PFLP, which claimed 'complete responsibility' for this 'brave operation'. The Japanese were reportedly told 'to kill as many people as possible at the airport, Israelis, of course, but anyone else who was there'.

The most famous incident of all occurred the following September, at the Olympic Games in Munich. Eight Palestinians belonging to Black September were spotted at 4.30 a.m. scaling the high wire-mesh fence that surrounded the Olympic village, but it was assumed that they were athletes returning from a night on the town. The men entered the Israeli compound through an unlocked door, killed a member of the team who got in their way and managed to capture nine others. Within hours they had specified their condition for the release of their hostages: the freeing of over 200 of their comrades then held in Israeli prisons. The authorities in Tel Aviv refused to negotiate. The West Germans, caught in the middle, offered various alternatives and eventually the hostage-takers agreed to forsake the compound for a guarantee of safe passage to Cairo. This was a trap, but one which was imperfectly set and bloodily sprung: in a gun battle at the airport, five of the Palestinians, all of the hostages and a German policeman were killed. No Israeli detainee was released.

In their 'will', published in Damascus, the dead terrorists wrote of their desire for the world to 'know of the existence of a people whose country has been occupied for twenty-four years, and their honour trampled underfoot.

. . . There is no harm if the youth of the world understand their tragedy for a few hours.'[8]

Within two months the seizure of a West German Lufthansa airliner with twenty passengers and crew on board led to yet another hijack drama. This one was resolved only when the German authorities agreed to release the three Black Septembrists who had survived the Munich operation. Meanwhile, Israel exacted revenge by launching aerial strikes against Syria and Lebanon in which hundreds of civilians were reportedly killed.

After Munich the PLO and its associated factions plummeted into bloody chaos. In December 1972 the Israeli embassy in Bangkok was seized and six of its occupants were held hostage for nineteen hours. In March 1973 Black September took over the Saudi Arabian embassy in Khartoum and shot dead three diplomats who were unfortunate enough to have been attending a party there at the time. The three were the US ambassador, Cleo Noel, and the US and Belgian chargés d'affaires, George C. Moore and Guy Eid. A Japanese jumbo jet was hijacked and destroyed in July 1973, apparently to punish the Tokyo government for having paid 6 million dollars to Israel in compensation for the Lod airport killings. A machine-gun and grenade attack on Athens airport the next month resulted in five deaths and fifty-three other casualties; the men responsible were later freed by the authorities after Greece had been threatened with further attacks. A series of hijacks followed, occurring in an apparently random way all round the world.

New heights of brutality were reached at Rome airport on 17 December 1973. Five Palestinians opened fire in the lounge before making their way to a Pan Am Boeing 707 which was preparing to take off for Beirut. They threw incendiary devices into the plane and twenty-nine people died in the ensuing blaze. They then hijacked a Lufthansa jet, took a group of Italian hostages, killed two more men and flew to Athens. One of the hostages was shot dead and dumped on the runway, after which the plane went via Damascus to Kuwait, where the men finally released the remaining hostages and gave themselves up. Unsurprisingly perhaps, no group claimed responsibility for this brutal episode.

The new year started much as the old one had ended. In January 1974 a combined PFLP and Japanese Red Army operation in Singapore and Kuwait involved the hijacking of a ferry, an attempt to blow up an oil refinery, the seizure of an embassy and the holding of numerous hostages, including the Japanese Ambassador to Kuwait. A British Airways jet was hijacked and destroyed at Amsterdam's Schiphol airport in March. Later in the year a series of car bombs damaged Israeli-owned premises in Paris. The contagion of violence seemed set to continue indefinitely.

A number of incidents demonstrated that the new callousness of the fedayeen could be brought right to the heart of their enemy. In April three members of the PFLP-GC stormed an apartment building in the town of Kiryat Shmona, close to the Lebanese border. Eighteen people, including eight children and five women, were killed in the incident and the three men themselves also died when the explosive-laden knapsacks they were carrying ignited on being hit by Israeli fire. The authorities alleged that the men had shot their victims indiscriminately; the PFLP-GC responded that they had been taken hostage, dying only when the authorities stormed the building. In retaliation the Israelis launched raids on six villages in Lebanon in the north and west of Kiryat Shmona. The number of casualties from these incursions was never confirmed, though it was alleged that there were some deaths.

In May twenty-five Israelis, twenty-one of them teenage schoolchildren, died during an attack on a school in the village of Maalot launched by the Popular Democratic Front for the Liberation of Palestine (PDFLP), an organization headed by Nayif Hawatmeh. Retaliatory air strikes into southern Lebanon the following day were reported to have killed twenty-one and injured 134. In June three women died in a raid on a kibbutz in northern Israel and a family was killed in a similar incident two weeks later in another border town. In both cases, the Palestinians involved also died and heavy raids into Lebanon followed. After the second of these Palestinian actions, Israeli naval commandos participated in a covert foray into the southern Lebanese ports of Tyre, Sidon and Ras a-Shak. The men were taken to the area in Israeli missile boats, came ashore in rubber rafts, blew up thirty fishing vessels belonging to the locals and returned to their ships undetected. A leaflet left behind by the raiders warned villagers that they would not be permitted to carry on their traditional fishing off the Mediterranean coast if the Palestinians persisted in raiding Israel from Lebanese bases.

After six years of escalating violence, it was becoming difficult to distinguish the methods of one side from those of the other. But what was political terror achieving for the Palestinian people? The answer that Yasser Arafat gave to this question led the PLO in new directions in 1974, a year of pivotal importance in any history of the tactic of political terror.

5   A War with Words

By 1974 the PLO could not deny that international terror had occurred, nor that it or other Palestinian factions had been behind much of it. However, the organization sought to take advantage of the attention such violence had won for it to move the debate on to a more general level. In a speech to the United Nations in November of that year, Yasser Arafat may have declared that he came 'bearing an olive branch and a freedom-fighter's gun' and dramatically called upon his audience not to 'let the olive branch fall from [his] hand', but his main thrust was the Palestinian problem. He argued that it was the result of a 'Zionist scheme' to bring Jewish immigrants into his country. The Israelis had launched a series of aggressive wars against the Arab nations, whose only alternative now was 'to expend exhaustive efforts in preparing forcefully to resist [another] barbarous invasion, and this in order to liberate Arab lands and to restore the rights of the Palestinian people'. He went on to call on Jews to 'turn away from the illusory promises made to them by Zionist ideology and Israeli leadership', neither of which offered more than 'perpetual bloodshed, endless war and continuous thralldom'.

Recrossing the Rubicon

The year of Arafat's United Nations speech was one of tremendous importance for the PLO, marking as it did the point at which they first attempted to transcend their international terrorist image. In the aftermath of the October 1973 war the oil weapon had emerged as a potent counter to Israel's political clout and technological might. Egypt was beginning the slow process of rapprochement with Israel which was eventually to culminate in the Camp David Agreement in 1978. Compromise was in the air and Yasser Arafat was quick to sense this change in the political atmosphere. Moreover, it was apparent to the senior leadership of the PLO that whatever value international terrorism may once have had, it was now far outweighed by the near-universal opprobrium that the tactic was attracting. In February 1974, therefore, the Central Council of the PLO met in Damascus and, under Arafat's guidance, agreed a new 'Provisional Programme', the details of which were then approved at a full meeting of the Palestinian National Council the following June. The revolution in PLO thinking involved in this policy was breathtaking. Whereas in the past the organization had committed itself to the wholesale destruction of the State of Israel, now it confined itself to calling for a new Palestine to be created out of any land that could 'be wrested from Zionist occupation'. In practice this meant the territories taken over by Israel during the Six Day War. The PLO were not officially accepting Israel, and rhetoric about the total obliteration of Zionism remained, as did violent manifestation of that ambition, but in practical terms the organization was according Israel de facto recognition. Henceforward the arguments were to be about borders, not existence.

Accompanying this new policy was a PLO drive to present itself to the world as the sole and exclusive representative of Palestinian interests, and in this they met almost immediately with a succession of diplomatic triumphs. On 14 October 1974 the United Nations General Assembly recognized the PLO as 'the representative of the Palestinian people'. Only four countries voted against the resolution: the United States, Israel, the Dominican Republic and Bolivia. The following week, the French Foreign Minister became the most senior European politician to meet Yasser Arafat, describing in enthusiastic terms his 'favourable and encouraging impression' of the PLO leader after the two men had met in Beirut. At the Summit Conference of the Arab League, held in Rabat at the end of October, King Hussein accepted a crucial resolution recognizing the PLO's right to represent the Palestinians in the occupied territories, which Jordan had lost in the 1967 war. The high point of this diplomatic offensive came on 13 November 1974, when, having been accorded all the dignities of a head of state, Yasser Arafat appeared at the United Nations General Assembly in New York and delivered his remarkable speech.

Arafat's 'freedom-fighter's gun' may have been a liberating weapon to some, but it was patently terrorist to others. His new respectability caused apoplexy and anxiety in certain quarters. The point was most graphically put by the Israeli representative at the United Nations, who declared that the UN had capitulated to 'a murder organization which aims at the destruction of a state member'. The point here was that the PLO had not forgone their assumed right to strike within Israel or the occupied territories. The Ambassador went on to castigate the General Assembly for having given credence to the 'murderers of athletes . . . [and] the assassins of diplomats in Khartoum'. The Israeli Prime Minister declared his refusal to 'negotiate with terrorist organizations'. The Israelis were not alone in their scepticism. Many Americans and Europeans pointed to the six years of terror which the Palestinians had brought to the Western world and asked about the morality of rewarding such deliberate bloodshed.

It was not unnatural that the main Western doubt about Yasser Arafat's role as a diplomat should have been prompted by his involvement in international terrorism. The PLO leader knew that he could not continue to be both a peacemaker and a condoner of the hijacking of aircraft and the murder of Western citizens. An opportunity to demonstrate a firmer line on such matters emerged a mere nine days after his moment of glory in New York. On 22 November 1974 four Palestinians hijacked a British Airways jet in Dubai and forced it to Tunis via a refuelling stop in Libya. The incident was a brutal and at times bizarre event. Forty-seven hostages were on board, one of whom, a West German, was killed and another, an Indian stewardess, was shot in the back before the crisis was brought to a close. The men claimed to be members of the Martyr Abou Mahmoud Squad and they called on the UK government to 'declare its responsibility for the greatest crime in history, which was the establishment of the Zionist entity . . . which [has] brought tragedies and calamities to our region'.[1] More practically, they also demanded the release of a variety of Palestinians imprisoned in Cairo for offences ranging from the murder of the three diplomats killed in Khartoum in 1973 to the terrorist assault on Rome airport later that year.

The significance of the incident lay not in what was achieved (some of those whose release was sought were freed) but rather in the response that it provoked from the PLO. The hijackers were criticized as 'saboteurs who ha[d] no connection with the Palestinian organization' and had to be punished for their misdeeds. Following this lead, the action was denounced by the majority of Arab states, and the Tunisian government, having resolved the crisis by offering asylum to the hijackers, promptly declared this oral undertaking to be non-binding and arrested the men. The PLO were eventually given custody of them and, in a highly publicized move in early 1975, declared that it had sentenced them to long jail terms. Arafat was said to have ordered an end to acts of terrorism in foreign countries and restricted the PLO to attacks within Israel and the occupied territories. The new policy was seen in operation again in 1975, when four Palestinians who stormed the Egyptian embassy in Madrid were turned over to the PLO by the authorities in Algiers, to where the gunmen had been allowed to go. Journalists were shown around a PLO prison where 'international terrorists' were being held and the organization proudly displayed the new provisions of its criminal code, under which hijacking that resulted in loss of life was to be regarded as a capital offence.[2]

The Dissenters

In recrossing this Rubicon of international terror, Arafat lost some of his more extreme troops; they preferred to stay and fight their version of the enemy on foreign soil. The PLO offers a graphic example of the general truth that once the taboo against terror is breached, a faction determined to terrorize ad infinitum is inevitably spawned, regardless of how the views of the mainstream might moderate. For such groups, terror stops being political and becomes a kind of bloody existentialism.

The British Airways hijack had been organized by a man who was in time to become the epitome of terror: Abu Nidhal. He savagely castigated the PLO for making policy changes which, he maintained, amounted to a sell-out to Israel. Nidhal was not alone. George Habash's PFLP viewed the Madrid embassy siege as a reaction to the treacherous politics of President Sadat and the 'surrender policies' of his Egyptian administration. Both his organization and the PFLP-GC, led by Ahmad Jibril, withdrew from the Executive Committee of the PLO, the PFLP declaring that Arafat had deviated 'from the revolutionary course'. In Habash's eyes there was to be no let-up in the struggle until all of Palestine was 'liberated', Israel was destroyed and King Hussein was overthrown in Jordan. These extremists had important backers among the Arab states. The Iraqi-sponsored PLO faction, the Arab Liberation Front, also withdrew from the Executive Committee, and General Gadaffi in Libya was vocal in his support for their line. The differences between the PLO and these various factions were basically political, but their most obvious manifestation was in the continued support that the factions gave to international terror.

The rest of the 1970s saw a continuation of such violence, at a much less intense level than before but enough to embarrass the PLO severely in its new role as the official government of a quasi-authentic country. In 1976, the PFLP hijacked a Dutch KLM aircraft en route from Malaga to Amsterdam, but the passengers and crew escaped unharmed. A scare over the poisoning of exported Israeli oranges caused alarm in 1978, especially when a group with the ominous title the Arab Revolutionary Army Palestine

Command claimed responsibility, but no more than a few Western consumers suffered any physical ill-effects. The amount of actual violence may have decreased, but the gory theatre remained, giving a false picture of a region still in the thrall of Palestinian terror.

The PFLP was implicated in two of the three great dramas which punctuated the mid-1970s. First, in 1975 six pro-Palestinian commandos burst into an OPEC meeting in Vienna, killing three people and wounding seven others. They seized seventy hostages, including eleven leading oil ministers, demanded the use of an airliner and led the authorities a merry dance between Austria, Algeria and Libya before releasing all of their captives and surrendering to the Algerian authorities. The Arm of the Arab Revolution claimed credit for the attack, though this was widely believed to be a cover for the PFLP. The action was hugely successful, netting the organization responsible some millions of dollars by way of ransom from Saudi Arabia and Iran.

However, the following year the second cause célèbre involved a dramatic rescue by Israeli defence forces of 103 passengers and crew held hostage in an Air France airliner at Uganda's Entebbe airport. Seven hijackers (alleged once again to be PFLP operatives), twenty Ugandan troops, three hostages and an Israeli commando, Jonathan Netanyahu, were killed during the Israeli assault. (Five weeks later two gunmen shot and killed four people and wounded over thirty when they opened fire indiscriminately on passengers waiting to board an El Al Israeli airliner at Istanbul airport. Turkish officials later reported that the two men had been PFLP members instructed to kill as many Israelis as possible in retaliation for the Entebbe raid.)

The third great terrorist event of the period occurred in October 1977 and was once again a rescue, this time by West German forces, of eighty-seven passengers and crew held captive aboard a Lufthansa airliner in Mogadishu, Somalia. The terrorists involved had demanded the release of members of the West German Red Army Faction, though they were later identified as belonging to the PFLP-Special Operations. This had been terrorism of a most callous sort: the hostages were holidaymakers returning from Majorca and the captain of the flight was shot dead in full view of the passengers and left lying in the plane for hours before being dumped on to the runway.

All these attacks were condemned by the PLO, immediately and unequivocally. However, to add to their troubles, the late 1970s also witnessed the resurgence of ancient inter-Arab rivalries, which often manifested themselves in acts of violence which appeared as yet further proof that the whole of the Arab world was addicted to terror. The hijack in 1976 of an Egyptian airliner with 102 passengers and crew on board looked very much as though it was part of a Libyan dispute with its neighbour, but this did not prevent one of the groups that claimed credit for the assault describing itself as the Palestine Revolution Movement.

The most damaging quarrel was between Iraq and Syria, ostensibly over the latter's intervention in Lebanon in 1976 but in reality about which of these two minor powers was to be master in its own backyard. Iraq's Black June movement, also revealingly but, from the PLO point of view, unhelpfully known as the 'Al Fatah Organization – Iraqi Branch', attacked Syrian embassies in Rome and Islamabad in October 1976, and in November stormed the Intercontinental Hotel in Amman. Hundreds of foreign guests were held hostage in the second of these incidents and eight people died before an assault by the Jordanian army brought the incident to a close. Within a month a bomb at Baghdad airport had killed at least three and injured over 230. The Iraqis blamed the Syrians and Black June stepped up its campaign during 1977. A series of car bombs in Damascus in July killed eight people and injured over sixty. A minister in the government of the United Arab Emirates was shot dead in Abu Dhabi airport in October, apparently having been mistaken for the Syrian Foreign Minister, Abdel Halim Khaddam. In December a car bomb in London killed the Syrian embassy's medical attaché and his driver.

Far from being involved in violence of this sort, the PLO found that its officials abroad were prime targets for assassination. Their potential assailants were too numerous to count. From time to time they included not only Israeli hit squads bent upon revenge for earlier atrocities but also the Abu Nidhal gang, killing on behalf of one or other of the rejectionist groups, and Arab states like Syria, displeased with the organization's role in the Lebanon. Successive PLO representatives in Paris were murdered, in 1972, in 1977 and again in 1978. During this period their senior officials in Kuwait and Belgium also died and their offices in Pakistan were attacked. In January 1978 the head of the PLO's London office, Said Hammami, was shot dead in his office by an Arab gunman. Hammami had consistently abjured the use of terrorism and had advocated some form of peaceful coexistence with Israel. The Voice of the Palestinian Revolution claimed responsibility for his assassination.

The PLO's representatives around the world can hardly have enjoyed the irony that their main task as publicists for the PLO involved them in daily denials of their terrorist inclinations, at exactly the time when they were themselves in acute danger of terrorist attack, more so perhaps than any other contemporary group. For the pressure on the PLO to live down their international terrorist links continued throughout the 1970s and 1980s, despite these murderous assaults, the Provisional Programme and Arafat's own public declarations against and disavowels of such violence.

The Alibi of Terror

The Israelis were chiefly responsible for furthering the association between terror and the PLO. Arafat's continued commitment to armed action within Israel and the occupied territories left him vulnerable on this front, while the killing of Israeli civilians continued throughout the decade. The strand of flexibility in the organization epitomized by Said Hammami was not taken seriously by them. Their efforts were geared to reducing the whole Palestinian movement to the common denominator of the last atrocity. When the PLO secured the rights of a United Nations member nation in 1976, Israel's most senior delegate denounced the organization as a 'loose coalition of feuding terrorist gangs'. And when in 1977 the French authorities held in detention but then expelled from the country a senior PLO executive whom the Israelis suspected of having been involved in the Munich Olympic killings, the Israeli government recalled its ambassador from Paris, expressing its concern that the incident amounted to 'abject surrender to the . . . threats of terror organizations'.

Academic literature provided another forum in which the same points could be made: the very existence of textbooks on terrorism directed public anxiety about violence down the route favoured by the Israelis. *Terrorism: The PLO Connection* emerged as late as 1989, with its authors, Yonah Alexander and Joshua Sinai, describing the PLO as 'the leading international terrorist group' of the past twenty-five years.[3] At the Washington conference of the Jonathan Institute, a private research foundation dedicated to the memory of the Israeli commando who died at Entebbe, Moshe Arens, a minister in the Israeli government, asserted that the PLO was the 'umbrella organization of virtually all Arab terrorist groups'.[4]

A fresh boost to Israeli determination to heighten anxiety about PLO terrorism came in the early 1980s, when Arafat's organization suddenly found itself being named as the junior partner in a liaison of international terror with Brezhnev's Soviet Union. The frenzy over the USSR as the 'master terrorists' of the world may now seem curiously dated, but it was real enough when Alexander Haig, at his first press conference as the new president's Secretary of State, declared in his inimitable style that the Kremlin 'today are involved in conscious policies, in programs, if you will, which foster, support and expand this activity, which is hemorrhaging in many respects throughout the world today'.

Many books dealt with this question of Soviet involvement, some with evocative titles like *The Soviet Strategy of Terror* and *The Grand Strategy of the Soviet Union*. The then Director of the CIA, William Casey, contributed an essay with an appropriately Delphic title, 'The International Linkages – What Do We Know', to the excitingly named volume *Hydra of Carnage*.[5] Connecting the Kremlin with terrorism suited the strategy of the first Reagan administration, since it helped to build up concern about the Soviets, which in turn made the greatly increased defence spending envisaged by the White House more widely acceptable. The only difficulty was that there was little direct evidence of Soviet involvement in actual terror acts.

It was known, though, that the USSR supported the PLO, so protagonists of this version of the international conspiracy theory tended to concentrate on this. As a result of this search for implicatory evidence against the USSR, the PLO found that every aspect of their organization was being placed under scrutiny. One book, *The War Against Terrorism* by N. C. Livingstone, which was published at the height of the panic in 1982, opened with the following memorable lines:

Among the Palestine Liberation Organisation (PLO) and the Popular Front for the Liberation of Palestine (PFLP) rank-and-file in southern Lebanon these days, the most prestigious badge of distinction that can be worn – weather permitting – is a Soviet-made fur hat. While not of the haute couture variety, Soviet fur hats are the latest thing in revolutionary chic, for possession of one in many parts of the world usually indicates that the owner is a graduate of one of the elite schools and camps operated by the USSR and its allies that train and indoctrinate terrorists and other revolutionaries. With each passing month, more and more fur hats appear in embattled Lebanon and, for that matter, in dozens of other locations around the world. Ironically, they may soon lose some of their prestige value as they become too commonplace.[6]

A linkage between communism and the PLO was something that the Israelis had been trying to contrive for years. That it should have been fostered, indirectly, by the Reagan administration was an unexpected bonus. Few commentators paused to consider whether the PLO of the 1980s was the terror organization which they were presumed to be.

From the Israeli point of view, the advantages to be derived from continuing to link the PLO with terror and terrorism were many. The battle for the support of Western public opinion would be more than half won if Arafat and his cohorts could be equated with the Red Army Faction, the Red Brigades, the IRA, ETA and all the other subversive groups which were then plaguing the European democracies. There was genuine and popular revulsion in the West against the terror tactics employed by such factions, and the Israelis hoped that the anathema would spill over to encompass their particular *bête noire*. The Palestinian rejectionists had done the Tel Aviv strategists no end of service in this regard. Their erratic international violence had obscured the fact that the PLO were no longer 'international terrorists' and their histrionic interventions at Vienna, Entebbe and Mogadishu had involved not only German ideological terrorists but also such popular hate figures as Idi Amin and the dreaded Carlos, an obscure South American popularly believed to be 'the terrorists' terrorist'.

The idea of a malevolent Arab presence in the world, and the spectre of a communist-inspired subversion, was useful for more than propaganda reasons. It allowed the PLO, and indeed the whole Palestinian cause, to be presented as a threat not just to Israel but also to the West as a whole. It was in this vein, for example, that Israel's Ambassador to the United Nations, in a book entitled *Terrorism: How the West Can Win*, described the 'war against terror' as 'part of a much larger struggle, one between the forces of civilization and the forces of barbarism'.[7] It was time for the West to 'unite and fight to win the war against terrorism'. This was 'the challenge facing the democracies, and the democracies alone can meet it'.[8] The Jonathan Institute, which held large conferences in Jerusalem in 1979 and in Washington in 1984, called for the 'need for a better understanding of terrorism and for mobilizing the West against it'.[9]

The message being conveyed was that in this war against a vicious, irrational and, above all, uncivilized foe, the West would often have to hit back hard. In this context the West usually meant the Israelis. The spectre of PLO terrorism proved itself to be an invaluable ally to the Israeli governments of the 1970s and 1980s in its role as a ready-made excuse and rhetorical cover for tough military action.

Initially, as in previous years, the Tel Aviv authorities reacted to PLO attacks within Israel by launching air or naval assaults on southern Lebanon, supposedly aimed at the Palestinian camps where the fedayeen were believed to be based but often hitting the villages of the local Islamic

Shia population. Then in late 1974 the army declared that they did not feel compelled to wait for violent incidents before carrying their war on terrorism into Lebanon. Their military incursions often involved the demolition of houses, the blowing up of bridges, the destruction of crops and the seizure of villagers for interrogation. Clearly the Israeli action was designed to intimidate the Lebanese authorities into expelling the PLO from its territory in the way that King Hussein had done in 1970. However, it should have been obvious that such a strategy was likely to fail because the Lebanese central government was not sufficiently strong to execute it even if it had been inclined to adopt such a policy.

The Invasion of Lebanon

With the election of Menachem Begin at the head of a new hard-line government in 1977, the fight against terrorism became the cover for a new and even more ambitious and expansionist military plan. There had long been a fantasy about Lebanon percolating just below the top layer of Israeli politics, one which had briefly surfaced in the mid-1950s. It involved the establishment of a Christian Lebanese state which would then be neutral towards or even favourable to the Israelis. The anxiety caused by the existence of large camps of Palestinian refugees in the country now made this appear more attractive than ever. To the manifold other benefits of such a new regime could be added the extirpation of the PLO.

There were two problems with this scenario. First, it was clear that no such Christian state was likely to emerge from Lebanon of its own accord. Riven by civil war, the country was bitterly divided. However, this did mean that it was also vulnerable, so the new Begin government set its sights on an invasion of Lebanon. The hope was that a decisive move into the country would bring about a restructuring of its affairs that the Israelis judged to be in their interest.

Second, it was quite obvious that Lebanon, caught up in its own tragedy, posed no security threat to Israel. This would make any invasion an obviously aggressive act and therefore unlikely to be defensible before world, and in particular US, opinion. Even the PLO had greatly scaled down attacks into Israel from 'Fatahland' in southern Lebanon, since Arafat was anxious not to loose the one part of the world which, thanks to the anarchy in Beirut, he could quite safely call his own. So the challenge for Begin was to contrive an excuse for his planned interference in his northern neighbour's affairs, one that would justify an intervention more dramatic than any dared in the past, even by Israel's most hawkish politicians and generals.

Terrorism provided the ideal pretext. On 11 March 1978 Fatah operatives carried out a particularly meaningless and murderous assault. They landed on the coast twenty miles south of Haifa, killed a US tourist, shot dead the occupants of a taxi, commandeered a bus and set off for Tel Aviv with its passengers as hostages, firing randomly at the passing traffic. After a shoot-out with the authorities brought the incident to a bloody close, twenty-five civilians had died and over seventy had been injured. Nine of the eleven commandos also died. At a press conference the following day, Prime Minister Begin promised retribution. Four days after the raid 20,000 Israeli troops crossed into Lebanon. They quickly took control of all the country south of the Litani, a river about one-third of the way from Israel to Beirut – an area of some 425 square miles. The main victims of the invasion were not terrorists but rather the local Palestinian and Shia communities. The United Nations were later to estimate that about 100 Arab villages had been attacked, leading to the total destruction of 2,500 houses and severe damage to a further 5,200.[10] The same body estimated that quarter of a million inhabitants had been made homeless.[11] The number of people killed by the Israeli army was estimated to be in the region of 2,000.[12]

The ratio of fatalities was fifty-four dead Arabs for every Israeli. However, other than as an act of disproportionate retribution, the invasion was not a success. It did not destroy the PLO, whose fighters simply gave way in the face of the overwhelming military superiority of the invader and withdrew to safety further north. The international outcry that inevitably followed culminated in a United Nations Security Council resolution calling upon Israel 'immediately to cease its military action against Lebanese territorial integrity and withdraw forthwith its forces from all Lebanese territory'. This was eventually complied with, but not before the Israelis had organized and armed their own maverick militia under Sa'ad Haddad to police a strip of Lebanon along Israel's border, which they then alternately described as their security zone and (more exotically) as Free Lebanon. North of Haddad's zone, United Nations forces struggled to achieve the impossible task set them by the Security Council of 'confirming the withdrawal of Israeli forces, restoring international peace and security and assisting the government of Lebanon in ensuring the return of its effective authority in the area'. And even further north was the new base of the PLO, still, as far as the Israeli authorities were concerned, frustratingly situated within Lebanon and a constant reminder to them that the main purpose of their invasion had not been achieved.

This was not to say that Israel stopped aiming for the total victory that had so far eluded them. In 1981 the Begin government began their war on the PLO all over again. The pattern was the same, but the price of an Israeli life continued to inflate. During ten days of hostilities in July, six Israelis were killed and this resulted in the death of an estimated 500 Palestinians and Lebanese. In one incident alone 300 died as Israeli jets bombed a number of apartment blocks in the Fakhani quarter of Beirut. Eventually a ceasefire was brokered by the US Special Envoy, Philip Habib. It subsequently transpired that at least some senior Israeli military planners viewed this breakthrough with disappointment since it deprived them of the *casus belli* they desired.[13] Their frustration was increased as eight months passed without any incident which the Israelis could claim to be a breach in the truce by the Palestinians. Their patience snapped when an Israeli officer was blown up by a land mine while patrolling in Haddad's 'Free Lebanon'. In the retaliatory air strike that followed on 21 April 1982 Palestinian positions between Sidon and Beirut were bombarded, with about twenty-five people being killed and another sixty injured. Then, after two children had been injured in a bomb attack in Jerusalem, the Israelis killed six and injured another twenty in southern Lebanon. The PLO did respond this time, with some erratic shelling which did no great damage and caused no casualties. Nevertheless, on account of these 'terrorist' violations, the Israeli government declared the ceasefire to be at an end.

On 4 June 1982 the key escalatory event occurred when the Israeli Ambassador to Britain was shot and seriously injured in London. The Abu Nidhal group were responsible for this attempted murder. Menachem Begin declared that 'this put an end to a long period of Israeli restraint', and promptly launched extensive air raids on Palestinian camps in Beirut, during which over 100 people were reported to have died. Retaliatory attacks by the PLO into northern Israel claimed a total of four victims but these 'terrorist attacks' were used as the excuse for the extraordinary Israeli action which then ensued. This was Operation Peace in Galilee, launched on 6 June 1982. The Israeli army swarmed in their thousands into Lebanon and attacked on three fronts: the Bekaa valley, Beaufort Castle near the Litani river and the coastal road near Tyre. They also launched aerial and naval assaults on other Palestinian positions. The towns of Tyre and Sidon fell after strong resistance from the fedayeen. In the Bekaa valley resistance was less fierce and it soon became evident that the Syrians did not wish to embark on full-scale war with Israel. They retreated further up the valley and had agreed a ceasefire by 11 June. Well before this, Israel's vast military superiority over the PLO had begun to tell. They outnumbered the opposition ten to one and their army had quickly swept past the 25-mile limit beyond which they had promised the Americans they would not go. Within four days they had linked up with their Christian Phalangist allies and were overlooking the final enclave of Palestinian resistance, west Beirut. Speed had been of the essence, but at a price. Rather then engage in difficult and dangerous face-to-face assaults, the Israelis had simply bombarded into oblivion the towns and villages that stood between them and their final goal. 1,000 buildings in Sidon were completely destroyed and another 1,500 were damaged. In Tyre and Sidon alone, twenty-seven schools and thirteen hospitals were bombed. Palestinian refugee camps in southern Lebanon were completely flattened, by aerial bombardment or, if that had not done the job, by Israeli bulldozers afterwards.

The Siege of Beirut

On 10 June the Israelis laid siege to Beirut, with the intention of eradicating for ever Palestinian nationalism. The Defence Minister, Ariel Sharon, told the Knesset that 'the PLO must cease to exist'. As in their drive to the city, the military eschewed the use of any tactics that might expose them to serious risk. Instead, they launched a bombardment of the city which continued, with only a couple of short respites, from 13 June to 12 August. The tactics used included 'air raids, naval bombardment, heavy artillery barrages (155-mm guns and 121-mm howitzers) and fire from tanks, mortars and rocket launchers'.[14] The weapons employed were indiscriminate, highly effective and extremely vicious. Suction bombs imploded rather than exploded and therefore caused whole buildings to collapse inwards. Phosphorous shells inflicted profoundly severe and agonizingly fatal internal burning; the correspondent for *The Times* reported how two five-day-old twins killed by such a bomb had smouldered in the mortuary for hours. Cluster bombs were the most devastating of all, and they were used by the Israelis despite an agreement with their supplier, the United States, that they should be employed only in a defensive capacity in a war with two or more Arab states. For much of the two-month siege the authorities did not permit international organizations such as UNICEF or the Red Cross to enter the western part of the city to assist in the treatment of its inhabitants.

It is impossible to know how many people were killed during Israel's invasion and subsequent siege of Beirut. Local estimates put the figures in the region of 18,000 dead and 30,000 wounded. What is clear is that practically all the casualties were Palestinian or Lebanese and that of these by far the majority were civilians. On 21 August the PLO agreed to leave Beirut, in order, they said, to save the city from further depredation. Arafat had survived, but by the end of August he was gone, leading his force of about 10,000 followers into yet another enforced exile.

The Lebanese Muslims and Palestinian refugees who remained in west Beirut were apprehensive about how they would fare under the new dispensation, now that they had lost their PLO protectors. Even the multinational force that had been involved briefly to oversee the fedayeen evacuation had left ahead of time. On 23 August the hard-line Maronite Christian and Phalangist leader, Bashir Gemayel, was elected President of Lebanon. Here was the clearest indication yet that the Begin dream of a Christian ally to Israel's north may have been coming to fruition. However, Gemayel began to show streaks of independence which did not augur well for his new Israel-designated role as a Lebanese quisling. He was killed on 14 September in a huge bomb explosion at the Phalangist Party head-quarters.

The day after Gemayel's death the Israeli army moved into west Beirut in violation of the agreement under which the PLO had withdrawn. They encountered only token resistance and suffered very few casualties. They then asked the Christian Phalangists to enter two Palestinian refugee camps, Sabra and Chatila, and hunt down the 'terrorists' that remained there. The man given the responsibility of overseeing the operation had seen members of his own family and his fiancée killed by Palestinian fighters in Damour. Some of the men under his command had been involved in a massacre of over 1,000 Palestinian refugees at the Tal Zaatar refugee camp in 1976. For two days, the Phalangists rampaged through Sabra and Chatila, engaged in an horrific pogrom:

Anything that moved in the narrow alleyways the Phalangists shot. They broke into houses and killed their occupants who were gathered for their evening meal, watching television or already in bed. Sometimes they tortured before they killed, gouging out eyes, skinning alive, disembowelling. Women and small girls were raped, sometimes half a dozen times, before, breasts severed, they were finished off with axes. Babies were torn limb from limb and their heads smashed against walls. Entering Akka hospital the men assassinated the patients in their beds. They tied other victims to vehicles and dragged them through the streets alive. They cut off hands to get at rings and bracelets. They killed Christian and Moslems, Lebanese as well as Palestinians. They even killed nine Jewesses who, married to Palestinians, had been living in the camps since 1948.[15]

Throughout this period the Israeli army stood by, within yards of these events. They prevented panicking inhabitants from escaping and, during the night, they lit the sky with flares so as to make the Phalangists' job easier. When it was all over, they lent them bulldozers so that they could bury the bodies more effectively. It is not known how many people died during those two days and nights of terror, but a number of estimates put the figure at over 2,000.

Conclusion

The Israeli campaign in Lebanon is not usually mentioned in books on terrorism, which are more concerned with cataloguing minor incidents of Palestinian subversion within Israel. After all, these fall clearly within our Western definition of terrorism. Nowhere have words been more dreadfully abused than in their use within the context of the Middle East. Operation Peace in Galilee was intended to put an end to the very occasional fatalities which the Israeli Ambassador to the United Nations had described at the time as 'constant terrorist provocations since 1981'. By the end of 1982 the Tel Aviv authorities were still singing the same tune, but those inhabitants of Lebanon who had survived real terror had a different view of who the genuine terrorists were. By then, a whole new anti-Western phenomenon had been ushered into Lebanon from Iran. The Islamic fundamentalism that it preached, and the anti-Americanism that it practised, were to become the terrorist obsessions of the 1980s. In the pantheon of super-terrorists, Arafat was replaced by the Ayatalloh.

6 War with the Shadows

With the arrival in Beirut of the Israeli army in 1982, conflict in the Middle East took a fresh turn. The Palestinian question was superseded by new problems which began very quickly to affect the regional interests of Israel and the Western powers. Accordingly, the meaning of terrorism found itself undergoing several fresh transformations to make it fit this new and broader range of enemies. The story starts, however, not in Beirut but in Tehran, with the Shah of Iran.

The Resurgence of Islam

In many respects, the Pahlavi dynasty that ruled Iran for fifty-eight years was an invention of the West. The British encouraged one of their local supporters, Reza Khan, to lead a coup d'état against the established order in the country in 1921, and they had him removed from office twenty years later when he apparently refused to allow Allied supplies through to the Soviet front. His son, who took over from him at this point, proved more amenable to Western interests, particularly in relation to Iran's gigantic oil reserves, the crucial value of which was coming to be realized. After the war the fact that the British-owned Anglo–Iranian Oil Company had sole rights to the oil caused growing local resentment. This culminated in the nationalization of the whole industry soon after Mohammed Mossadeq became Prime Minister, in 1951. This action was taken against the wishes of the Shah, who found as a result that his position as leader was increasingly unsustainable. However, his pre-eminence was restored in a coup in 1953. This putsch ousted Mossadeq from power and, being CIA-inspired, it served thereafter to underline the Shah's dependence on the West. By 1976 Iran was the largest single buyer of US arms in the world, with total purchases from this source alone in the years 1972–6 coming to $10.4 billion. Apart from Israel, with which the Shah had developed a close relationship, Iran had become the key regional power protecting Western interests in this most sensitive part of the globe.

The vast majority of Iran's population, which in the mid-1970s stood at over 33 million, were followers of the Twelver branch of Shia Islam, which had been the state religion in the country since the sixteenth century. Over time it had come to stand for a type of Islamic fundamentalism which both revelled in old-fashioned Muslim values and held the rival world-views of communism and capitalism in equal contempt. The Shah's policies of rapid modernization and industrialization, fuelled by a constant flow of oil, had achieved a high degree of speedy economic growth, but at the expense of further widening the gap in thinking between his westernizing ways and the traditional views of his subjects.

In particular, he saw the old religious leaders as symbols of an antiquated nation which he wanted to bring to an end. Accordingly, the mullahs lost property in various land reforms that reshaped ownership in the country, and other advances pioneered by Tehran sought to reduce their hitherto unequalled influence in the social, legal and educational life of the nation. The tensions that this created were held in check by the US-trained SAVAK, the security and intelligence arm of government, which administered what was fast becoming a virtual police state. Despite such policies and the widespread repression, Islam enjoyed a strong resurgence. The seminaries were full and the places of worship were thriving. Ancient Islamic institutions remained well supported by the people, whose voluntarily paid tax compensated for the pattern of neglect that had been contrived by the government. Indeed, by the late 1970s Islam and the mullahs had become the focus for opposition to the increasingly unpopular domestic and foreign policies of the government.

Viewed in this context, the reassertion of Shia ascendancy reflected in the triumph of the Ayatalloh Khomeini and the exile of the Shah in 1979 may not have been altogether surprising, but it was none the less an unqualified disaster for the West. Not only was the new government fundamentalist in its Islamic perspective; it was also convinced that there was no room at all for any difference between church and state. The whole edifice of Pahlavi achievement was completely thrown out. Soon the new state revealed itself to be uncontent with domestic triumph alone and determined to export its Islamic revolution around the Muslim world.

One feature of the subversion that had brought down the Shah was the virulently anti-Western – and in particular anti-American – atmosphere that had been prevalent in Tehran during 1978. The successful revolution made the expression of such hostile sentiments part of official policy. The chaotic and vehemently xenophobic vigour of the revolution was crystallized in the storming of the US embassy in November 1979 and in the seizure by radical students of US personnel found there. In all, fifty-two Americans were held hostage in Iran for a total of 444 days. Their incarceration dominated the Washington political agenda throughout the election year of 1980. The failed rescue mission in April cost the lives of eight men and seemed to symbolize the United States impotence in the international arena. Vietnam at least had been a proper war. Now here was the world's greatest power being 'humbled' by a bunch of students, some Muslim fanatics and a regime that was already being described in some quarters as little more than a gang of 'international terrorists'.

It was an understandable insult, but was it a correct description? The new President certainly thought so. Welcoming home the hostages on 27 January 1981, just one week after he had assumed office, Ronald Reagan said: 'Let terrorists beware that when the rules of international behavior are violated, our policy will be one of swift and effective retribution.' The atmosphere of crisis was fuelled by a quick succession of incidents. On 30 March Reagan was shot and injured outside a Washington hotel. It was not a terrorist bullet, but it was a reminder of the president's vulnerability. On 13 May Pope John Paul was nearly assassinated in St Peter's Square and it was soon suspected that there had been Bulgarian or even KGB involvement. On 6 October the Egyptian President, upon whom the United States pinned so much of its Middle Eastern policy, Anwar Sadat, fell victim to a brutal and public gun attack while watching a military parade in Cairo. The United States immediately suspected Libya, two of whose pilots had attacked US navy fighter jets the previous August and been shot down in retaliation, although it later transpired that Muslim extremists had been responsible.

With Iran firmly in his mind, President Reagan's new Secretary of State, Alexander Haig (who had himself nearly been blown up by a terrorist bomb in 1978 while serving as NATO's top military commander in Europe) declared shortly after entering office: 'International terrorism will take the place of human rights as our concern, because it is the ultimate abuse of human rights. And it's time that it be addressed with greater clarity and greater effectiveness by Western nations and the United States as well.'[1]

Exporting the Revolution: Amal, Islamic Amal and Hezbollah

The first test of America's determination to resist 'international terrorism' came in Lebanon. By late 1982 it was not the country it had been even twelve months previously. The Begin and Sharon plan had turned into a nightmare. The Israeli invasion had not brought peace to Lebanon; rather it had complicated its political mosaic even further, by unchaining new forces of brutality. These emerged not only as a reaction to the heights of violence that the invading army had inflicted during the siege of Beirut but also as a consequence of the behaviour of the occupying forces in southern Lebanon. The indigenous population there was mainly composed of Shia Muslims. As the main victims of the PLO's quarrel with the Israelis, through the latter's reprisal air attacks, they initially welcomed the invaders as the guarantors of an enforced tranquillity in the region. Over a short time, however, the casual ill-discipline and occasional ugliness of the Israeli army and its plethora of allied militias changed the political atmosphere. As the Israelis were forced to give ground further north, so the alienation caused by their behaviour in the south intensified.

There were other complicating factors as well. The Shias of southern Lebanon had long been the poorest group in the whole country. In a nation dedicated to prosperity through the protection of vested interests, they were the forgotten people, the religious group that had perennially lost out. As befits the holders of such a lowly status, there was little political organization in the south. The Movement of the Deprived had been established in 1975 by Imam Mousa Sadr and it was dedicated to the assertion of the rights of the Shias. Its military wing, the Battalions of the Lebanese Resistance, became well known as Amal and was headed by a lawyer, Nabih Berri.

If Israeli attack, and finally occupation, had provided the stimulus to the growth into a political organization of a body like Amal, then the Iranian revolution provided the essential inspiration for two others. Since 1979 Tehran had coveted Lebanon as an ideal spiritual market into which to export its worldwide Islamic revolution, but Syria resisted its move into the country. President Assad considered the place his fiefdom and was worried about how contagious Iranian fundamentalism might prove to be. In the chaos caused by the 1982 invasion and Israel's attack on Syria, however, Assad chose to allow through into Lebanon contingents of Iranian Revolutionary Guards. Two new Shia groups promptly emerged: Islamic Amal and Hezbollah. Islamic Amal was led by a former teacher, Hussein Mussawi, and, as the name suggests, broke away from Berri's Amal on the grounds that it was not sufficiently Islamic. Hezbollah, or the Party of God, was also avowedly Islamic in intentions, and was very close to Tehran in its politics. Its spiritual leader was Sheikh Mohammed Hussein Fadlallah, whose book *Islam and the Logic of Force* was influential in the evolution of its thinking. The West has come routinely to regard all three groups as 'terrorist'. It is worth underlining, therefore, that they emerged as the defenders of the Lebanese Shias and that they gave their communities organizational and structural support which had hitherto been almost totally lacking. Because of this, the three quickly gained a widespread following in many parts of the country, but particularly in the south.

Meanwhile, events were also moving fast in Beirut. Immediately after the terrible massacres at Sabra and Chatila in 1982, the multinational force returned to the city to offer what could cynically be described as posthumous protection to the Muslims and Palestinians left alive. Though initially the US, French and Italian soldiers were welcomed as saviours by the survivors, the policy decision to return was to have tragic consequences. Viewed from the Shia perspective – a perspective that many of the rest of the Lebanese Muslims came to share – the multinational force in Beirut looked to be anything but the trumpeted guarantor of a peace.

Apart from preventing new atrocities by the Christian Phalangists, the force, or MNF as it quickly came to be called, had as its vaguely defined strategy the restoration of the authority of the Lebanese government. The neutrality of this ambition was more apparent than real, for the political system in Lebanon had been weighted in favour of the Christians since the country had been founded in 1943. Under the scheme then adopted, the president of the country was always a Christian. The Muslims were restricted to the less powerful post of Prime Minister (to be held by a Sunni) and the almost purely honorific position of Speaker of the Chamber of Deputies (to be held by a Shia). Parliamentary representation was fixed to guarantee the Christians a majority, regardless of whether they secured most of the votes at election time. This structure had persisted despite demographic change and the probability that the Christians had over time become a minority in the country they controlled. It was impossible to prove this latter point, since there had been no official census since independence, and no government estimate of the population had been made since 1956. To many Syrians and Lebanese Muslims, the nation looked like a ruse to extend the power of the ancient Maronite Christians of Mount Lebanon over as much of 'Greater Syria' as possible.

After the assassination of the President-elect, the Christian Phalangist leader Bashir Gemayel, what little central authority that remained in Lebanon devolved to another Christian, this time Bashir's brother, Amin Gemayel. The Christians, with Bashir prominent among them, had not fought against the Israelis and – to start with at any rate – had colluded with them in the dream of a PLO-free Christian Lebanon. It had been the Christian Phalangists who had revenged Bashir's death in the camps of west Beirut. This was the central authority that the MNF was perceived to be seeking to restore. It was odd that the forces who came to protect west Beirut should have as their final goal the creation of the conditions within which such an atrocity could be repeated.

In December 1982, while the US marines who formed part of the MNF were digging in in Beirut, Congress raised US military aid to Israel by $300 million, to a total of $1.7 billion for the fiscal year 1983. A further $250 million was made available by way of soft loans.[2] The new Islamic forces in Lebanon were infuriated that the main supporters of Israel and of the Christian government in Lebanon should also have the effrontery to pose as their protectors. It was not a role that could be maintained for long.

Fighting an Invisible War

In 1983 the rival imperialisms of the United States and Iran fought out their struggle in Lebanon. On one side was the 'great Satan'; on the other were the 'international terrorists'. Buoyed by the support they were receiving from the MNF, the Christian Phalangist government began to harass the Muslim and Palestinian sectors of west Beirut. A car bomb nearly killed the Druse leader, Walid Jumblatt. The Israelis engaged in confrontations with the US marines. Then, in March 1983, a series of attacks were launched against the MNF. Ten Italians were wounded, two seriously. Five Americans were injured when a grenade was lobbed on to their patrol from the upstairs floor of a house they were passing. The French were left unharmed only because the grenades aimed at them failed to explode. The attacks were claimed by a new and mysterious group, Islamic Jihad, meaning Islamic Holy War. On 18 April a van packed with explosives blew up in front of the US embassy, killing sixty-three people and wounding another 100. Seventeen of the fatalities were Americans, and almost the whole CIA operation in the region was wiped out by the assault: they had been having a strategy session inside when the bomb went off. Islamic Jihad declared the attack to have been 'part of the Iranian revolution's campaign against the imperialist presence throughout the world'.

During the summer of 1983 the MNF became even more embroiled in the unedifying and difficult task of propping up the authority of what was still theoretically the government. Israeli forces withdrew from key strategic positions around Beirut and in the mêlée left by their departure, the MNF ended up firing rounds in support of the Phalangists. The Amal leader, Nabih Berri, warned that the marines had 'turned into a fighting force against Muslims in Lebanon' and Walid Jumblatt declared ominously that 'the mere fact that they are providing the Lebanese factional army with logistic support, expertise and training is enough for us to consider them enemies'.[3]

The inevitable escalation came in the middle of September, when the Sixth Fleet began shelling Souq al-Gharb in support of Gemayel, after it had become apparent that without such an intervention the Druse would have wrested key areas from Christian control. Islamic Jihad struck back at their new foreign foes with devastating effect. On 23 October 1983 suicide bomb attacks were launched on the headquarters of the US and French battalions. In the first incident 241 men died; in the next fifty-nine. They occurred within seconds of each other, early on a Sunday morning, and they permanently transformed the politics of Lebanon. The French had hardly lost a soldier in combat since the Algerian war. Not even the Americans had suffered this badly from a single strike throughout the entire Vietnam war. Now these terrible blows had struck at a mission that was even less well understood than either of those earlier military failures.

Perhaps because of this the attacks achieved their purpose. Within six months the MNF was effectively out of Beirut. After its initial welcome the value of its presence had become increasingly unclear and now the cost of keeping it in place had become too high. The defeated nations pulled out in a welter of bad temper. President Reagan launched the invasion of Grenada two days after the marines were blown up, a politically well-timed diversion for an anxious US public. In November the French launched an aerial attack on the Sheikh Abdullah barracks near Baalbek, the place where they believed the suicide bombers had been prepared for action by Iranian Revolutionary Guards and Islamic Amal. The planes seem however, to have missed all their targets.[4] Sixteen months later, a huge car bomb exploded in the vicinity of the offices of Sheikh Fadlallah, which were situated near the Bir al-Abed mosque in the suburbs of Beirut. Eighty people died in the blast and over 200 were wounded. The Americans had put it about that Fadlallah had blessed the bombers before their assault on the US marines and the *Washington Post* later alleged that the CIA had planted this car bomb in the hope of assassinating him. In February 1984 the final evacuation was marked by a bombardment of the Lebanese coast by the huge, forty-year-old battleship *New Jersey*. The shells from its 16-

inch guns created craters 5 feet deep and up to 15 feet across. Each round was as heavy as a small car and casualties must have been suffered in the vulnerable villages along the coast.

The car bomb assaults on the US and French forces have achieved macabre fame as two of the worst terrorist atrocities ever committed, and they have always been regarded as quintessential terrorist acts. Clearly both attacks were violent, indeed terminal, blows against the Western forces stationed in Beirut, and involved killing and maiming on a grand scale. But, then, so do all wars and many forms of conflict.

Horrible though the attacks on the Americans and the French were, none of the elements of pure terror was present. The bombs were targeted on a particular class of person: soldiers in the MNF stationed in Beirut. They were not intended to terrorize but rather to compel an evacuation of these forces so as to isolate the Phalangist armies in the city and facilitate an eventual takeover by the forces of Islam. Furthermore, to talk in 1983 of an established authority in Lebanon which the bombers could be said to be subverting was to miss the point, for there was no such government operating in the country at the time. Lebanon was in a state of effective civil war and all sides were tussling with one another for their survival. The fact that the Western powers chose to call one of the factions a government did not make it sovereign or its opponents subversives. The constitution of Lebanon had been transcended by the hugeness of the crisis. Indeed, it could be said that the shelling by the *New Jersey*, the bomb attack on Bir al-Abed and the French assault on Baalbek had more of the characteristics of pure terror than the action of the Islamic Jihad. But this is just name-calling and misses the point. In the Lebanon of 1983–4 instability had reached that point where terror violence becomes just another tactic in the armoury of militias, factions and interested foreign governments. If the idea of terrorism in its Western sense had ever had any meaning in Lebanon, it suffered a blow the moment the Israelis invaded in 1982. From then on the conflict was too viciously grand to preoccupy itself with what is, after all, only one way (and not a particularly effective way) of causing death on a massive scale.

Western Vulnerabilities

Despite the complexity of the situation in Lebanon, the label 'terrorist' continued to exert a powerful grip on the imagination of the West in general and President Reagan and the Americans in particular. The way in which pure acts of terror bewitch liberal sensibilities through the intentional brutalization of indiscriminately chosen, innocent individuals has already been mentioned. The wide publication of photographs of such victims, together with interviews with their distraught families, achieves a large impact and therefore (in a democracy) an influence over policy which may be disproportionate to the harm that is being done, terrible though that harm might be. It was not surprising, therefore, that, quite apart from the low-intensity warfare at which they had shown themselves to be adept, Islamic Jihad should have chosen this method as well. It was another way of fighting 'imperialism', and bringing home to the general public other violence which, they believed, the West, blinkered by its obsession with terrorism, was resolutely ignoring.

The most dramatic event of this sort was the hijacking in June 1985 of TWA flight 847 en route to Rome from Athens, with 153 passengers and crew on board, 135 of whom were American. The affair followed the usual logic of such occasions. The flight was diverted to Beirut, where seventeen women and two children were released. After a stopover in Algiers, where more passengers were allowed to leave, the plane returned to Beirut, where a young member of the US navy, Robert Stethem, was badly beaten and then shot dead. His body was dumped on to the tarmac. When the authorities in the control tower remonstrated with the hijackers about the killing, one of them answered back, 'Did you forget the Bir al-Abed massacre?' After the men had taken on further reinforcements and made another trip to and from Algiers, matters finally came to a head in Beirut. By this time, the majority of the remaining passengers had been taken off the airliner and spirited away into the suburbs.

The Amal leader, Nabih Berri, had taken control of events. The hijackers, who were members of Islamic Jihad, had originally called for the release of seventeen prisoners held in Kuwait for complicity in a series of suicide attacks on various targets in that country in December 1983. Fourteen belonged to an Iranian-backed group based in Tehran called Al-Dawa and the remaining three were reputed to be Lebanese members of Hezbollah. The authorities in Kuwait were not inclined to bend to pressure for their release, and Berri did not push these demands very hard, not least because they were those of a rival Shia group. Instead, he concentrated on that part of Islamic Jihad's ambitions which coincided with his own. This was the demand for the freeing of over 700 southern Lebanese Shia prisoners whom the Israelis had taken captive and then transferred to jails in their own country. The detainees had simply been arbitrarily rounded up and their transfer into Israeli territory was in breach of international law. They looked rather more like hostages than prisoners; this is what they would have been called if they had been Westerners and their jailers Arab.

Berri cleverly exploited the apparent moral equivalence between these people and the TWA passengers. He spoke of the Shias having been 'kidnapped on and taken from Lebanese territory' and of Israel having 'violated the law . . . just as does any hijacking operation'.[5] At a press conference staged by Amal, one of the US passengers spoke of the Lebanese 'hostages' who have 'as equal a right and as strong a desire to go home as we do'.[6] Many days of drama along these lines ensued before the TWA Americans were handed over to the safekeeping of the Syrian army, and sent to Damascus and freedom.

The failure of the Islamic fundamentalists to secure their initial goal, the freeing of the Kuwaiti seventeen, was to lead to another hijack three years later, this time of a Kuwaiti jumbo jet en route from Thailand to Kuwait. That operation, which dragged on for over two weeks and involved fatalities among the passengers, was more brutal and more professionally executed than the TWA affair, but its only success was that the perpetrators escaped punishment. In contrast, the hijacking in 1985 could claim to have worked on two counts. First, over the following two months the Israelis did indeed release their Shia detainees, or 'hostages', into the hands of the Red Cross, just north of their border with Lebanon, though whether this was part of the deal which ended the crisis is still debated. Second, and just as importantly, the incident captured the attention of the world in exactly the way that the terror method strives to do; and having done that, it went on successfully to focus that concern not only on its own actions but also on the conduct of its enemy.

The criticisms that subsequently poured from Western terrorism experts and specialists about the undue attention the media, and in particular the television networks in the United States, gave to the hijackers miss the point that, apart from providing compelling human-interest drama, Islamic Jihad and Nabih Berri did have something interesting to say. Who in the West would have bothered with the fate of these southern Lebanese Muslims had not the lives of Americans been put in the balance against theirs? There is no point in blaming the messenger for revealing something that you would rather was kept secret. If ethical games have to be played, then surely in the scale of moral wrongdoing surrounding the TWA affair it is the case that the journalists came a poor third behind both the killers of Robert Stethem and the jailors of the Shia civilians?

The Libyan Sideshow

The TWA affair apart, 1985 saw further disturbing signs of a resurgence of the sort of international terrorism that was sufficiently bloody to be reminiscent of the peaks of 1968–74. In November 1985 an Egypt Air flight bound for Cairo from Athens was hijacked. After a fight in the cabin in mid-air had led to an emergency landing in Malta, the gunmen began to shoot the passengers (Israelis and Americans first) when they were denied fuel by the airport authorities. The Egyptian commandos standing by stormed the plane, but the action was a tragic failure, with nearly sixty people dying in a gun battle before they could gain control. Then in December 1985 came a repeat of what was one of the most terrifying of all terrorist actions: the arbitrary gun attack on an airport lounge. In two such assaults, launched simultaneously on the El Al desks at Rome and Vienna airports, twenty people died, including four of the seven gunmen involved. Five of the dead were American. Both of these incidents were traced back to the Fatah Revolutionary Council, a Palestinian rejectionist faction run by the notorious PLO renegade Abu Nidhal.

This man had for years operated under the protective umbrella of one or other of the Arab states, committing acts of violence on their behalf in places around the world where it would have been embarrassing for them to have had their complicity in such acts revealed. But Nidhal's promiscuity as a hired killer made it difficult to establish exactly for whom he was now operating. Iraq had been his patron in the 1970s, and there were allegations that the killers at Rome and Vienna had trained in Lebanon and travelled to Europe via Damascus. On the other hand, it was said that Nidhal spent most of his time in Iran.

President Reagan chose to focus US wrath on none of these countries, but rather on General Gadaffi of Libya. There was no doubt that Gadaffi was a dangerous man. He had been involved in violent subversion beyond his own borders and had waged a campaign of assassination against Libyans exiled abroad for opposition to his rule. He had been one of the most vocal of the rejectionists of the PLO's conciliatory line towards Israel, on occasion putting his rhetoric into violent practice, and had provided a base for the training of all sorts of unsavoury commando units. Gadaffi had engaged in violent squabbles with Egypt and had conducted military adventures of his own in neighbouring Chad. But with a population of no more than $3\frac{1}{2}$ million, the General was then, as he is today, a minor tyrant ruling over a tiny, backward country, but someone who can protect his people (and himself) from economic reality through the shrewd use of substantial oil revenues. It may be entirely appropriate to draw attention to the ruthlessness of the Libyan regime's involvement in 'international terrorism'. However, it is going rather far to create a vision of Gadaffi as the evil emperor of terror. Yet this is exactly what the US administration chose to do at the start of 1986. It was as though it had finally found a target upon which to vent all the impotence and rage of three years' frustration.

President Reagan had always had something of a fixation about Gadaffi. In his filmic approach to right and wrong, here was the familiar 'bad guy'. Soon after taking office, his administration closed down the Libyan mission in Washington and expelled all its serving diplomats. Then came an aerial fight over the Gulf of Sidra during which two Libyan planes were shot down. Hit squads were said to have entered the United States, and on 9 December 1981 the Deputy Secretary of State called upon 'all Americans to leave Libya as soon as possible'. On that occasion he invalidated all US passports for travel to the country. In 1982 the administration made strenuous efforts to enforce a series of economic sanctions against Libya, but when this policy met with little success, the campaign somehow faded away. Now it was revived with renewed vigour. Shortly after the Rome and Vienna attacks, the President declared Libya to be a 'threat to the national security and foreign policy of the United States'. On 7 January 1986 all Americans still living in Libya were ordered to leave immediately and President Reagan warned at a press conference that 'if these steps do not end Gadaffi's terrorism, I promise you that further steps will be taken'.[7] In late March the Americans conducted naval manoeuvres inside the disputed Gulf of Sidra and there was a brief engagement between the two forces.

Two incidents on successive days in early April provided the last straw for the Reagan administration. First, an explosion on a TWA flight from Rome to Athens blew a hole in the plane's fuselage; four Americans were sucked through and fell to their deaths. Second, a bomb explosion at the La Belle Disco in West Berlin killed three people. The club was regularly frequented by US service personnel, two of whom were among the fatalities. In so far as any blame could be allocated, the Syrians appear to have been implicated in the first of these attacks and they were, and still are, suspected by many of having orchestrated the second. It is certainly true that Syria, whose motive may have been to isolate the PLO, was actively engaged in acts of terror in Europe during the mid-1980s. This was subsequently clearly established when a Syrian surrogate was sentenced to forty-five years in jail in London in October 1986 for having arranged to blow up an El Al jet carrying 380 people. His plan had been foiled only when airport security found the bomb in the luggage of his pregnant girlfriend, whom he was allowing to go unwittingly to her death. Other incidents in Spain and Italy raised questions of Syrian involvement. However, the US administration, relying on intelligence data, declared the Berlin disco explosions to have been the work of the Libyans. Shortly afterwards, on 15 April, US warplanes retaliated for Libya's involvement in international terrorism by bombing Tripoli and Benghazi.

The raid was said to have been precise in its aim, but many of the targets appeared to have been missed. Certainly, a number of residential areas were damaged and there were fatalities. Four 2,000-lb bombs fell on the suburb of Bin Ghashir, causing more devastation than even a series of car bombs could have done. An attempt was made to blow up General Gadaffi's private residence and it was later claimed that his fifteen-month-old adopted daughter had been killed and that two of his children, aged three and four, had been injured. The exact total of casualties is not known but it was in the region of thirty-seven dead and ninety injured. If these figures are accurate, President Reagan had caused the death of more Libyans than Gadaffi had killed Americans. The justification under international law claimed for its actions by the administration was 'self-defence'. However, acting so as to prevent the occurrence of imminent violence falls under the category of self-defence, whereas punishing someone for having done something falls under the category of retribution or retaliation. President Reagan's action belonged to the second of these categories, not the first. The only defence claim that could be raised was in relation to some unspecified type of violence against unspecified victims in some unspecified place at some unspecified time in the future.

With the raid, the word 'terrorism' lost even more of the credibility that it might have had in its application to Middle Eastern affairs. The European and US political and academic response to the attack demonstrated the lack of even-handedness in Western definitions of the subject. For why was the air strike not viewed as an act of terrorism? If it had been an assault by a substate subversive group, it would have fallen squarely within traditional definitions. Thus, if the PFLP had attacked Tel Aviv in this way, it would have been so defined. If such a group's attack had been supported by a state, it would then have been called 'international terrorism'. The Americans escaped this categorization for the same reason that Israel invariably does: their violence was authorized by a government and was executed by the *official* armed forces of a state. The reward for using their full power in this way – with all the greater efficiency in terms of killing that it implies – is to have the label 'terrorist' rendered inapplicable to them. It is doubtful whether the West could have brought itself to castigate the action as terrorist even if the Americans had somehow (and improbably) contrived to have the work done on their behalf by some freelance militia – say, a Christian Phalangist commando unit based in Beirut. It is equally improbable that, had General Gadaffi 'defended himself from further attack' by bombing the White House, there would have been any hesitancy in declaring the action that of an 'international terrorist'. But it is instructive to recognize that, in theory at least, the Western categorization as 'terrorist' seems to depend on just these points.

In truth, the label 'international terrorist' has ceased to have a coherent meaning. Logic has taken second place to politics. In his penetrating study of the subject, Professor Grant Wardlaw is highly critical of the way the data on international terrorism has been employed:

[W]hat is noteworthy is that, for those terrorist acts which might reasonably be thought of as having major implications for international relations, the evidence for Libyan involvement is not generally of a significantly better quality than that available for, say, Syrian sponsorship. That is, it is based on similarities, known connections between individuals and organizations, reasonable assumptions, and an informed opinion about what the sponsor would hope to gain by the act. By the very nature of such information, assertions based on it are liable to one of two errors of interpretation. Either the evidence is downplayed because of the difficulty of proving the connections and of the difficult political consequences which may ensue, or it is overplayed as every possible inference and hint of conspiracy is given full rein. What seems to determine the end of the spectrum to which evaluation of the evidence will go is a complex combination of the presumed political fall-out of determining sponsor status, and the ease and relative safety with which an accuser can take action against an accused.[8]

General Gadaffi, therefore, was not just the 'bad guy'; he was the accessible 'bad guy': 'It seems, on the face of it, that what distinguished Libya in American eyes was its foolhardy bragging about support of terrorism. In fact, its relative weakness made it the ideal sponsor of which to make an example through retaliatory measures.'[9]

The exasperation of the serious academic at the capture of his subject by the politicians comes clearly to the surface in Professor Wardlaw's analysis of the US approach to states said to be supporting terrorism:

The list of such countries continually grows and changes, with the changes often appearing to be related directly to the political needs of the US. Thus, Syria was identified as a direct supporter of terrorism in an official statement of March 1985, but was conspicuously absent from those supporters identified in President Reagan's speech of July 1985. This speech followed the release, facilitated by Syria, of American hostages taken during the hijacking of TWA Flight 847 in June 1985. However, Syria again resumed its high profile on America's list of terrorist sponsors following Great Britain's call for action against Syria as a result of evidence of continuing Syrian involvement in acts of international terrorism.

The case of Syria illustrates how the concept of state-sponsored terrorism and the evidence for it, lacks clarity and is used politically. In June 1986, US officials concluded that 'although Syria's involvement in terrorism may be 'much more professional, much more deadly' than Libya's, the evidence remains murky about Syria's direct links to recent acts of violence'. Yet only five months later the State Department was confident enough of the evidence to release a list of 46 terrorist incidents claimed to have links to Syria. In an accompanying statement, the Department said that the list was 'not intended to be all-inclusive but is illustrative of Syria's involvement in and support for terrorism and terrorist groups'.[10]

The reluctance to act in relation to Syria lay not only in the fact of its strategic importance in the Middle East but also in what the United States understood to be its power to control or at least to influence events surrounding the Western hostages held in Beirut. Exactly the same involvement immunized Iran from attack. Gadaffi had no such protective currency. Before considering the taking of these hostages and the effect it eventually had on the Reagan administration's already bizarre doubletalk about terrorism, we may observe one final irony about the US raid on Tripoli: Gadaffi was bombed not so much because he was a 'terrorist' but rather because, without any hostages, he had not been 'terrorist' enough.

The Hostage Crisis

Hostage-taking has been endemic in Lebanon since the civil war of 1975–6. However, Westerners were not vulnerable until the Israeli invasion in 1982. Even then, very few were abducted for some years. The acting President of the American University in Beirut, David Dodge, was kidnapped in 1982 and held for several months, apparently in Iran, before being freed. It seems that he was taken in order to compel the release of three Iranian diplomats who had been seized earlier by Christian Phalangists, although a bargain on these lines does not appear to have been concluded; indeed, the terms (if any) that secured the American's liberty have never been made public. While the marines were drawing their Lebanese nightmare to a close in early 1984, Dodge's replacement at the University, Malcolm Kerr, was shot dead on his own campus by Islamic Jihad. The CIA's station chief in Beirut, William Buckley, was abducted by the same group in March of that year (he was later to die in captivity as a result of severe maltreatment by his interrogators). Two other men taken in 1984, an American academic, Frank Regier, and a French construction engineer, Christian Joubert, were freed after the intervention of Nabih Berri's Amal organization, although another, the American pastor Benjamin Weir, was seized in May 1984. A British reporter, Jonathan Wright, was abducted in August but he escaped after only nineteen days and in February 1985 another newsman, Jeremy Levin, managed to free himself after nearly a year in captivity. By the time of his return, Weir's continuing incarceration, together with the abduction of two more Americans, Peter Kilburn, a librarian at the American University, and Father Laurence Jenco, a Catholic priest, had shown the kidnappings to be more serious than a passing phase in Lebanon's continuing anarchy.

Whether coincidentally or otherwise, the real escalation came in March 1985, after the Bir al-Abed car bomb attack on Sheikh Fadlallah had killed eighty people near the office of the Hezbollah spiritual leader. The CIA were blamed for this atrocity, and within a week of its occurrence two British industrialists, Brian Levick and Geoffrey Nash, were kidnapped, only for both men to be released when their captors realized they were not from the United States. Two French citizens were dealt with likewise at the same time. Eight days after the car bomb, the Beirut bureau chief for Associated Press, the American Terry Anderson, was abducted, as were two French diplomats, Marcel Fontaine and Marcel Carton, neither of whom was released quickly, as their compatriots had been. A British writer working with the United Nations, Alec Collett, was also taken. In May two more Frenchmen, Michel Seurat (who was later to die in captivity) and Jean-Paul Kauffmann, a journalist, were abducted, as was another American, the Director of the American University hospital, David Jacobsen. In June the Scottish-born Acting Dean of Agriculture at the same university, Thomas Sutherland, was kidnapped. In September an Italian businessman disappeared. It soon became apparent that Islamic Jihad or Hezbollah were behind the vast majority of the seizures, though Alec Collett appeared to have fallen into the hands of the Abu Nidhal organization.

The list of hostages continued to grow with merciless abandon through 1986 and afterwards, though now such vaguely named groups as the

Revolutionary Justice Organization and the Islamic Holy War for the Liberation of Palestine had emerged to share the responsibility, although it was probable that both had links with Hezbollah. A French businessman, Marcel Coudari, was taken in February 1986 and held for nine months; three Spanish embassy officials spent short periods as hostages at the same time. In March 1986 a four-man French television crew was abducted, as were two British academics, Leigh Douglas and Philip Padfield. Other French citizens to be kidnapped at this time were a teacher, Michel Brian, and a car dealer, Camille Sontag, though both were released by the end of the year. (As though to compensate, the French journalist Roger Auque was taken early in 1987.) Shortly after the United States' Libyan raid, which had been launched from air bases in England, two British passport holders, Brian Keenan and John McCarthy, were seized, the latter while on the road to Beirut airport and safety. In January 1987 two West Germans, Rudolf Cordes and Alfred Schmidt, were abducted. By the end of that year, all Westerners in Lebanon had become targets, regardless of their job, their nationality or their political views, and all such foreigners had reason to fear being whisked away into the bleak oblivion of Beirut or its southern hinterland.

Kidnapping is always a gruesome experience, but for the victims of Islamic Jihad and Hezbollah, it has been peculiarly awful. As those who have emerged alive have testified, the hostages are held in squalid surroundings, with little consideration being given to their personal wellbeing or the fears and concerns of their grieving families. Sensory deprivation is the norm and the victims can go months without making any visual or aural contact with a living soul other than their jailors. No relationship is allowed to develop between the captor and the captive. The hostages are denied all contact with the outside world, yet are often required to record or write extravagant and ungrammatical demands on their captors' behalf. David Jacobsen had to write a letter comparing his allegedly neglected plight with that of a US journalist who was then being held in the Soviet Union and for whose release the Americans were at the time furiously working. Jacobsen's captors beat him for sending coded messages when their own misspellings were analysed by the world's press.[11] Over the whole period of detention lie two dreadful realities: release may never come and death is not much less likely than the next meal. Like the urban guerrillas of Latin America and George Habash's PFLP during its time of maximum destructiveness, the kidnappers in Beirut have forgotten the man in their hatred of the nation from which he comes. Such dehumanization leads to brutalization and turns the life of a hostage into a long, uncertain vacuum of fear.

The taking of Westerners in Lebanon fulfils many of the criteria of pure terror. The class of person vulnerable is very wide, and the choice of victims within that group appears to be quite arbitrary. The experience is terrifying for the individual hostages, their families and their friends. The plight of the victims, whose faces and whose dependants appear regularly in the media, grips Western attention in much the same way as do plane hijacks or embassy sieges. The purpose of these acts of terror, however, is not necessarily to achieve a platform for the communication of a grievance, though this may often be a consequence. As we would expect, Lebanese hostage-taking is more complex than simple analogies with other jurisdictions would allow.

Various motives for the seizures are discernible. First, and it is not to be underestimated, there is the financial factor. It seems clear that at least some of the later kidnappings were the work of freelance groups intent upon ransoming their hapless Western prizes to the highest bidders. The fate of their victims would then depend on the outcome of the auctions. Quite apart from such independent operations, it seems that the politically motivated kidnappers are also not immune to the right financial offer. It has been widely reported that Alfred Schmidt, one of the two West Germans taken in 1987, was released after the payment of a substantial ransom and the provision of medical supplies to Shia communities in southern Beirut. The Bonn government denied direct involvement but the possibility of a private financial package remained.

Second, a hostage can be punished for what his captors or his buyers regard as the misbehaviour of his government. Thus, after the bombing of Tripoli, the two British teachers abducted just a couple of weeks before, Leigh Douglas and Philip Padfield, were killed, as were both Alec Collett and the American Peter Kilburn. It was the kidnappers' way of retaliating against President Reagan and Mrs Thatcher.

The third motive, which is the most prevalent, regards the seizure of hostages as a bargaining chip in a battle to secure defined aims from Western or Arab governments, or the Israelis. Many of the early hostages, including the Reverend Benjamin Weir and Terry Anderson, were taken by Islamic Jihad in order to compel the release of seventeen Al-Dawa and Hezbollah prisoners held in Kuwait on bombing charges (these were the same detainees whose freedom had been called for by the hijackers of TWA Flight 847).

The demands of the kidnappers have, however, changed over the years. The release of the Iranian diplomats taken in 1982 (the event which motivated the Dodge kidnap) has been dragged out from time to time, despite the widespread belief that these unfortunate men have been dead for some time. More recently, the kidnappers have used their bargaining position to focus attention on conditions in Khiam prison. This notorious jail contains some 300 Lebanese Shias, held without charge or trial in unspeakable conditions of brutality by Israel's proxy militia, the South Lebanon Army. The inmates 'are forbidden to speak, and are drenched with cold water if they disobey. They are hooded whenever they leave the windowless, stone cells, which contain nothing but a plastic toilet bucket.'[12] Torture allegations are frequently made, and some of the detainees have been incarcerated for as long as the longest Western hostage, making the decision to contrive a linkage between their fate and the hostages' release understandable if not logical or excusable.

It remains to be seen how high a price the kidnappers can exact for the hostages that remain. Already, however, the unorthodox international diplomacy practised by Islamic Jihad has proved itself a most useful adjunct to Tehran's foreign policy. When they have picked their nationalities and their moment with care, they have achieved many small victories. The West German captives, for example, were taken to coerce the Federal Republic into resisting US demands for the extradition of Mohammed Hamadei, a man who had been detained by the Germans on suspicion of involvement in the TWA hijack. The Germans decided against extradition. Then, when Hamadei's brother was facing charges arising out of the kidnappings themselves, one of the German hostages was used by the extremists in order to intimidate the court into giving the man a light sentence. The blackmail did not work on this occasion, since the court handed down a long prison sentence, regardless of the jeopardy in which this placed the remaining hostage.

The French have also shown themselves inclined to regard the seizure of their citizens as more of an opening move in a bargaining game than an untouchable act of terror. In November 1987 two of their nationals, Jean-Louis Normandin and Roger Auque, were freed. Their liberty came at around the same time as the occurrence of a complex series of diplomatic manoeuvres: the sieges of the French embassy in Tehran and the Iranian embassy in Paris were lifted; an Iranian suspected of involvement in a bombing campaign in France in 1986 was permitted to return to Tehran; and a portion of France's long frozen debts to the Shah's Iran was repaid.

Many people suspected that these events were linked, especially when it was alleged that a very large sum of money was also paid over by way of ransom.[13]

Just before the French presidential elections of 1988 the three remaining French hostages, Carton, Fontaine and Kauffmann, emerged alive, and there was widespread suspicion at the time that a new secret deal had been successfully negotiated. After the earlier breakthroughs, the main tension in Franco–Iranian affairs now related to the long terms of imprisonment handed down by a French court in 1982 to a Hezbollah hit squad which had killed two French citizens during a bungled attempt to assassinate an exiled former prime minister of Iran. (A widespread bombing campaign that drove Paris into a state of panic in 1986 was thought to have been intended to put pressure on the government to release the men.) On the eve of the traditional summer holidays in 1990, two years after the release of the French hostages, President Mitterrand freed the hit squad and arranged for its speedy removal to Tehran. It seemed that hostage-taking had worked where explosives had not.

Not all countries have reacted with the non-violent diplomatic pragmatism of the French and the Germans. The British have made a public virtue of refusing even to talk to the hostage-takers and have thereby greatly reduced the chances of a speedy release for any of their own citizens. The USSR reacted in an entirely different way. When four Soviets were seized in September 1985, its response was alleged to have been to abduct a relative of one of the supposed kidnappers and mutilate him, sending bits of his fingers to his family. The three captives who remained alive (the fourth had been shot dead soon after they were seized) were quickly freed and the Soviets were not threatened again. In a similar vein, the Israelis have kidnapped two leading members of Hezbollah, Daud Qashfi and Sheikh Obeid, in the hope of securing the freedom of six Israelis believed to be alive in detention in Lebanon. Most extraordinary of all has been the conduct of the Americans. All the time that President Reagan was condemning 'international terrorism', exhorting the world to stand firm against this unique form of evil, castigating the Greeks and the French for weakness and orchestrating his assault on Libya, his administration was not only happily talking to the biggest 'international terrorist' of them all, the Iranians, but was also trading arms with them via Israel, in the hope that this would lead Hezbollah to release the Americans held hostage in Beirut.

Presumably the Iranians could not believe their luck. They took the guns and three Americans (Father Jenco, Reverend Weir and David Jacobsen) were freed. By the time the last of these men was out, Hezbollah had already restocked their supplies by grabbing three more Americans, Frank Reed, the Director of the Lebanese International School in west Beirut, Joseph Cicippio, the Financial Controller at the American University, and Edward Tracy, an author. The Arab Revolutionary Cells and the Revolutionary Justice Organization both claimed responsibility. So the number of hostages remained constant, the only difference being that Iran had secured tremendous supplies of weaponry from Washington. Islamic Jihad for the Liberation of Palestine then kidnapped three American professors at Beirut University College, Alann Steen, Jesse Jonathan Turner and Robert Polhill. Terry Waite, a British negotiator who had attempted to mediate between Islamic Jihad and elements within the Reagan administration, was also abducted.

Many members of Tehran's government would no doubt have been happy to see this sort of relationship with the United States continue, but it was spoilt by a leak to a Lebanese magazine. This led eventually to the revelations that were to become known to the world as the Irangate affair. The final irony lay in the involvement of the Contra rebels of Nicaragua. It transpired that the profits from selling arms to Iran were being diverted to fund the activities of a group of renegade subversives whose bloody conduct in central America made Islamic Jihad seem altogether squeamish. But they were not 'terrorists' because President Reagan was on their side.

A Confusion of Violence

Since the Irangate scandal, the violence in Lebanon has continued to defy categorization and has gone round and round in ever more brutal circles. The hostage crisis has been exacerbated by many new seizures and ameliorated by the occasional release or escape. There have been further killings of Westerners and numerous false dawns when it has seemed that the release of one or other of the remaining men was imminent.

Meanwhile, by the end of the 1980s factional fighting had gone through every conceivable permutation, as though the militias were anxious to demonstrate to the world the full extent of the anarchy they had achieved. One of the most ludicrous was the pointless conflagration which blew apart what remained of the Christian communities of east Beirut. The argument was between the maverick Christian general Michel Aoun and the 'official' forces of the State of Lebanon, represented by the Phalangist Samir Geagea and President Elias Hrawi. The bloodiness of this fraternal conflict was an eloquent comment on the brutalized, apolitical stupidity of these erstwhile allies; finding no one else they could fight, they fought each other. In west Beirut Amal shelled into even further oblivion the already destroyed, ramshackle camps into which the surviving Palestinians had huddled. Berri's militancy was a manifestation of Syria's strategic effort to destroy altogether the PLO presence in Lebanon. To this end there was also perpetual fighting between forces loyal to Yasser Arafat and the rejectionist Palestinian factions sponsored by President Assad, of which Saiqa, Fatah Uprising and the PFLP-GC led by Ahmad Jibril were the most prominent. Having survived these assaults, the PLO themselves led a determined campaign in the summer of 1990 to crush the Fatah Revolutionary Council (led by Abu Nidhal) presence in southern Lebanon.

With so many violent groups around it would have been surprising if some were not available for hire, and it now seems that the PFLP-GC, on loan to the Iranians, were behind the most serious atrocity yet to afflict the West as a by-product of violence in the Middle East. This was the December 1988 blowing up of a crowded jumbo jet, Pan Am Flight 103, en route from Frankfürt via London to New York. The plane crashed into the Scottish town of Lockerbie, killing many of its inhabitants as well as all the passengers and crew on board the flight. It was suspected that Iran, through the actions of its proxy, was exacting revenge for the shooting down of an Iranian airbus over the Gulf by a US cruiser earlier in the year.

Finally, in Beirut and to the south of the country, Amal fought with Hezbollah over which of the two groups should have the right to represent the Shia Muslims. The fact that each organization had its own state sponsor (Syria and Iran respectively) meant that the militia leaders involved could afford the luxury of intransigence. A point of difference between them lay in their attitude to Israel: Hezbollah was more hostile to its Jewish neighbour and therefore more inclined to launch bombardments and other attacks into it; Amal rejected this policy because of the retaliatory air raids it provoked from Israel. Many such aerial attacks by the Israeli defence forces occurred in 1989 alone, and at least some of these caused fatalities. By the end of the decade, therefore, the quarrel was exactly where it had been nine years before, except that Hezbollah had joined the Palestinians in the role of Israel's intractable, 'terrorist' neighbour. It was as though Operation Peace in Galilee had never been.

In another uncanny recycling of history, the PLO began in the penultimate year of the decade to seek through diplomacy the political breakthrough which their fedayeen warriors had never managed to achieve. The positive international response to their 1988 peace initiative was reminiscent of the heady days of 1974, but there were new and vital conciliatory elements to it. First, the PLO now accepted that there would be a 'two-state' solution to the Palestinian question, meaning that they now effectively recognized Israel's right to exist. Second, the initiative brought to an end all PLO cross-border raids into northern Israel from Lebanon. While this decision commanded the support of a wider range of Palestinians than had been the case in 1974, it was as true in 1988 as it had been then that a small number of rejectionists can do a lot of damage, especially if they are backed by the might of an Arab nation and enthusiastically talked up by Tel Aviv authorities intent on ignoring the changes within the PLO.

Just as in the 1970s, and with the same apparent inevitability, a series of violent acts put the organization's new diplomatic face under pressure. In July 1989, fifteen people died when a Palestinian passenger grabbed the steering-wheel of the bus he was travelling in and drove down a ravine. Islamic Jihad claimed responsibility for the attack. In February 1990 a machine-gun and grenade assault on Israeli tourists in Egypt left eight dead and nineteen wounded. In April a bomb attack on a Jerusalum market claimed one fatality. Finally, an attack on the Israeli coastline by Abu Abbas's Iraqi-backed Palestine Liberation Front (PLF) led the Americans to cease all diplomatic contacts with the PLO. Abbas was a particularly sensitive figure in US circles, because he had been behind the 1985 hijacking of the pleasure cruiser *Achille Lauro*, a classic act of terror during which a US tourist, the invalid Leon Klinghoffer, had been killed.

By the summer of 1990 the PLO had not seen any tangible returns for their two-year flirtation with appeasement. Their neutral position over Iraq's invasion of Kuwait may well presage a return to militancy.

Conclusion

The 'terrorism' of Abu Abbas undid Arafat in US eyes. The Bush administration used the term with as much conviction and as little regard for context as had the Reagan presidency before it. The manipulation of the word throughout the 1980s appeared to have had little detrimental effect on its political utility as an insult.

Despite the disasters of the decade and increased divisions within their own society, the governments headed by Yitzhak Shamir and Menachem Begin remained preoccupied with the terrorist label. They refused to countenance the possibility that the 'terrorist' PLO could be negotiated with. From 1987 Israel concerned itself with 'the war on terrorism' in the occupied territories. The rest of the world called it by its Arab name, *intifada*, meaning 'uprising', and saw the oppressed conditions in which the inhabitants of the West Bank and Gaza Strip were forced to live. Western public opinion refused to affix damning Israeli labels on youths whose only act of defiance was the systematic throwing of stones. This was terrorism to the authorities and it had to be dealt with militarily, not politically. Accordingly, in the first three years of the *intifada*, Israeli soldiers shot dead over 600 Palestinians. Stones were routinely met with rounds of live ammunition and rubber bullets. According to a Save the Children report published in 1990, 159 children were killed in the first two years of the revolt. The average age of the children shot dead was twelve and a half. The report stated that more than half of those killed were neither participating in nor in the vicinity of any protest activity. Save the Children also drew attention to the facts that nearly a quarter of all child deaths were the result of exposure to tear gas and three-quarters of these victims were infants. It estimated that in the two-year period under study 30,000 children (one-third of them under ten years of age) had needed medical treatment after beatings received in the course of the *intifada*. The Israeli Justice Ministry has drawn attention to its belief that 'children of all ages are recruited by the PLO and extremist Islamic elements to participate in street violence . . . Thus it is the inciters who must ultimately be held responsible for the injury and death of rioting children.'[14] In twenty years Middle Eastern 'terrorism' had come a long way.

7   The Pseudo-colonials

So far our journey through the complexities of violence and terror in the Middle East has led us to the depressing conclusion that the word 'terrorism' does not help us properly to understand the issues afflicting the region. However, this is not to say that it has no value anywhere else. Everything depends on context, and the manipulation of the concept in the Middle East should not prevent us from analysing other problems of violent subversion in terms of terror, if this is appropriate.

As has been stressed, the Middle East in general and the Palestinian question in particular are unusual in that 'terrorism' as the West understands it is but one element in a much larger equation of violence. Politically motivated violent subversion which is unconnected with the Middle East, however, usually occurs in liberal societies which are quite unused to bloodshed of this sort and on this scale. This was the point exploited by the PFLP in the early 1970s. Since then, such instability has persisted in Europe and has spread to the Indian subcontinent. In this and the following chapter, we consider the nationalistic violence of the Tamil Tigers in Sri Lanka, the militant Sikh groups in India, the Basque separatists in Spain and the IRA in Northern Ireland, attempting in each case to recognize linkages between them, without in any sense losing sight of the differences of their respective contexts.

For much of the developing world, the violence generated by guerrilla warfare remains respectable. The phrase evokes images of conflict which many new nations inextricably link with their own struggles for an escape from colonial rule. Thus in 1977 the United Nations concluded a protocol to the Geneva Conventions of 12 August 1949 which widened the definition of 'international armed conflict' to include 'armed conflicts in which peoples are fighting against colonial domination and alien occupation and against racist regimes in the exercise of their right of self-determination . . .'[1] This went a long way towards legitimizing genuine guerrilla campaigns. The protocol envisaged the application of the rules of humanitarian law to such conflicts as well as to the more widely accepted situation of war between nations. This reflected the respect in which genuine liberation movements, such as the ANC and the PLO, were held. Those special cases apart, however, few such relatively straightforward struggles remain today. The liberation wars being fought by Mozambique and Angola at the time the protocol was drafted have ended; the principle of national self-determination has won a comprehensive victory. However, this has not stopped a number of contemporary subversive organizations from conducting campaigns of violence in the manner of old-style liberation movements struggling to discard an alien or colonial yoke. The IRA and ETA see themselves as third-world fighters in a first-world context. In developing nations which have recently emerged from colonial domination, similar groups seek what they see as further decolonization within already decolonized countries. Their question for the indigenous leaders is a simple but challenging one: why stop at the borders inherited at the moment of freedom? The gist of the argument, consciously or unconsciously presented, is that the principle of self-determination which brought the country its freedom should now be applied with equal force to some community or group within the new nation which is distinguishable on ethnic, religious or linguistic grounds.

The Tamil Tigers

This separatist pressure has been particularly evident, to tragic effect, in Sri Lanka (formerly Ceylon), an island nation about the size of Ireland lying just south of India. The country has a population of some 16 millions, of whom about three-quarters are Sinhalese and rather less than one-fifth Tamils. These racial labels reflect a religious divide also, the Sinhalese being Buddhist and the Tamils being generally Hindu. The rest of the population is made up of a smattering of Muslims and Christians. The old Ceylon gave every appearance of having benefited from colonial influence, under first the Portugese, then the Dutch and finally (until independence in 1948) the British. The constitution promulgated by the new nation after the Second World War sought to preserve the tranquillity of the past by combining a Westminster style of government with guarantees of civil and cultural rights for the minority Tamils, who lived mainly in the north of the country, and who through a combination of competence and patronage had thrived in the colonial atmosphere. However, in the two decades that followed, successive administrations of a predominantly Sinhalese persuasion set out to redress the balance of unfair advantage which they believed the Tamils had achieved under British rule.

There was some truth in this point but it could not possibly have justified the enthusiasm which was brought to the task of relegating Tamil status within Ceylonese society. In 1956 the Prime Minister, Solomon West Ridgeway Bandaranaike, declared the Sinhalese tongue to be the national language and, when the Tamils demonstrated in protest, the forces of the state replied with aggressive repression. Quotas on Tamil employees were introduced into many walks of life, including government, education and the professions, with the result that by 1980 the Tamils held only one-tenth of the jobs in government, whereas twenty-five years before they had held nearly half. For a people who had once been the key bureaucrats of British rule, this was hard to bear.

During the late 1960s and the 1970s the economic situation declined and the hardship that this caused within the country threw into sharper relief the communal tensions that the political leaders of all the parties had so recklessly provoked. In 1971 a revolutionary organization on the Sinhalese side, the JVP, launched an insurrection which was suppressed only at a cost of at least 2,000 lives (the exact figure is uncertain). Shortly afterwards a group of Tamils calling themselves the Liberation Tigers of Tamil Eelam began to demand an independent state to the north and east. These Tamil Tigers, as they quickly came to be known, initially did little more than flex their military muscles with the occasional robbery and assassination, their most notable endeavour in these formative years being the killing of the mayor of the Tamil town of Jaffna in 1975.

The real escalation came in 1983. Thirteen Sinhalese soldiers were killed in an attack on Jaffna, after which 140 people, most of them Tamils, died in JVP-inspired riots in the capital Colombo and other cities. This disordered display of vengeance polarized the communities, just as the Tigers hoped it would. By 1985, armed, equipped and trained by the Indians, whose own large population of Tamils (encouraged by Mrs Gandhi) had begun to sympathize with their plight, the Tigers had grown into a formidable fighting force, capable not only of acts of sacrilegious terror (such as the murder of 150 Sinhalese at a sacred Buddhist shrine in May 1985) but also of military strategies which had brought much of the northern part of the island under their control. During 1986 and 1987 the spiral of violence gained a frenzied momentum of its own. The bombing of an aircraft in 1986 killed fifteen people, most of them tourists. Explosives on buses became a favourite ploy. In April 1987 the Tigers commandeered a group of buses travelling together, picked out the Sinhalese from among the passengers and shot all of them dead, not sparing even the women and children. The fatalities were in excess of 100, a level that was matched four days later when the Tigers set off an explosion at Colombo central bus station. In June of the same year twenty-nine Buddhist monks were killed in another bus attack.

This extraordinarily brutal strategy of provocation was reminiscent of the urban guerrilla theories of Latin America, though neither the writers from that region, like Carlos Marighela, nor the practitioners of such subversion, like the Tupamaros, could possibly have envisaged their being implemented in this homicidal fashion. Not for the first time, national fervour was proving itself a crueller taskmaster than the humanist radicalism propounded by scrupulous intellectuals. In Sri Lanka the tactic of destabilization, so savagely applied, had its desired effect. In the atmosphere of crisis and panic which the Tigers' brutality had engendered, the government launched a full-scale assault by land and air on the Tigers-controlled northern regions. This had the inevitable effect of drawing the Indians into the conflict: first, as the providers of humanitarian relief, and second, because the alternative was an invasion to protect their fellow Tamils, as the suppliers of troops invited in as peacekeepers by the Colombo authorities.

Initially the Indian involvement presaged a settlement containing much of what the Tigers had long been campaigning for. In return for a truce to be policed by Indian troops, the government promised Tamil autonomy for the north and east. The significance of this offer was that it extended to territories which were disputed between Sinhalese and Tamil and also covered the important harbour of Trincomalee. In addition, Tamil and English were to be made equal in status with the Sinhalese language.

Breathtaking in the range of its compromises, this 1987 Sri Lankan offer represents the furthest point a national government has ever gone in its attempt to satisfy the demands of a subversive group that had pushed its political goals to the surface through the systematic practice of terror tactics. Despite the unprecedented extent of this olive branch, however, the initiative was a failure. With reluctance, and under considerable Indian pressure, the Tigers accepted what was effectively their triumph, but the peace this brought was short-lived. Within two months, thirteen of their men committed suicide after being caught attempting to smuggle a large quantity of arms into Sri Lanka. The Tigers immediately called off their truce, and returned to killing with renewed vigour, and since then the situation on the island has continued to deteriorate.

The fighting has had many strands. First, the Tigers ruthlessly extirpated rival Tamil movements whose existence threatened their monopoly on subversive activity in the north. Even before the truce had formally ended, it was reported that they had killed over 100 members of such groups.

Second, they relaunched their guerrilla campaign and took control once again of Jaffna. This involved them in open conflict with the Indian troops, who at their highest point on the island numbered over 60,000. The Tigers held Jaffna against the might of this army for seventeen days, and in that and other confrontations inflicted fatalities on the foreign force which official estimates put at 530 in the first year alone. Indian efforts to train a rival Tamil force to counter the Tigers, and thereby facilitate a withdrawal of Indian forces, were unsuccessful.

Third, the Tigers continued their deliberate campaign of terror against the Sinhalese communities in those eastern provinces which had been included in the ill-fated government peace plan. On more than one occasion they entered Buddhist villages and shot every person they could find. In March 1988 they blew up a truck, killing nineteen people. In April a bus explosion led to twenty-six deaths. The list of atrocities includes far more than these gory highlights. The tactic worked, and by the summer of 1988 much of the Sinhalese population of Trincomalee had fled from the fighting. Provincial elections in November 1988 produced a Tamil administration in the north, but it existed only under the umbrella of Indian protection and within a year had little to govern, the Tigers having reasserted control over much of their notional jurisdiction. Having achieved their military goals, and retained popularity within the Tamil community, the Tigers announced in 1989 the setting up of a political wing, the People's Front of Liberation Tigers, to capitalize on the gains their violence had achieved. After a truce the fighting continued during 1990, with 538 people being reported killed in a ten-day sequence of atrocities in the eastern province. Many more died in a government assault on Jaffna, aimed at relieving the fort there, which had been besieged by the Tigers for three months.

Meanwhile, in the south the government's ill-fated autonomy plan of 1987, and its connivance at an Indian presence on Sri Lankan soil, immediately led to a renewal of JVP violence. In the six months after the signing of the accord some 200 officials, police officers and civilians were killed, and during 1988 an escalation of the JVP's war with the Sri Lankan army, together with strikes and a failure of public services, threatened to destroy altogether the nation's infrastructure and industry, its thriving tourism having already largely disappeared. Some estimates put the number of killings in the Sinhalese provinces during 1989 at over 5,000. The government has been accused by Amnesty International of being behind many of the fatalities in all parts of the country. The organization recognizes that the opposition groups 'have themselves committed atrocious crimes' but calls on the authorities not to 'use this as an excuse for brutality that violates basic rights'.[2]

Clearly Sri Lankan violence has involved some of the most extreme examples of intercommunal brutality that has ever been seen anywhere in the world. The conduct of both the Tigers and JVP seems at first glance to fall into most Western definitions of terrorism. The groups are substate, the killings are random, civilians are involved and the systematic nature of the atrocities strikes terror into the open-ended categories of innocent people on both sides who fear that they may be the next victims. And yet there is a key element missing. The vast scale of the violence and the barely comprehensible number of casualties indicate that there is something rather worse than classic terrorism going on here. For, as has already been mentioned, the essence of the act of terror is the use of symbolic violence in order to communicate a message to a wider audience. As Brian Jenkins from the Rand Corporation has remarked, the terrorists want people watching; they do not want people dead. This fits the hijack, the hostage seizure, even the attack on the airport lounge, but it is hardly relevant to killing on the scale that has occurred in Sri Lanka. The Tigers may be intent on terrorizing when they massacre an entire village, but the message is no more sophisticated than an intimidatory 'clear out or you will be next', aimed at the neighbours, not the US networks. The bloodshed may have coherent aims – the physical separation of Sinhalese and Tamil communities; the forced evacuation of Sinhalese villagers; the polarization of society; the provoking of government into overreaction – but the winning of a hearing and of public sympathy are distinctly not among them. The Tigers are making pogroms, not propaganda. Furthermore, they are a military force as well as the killers of innocent people: they have engaged government forces, resisted the Indians during the siege of Jaffna and retained physical control over large tracts of territory. If labels matter, it would be better to describe the Tigers as a guerrilla force that uses the tactic of terror as a means of extending control over its hinterland and as a strategy to destabilize the government which it opposes. They cause terror, and are – to that extent – 'terrorists', but to use the word, with all the Western academic theory that it carries with it, does not help achieve a better understanding of the breakdown of central authority in Sri Lanka.

Violence in the Punjab

There are some similarities between the instability in Sri Lanka and the violence in that other great area of unrest in the region, the Punjab in India. Like the Tamils, the Sikhs are a distinct people within their nation. The religion they follow dates from the fifteenth century and involves an amalgam of the Hindu and Muslim faiths. It accepts the monotheism of Islam but also believes in the Hindu notion of reincarnation, though without accepting the latter's caste system. Early in their history the Sikhs took root in the Punjab. The fifth guru wrote the key holy text, the Granth, while sitting by the banks of a large pool called Amritsar. In the middle of this sacred pool was built the Golden Temple, called Harimandir, or Temple of God. The tenth (and last) guru of the faith handed down the instructions which have over time confirmed the followers of his faith in their distinctive identity. All the men are required to allow their hair to grow and are also expected to take the name of Singh, meaning 'lion'. In this guru's time the men were also to carry a dagger on their person. These stipulations were designed to prevent the Sikhs from drifting back into Hinduism, and the coreligionists have indeed lived in harmony for centuries. When independence after the Second World War led to the partition of the Punjab between India and Pakistan, the Sikhs and the Muslims became embroiled in a most terrible series of mutually reciprocated atrocities, but the Hindus were not involved. For thirty-five years the Sikhs thrived in the new Republic. Unlike the Ceylonese Tamils, they were neither economically oppressed nor politically marginalized within the new dispensation. Far from it. By the start of the 1980s they had a secure and prosperous niche within the Punjab, where the fact that a majority of the people shared their faith provided yet further security and another point of difference with the vulnerable Hindu islanders to the south.

How such a successful situation could plummet into bloody chaos by the end of the decade can be no more than partly explained, and even then only by careful regard to local factors. There has always been a fundamentalist faction expressing the perennial fears of some Sikhs that their religion is being swamped by modernity. A language movement surfaced in the 1950s and in 1981 the Sikhs' political party, the Akali Dal, issued a series of demands for a greater say in the running of the Punjab. An extremist group, led by Sant Jarnail Singh Bhindranwale, emerged and, harking back to a 'golden age' at the start of the nineteenth century when the Sikhs had governed all of the Punjab, they began to demand ever-increasing powers on the Sikhs' behalf. In these early years Bhindranwale was actively encouraged by Mrs Gandhi, in the hope that this would damage the Akali Dal, which she thought of as her real political enemy in the state. Like her decision to arm the Tamil Tigers, this move was to have tragic consequences, for the extremists, once established, could not long be controlled. In time their increasingly ambitious programme included calls for an independent Sikh state of Khalistan, something which could never be accepted by the New Delhi authorities.

The strident certainty that suffused their demands made it only a matter of time before violence erupted. Indeed, as early as 1981 militant Sikhs had hijacked an Air India Boeing 737 with 117 passengers and crew on board, but the operation was not a success since the Pakistani authorities overpowered the gunmen involved shortly after the plane landed at Lahore. Such a conventional terror incident was not typical. The Sikh extremists did not grow into 'international terrorists' in the Middle Eastern mode. Their violence during the 1980s resembled more closely that of the Tigers, though they never came to assume the guerrilla status achieved by that group in northern Sri Lanka. In October 1983 a bus full of Hindus was stopped and the passengers massacred, and two weeks later a train was deliberately derailed, causing over 200 deaths. That autumn and winter journalists, politicians and police officers were regularly assassinated. Bhindranwale, who was by this stage in effective charge of the Golden Temple, issued orders to execute his opponents and these seemed to be carried out in an almost routine manner.

It is impossible to guess at how the military campaign would have developed if the government had not taken the course it did at this point. During the crucial early years when Bhindranwale was turning the Golden Temple into a fortress of extremism, the authorities had vacillated about how to respond. Then, when the upsurge of violence and Hindu rioting in 1983 finally made it clear to Mrs Gandhi that she had serious law and order problems on her hands, her needless and provocative decision to seize control of Bhindranwale's stronghold in the Sikhs' holiest shrine inflamed the situation.

Storming the Golden Temple in June 1984 transformed the political atmosphere in the Punjab. An army siege, followed by a full-scale assault with tanks and artillery and hand-to-hand fighting, eventually achieved its goal of ending the extremist Sikh presence there, but at a terrible cost. The pictures of the damaged temple, the destroyed sacred buildings, together with the high casualty rate (eighty-three government troops and 493 Sikh militants and civilians dead) and the death of Bhindranwale and other leading extremists, alienated moderate Sikh opinion and led to disturbances across the state. The following October Mrs Gandhi was shot dead by her Sikh bodyguards, and in the rioting that followed this assassination some 2,000 Sikhs were reportedly killed, allegedly without any effort to protect them being made by the authorities. By the end of 1984, therefore, this combination of action and reaction led to a difficult situation becoming almost uncontrollable. An attempt by Mrs Gandhi's successor, her son Rajiv, to conclude an accord with moderate Sikh opinion improved the atmosphere for a while, but within two years it had completely floundered amid allegations that he had not kept to his side of the bargain. Sikh prisoners had not been released as promised, the killers of Sikhs had not been brought to justice and the controversial transfer of an important city to the state of Punjab had not occurred. In an atmosphere of greatly increased instability, Rajiv Gandhi's government took direct control of the administration of the Punjab in 1987, thereby hopelessly isolating the moderates within the Akali Dal with whom the original deal had been made and unleashing the police for a further round of alienating counter-terrorist measures. The government's use of detention without trial and the suspicion that vigilante murder gangs roamed the streets with tacit official support estranged the ordinary Sikh communities even further.

This was the erratic political context – one moment conciliatory, the next vengeful and draconian – against which the violence from the end of 1984 has to be viewed. The escalation was dramatic. In 1985 an Air India Boeing 747 en route from Toronto to London exploded west of Ireland, killing 329 people. A few hours later a bomb went off in luggage which had been aboard another Air India flight. Sikh extremists were suspected of being behind both explosions. The rise in bloodshed within India in the latter half of the decade was horrendous: the estimates of the dead are of 609 in 1986, 1,566 in 1987 and as many as 2,000 in 1988. On one occasion a Sikh wedding was attacked and ten people killed; on another the audience at a Hindu festival was machine-gunned, with thirty-four fatalities; in a third incident extremists fired indiscriminately in the market town of Kaithal in Haryana, killing sixteen people outright. Many of these atrocities led to Hindu rioting, which played into the militants' hands.

There was no element of propaganda in any of this; it was all polarization and provocation. The violence against innocent civilians was intended to drive the local communities into rival camps and to provoke government overreaction, which would have the same effect. The long-term strategy was to create a state of intercommunal tensions and a situation of desperate insecurity in which the militants would then be able to emerge ahead of the moderate parties as the sole and authentic voice of the Sikh people.

The election of a new and conciliatory prime minister, Mr V. P. Singh, led to a brief lessening of tensions at the start of 1990, but the situation had deteriorated once again by the middle of the year. The offers of compromise made by Singh's government served only to emphasize that the years of violence had hardened the resolve of the militants to accept nothing short of Khalistan. This may be the final legacy of a Gandhi administration whose initial support and then passionate vindictiveness towards the extremists both gave them the importance they craved and undermined the moderate Sikh politicians, whose antagonism towards their violent coreligionists could have been utilized to end the trouble more quickly than any amount of firm police action. The conditions in the Punjab were not such that the extremists could have survived without the assistance of governmental overreaction. The most notable feature of the whole crisis has been the extent to which it has been mishandled by the central government, in particular by the two administrations headed by Mrs Indira Gandhi and, after her death, by her son Ravij. Their conduct amounts to an object lesson in how not to respond to violent subversion.

ETA

Europe too offers examples of subversion based on national or subnational aspirations, but they are uniformly less bloody than those to be found in either Sri Lanka or the Punjab. The violence is more often treated as symbolic, and is used to communicate a distinct message. As a result, the level of casualties is lower, but this, paradoxically, leads to an even more confident assertion of 'terrorism'. The violence of ETA in Spain and the IRA in Northern Ireland predates either outbreak in Asia and has proved extraordinarily intractable over the years. Both groups have resisted all political initiatives and every attempt at conciliation. Their violent instincts have survived intact the best efforts of the leaders of the European Community, perhaps the world's most sophisticated political entity, of which both places form a part. In the forward-looking Europe of 1992, ETA and the IRA are reminders of our past primitiveness.

The Basque region lies in the north-east tip of Spain and the south-west corner of France. Four of its provinces are Spanish (Alava, Guipúzcoa,

Navarra and Vizcaya) and three are French (Basse-Navarre, Labourd and Soule). The region was formally divided between the two countries in 1512, with Spain receiving the vast majority of the people and most of the land. Today the population of its four Basque provinces amounts to about $2\frac{1}{4}$ million, 65 per cent of whom are native Basques. These are a separate people with an ancient history and their own culture and language (not in universal daily use today). Over the years the region has enjoyed the economic advantages that follow from its status as an industrially advanced area in a generally backward country, and in the 1930s the Republican government allowed it a large measure of autonomy. The Basque Nationalist Party (PNV) was in control during the civil war. Many of fascism's most determined opponents were drawn from the region, a fact of which Franco was aware, not only when he oversaw the aerial destruction of the Basque city of Guernica (an act of barbarism immortalized by Picasso) but also when he set out to mark his assumption of total power with the extirpation of all traces of Basque nationalism. Vicious repression marked the General's long term in office and the Basque identity could survive only in exile. The PNV evacuated to France, where its leaders settled down for a long stay while they waited for better times in their native land. Inevitably, young Basque nationalists were not willing to accept their eclipse so phlegmatically. Their pressure for a stronger line culminated in 1959 with the formation of Euzkadi ta Askatasuna (Basque Homeland and Liberty) or ETA, a group determined to fight the fascists for Basque freedom.

The repressive atmosphere of Spain made this more an aspiration than an actual fact in ETA's early years, but when their first killing (of the chief of political police in the Guipúzcoa province) occurred, in 1968, the state's reaction was not only predictable but also, as events were to prove, politically inept. A nationwide clampdown followed by a massive security operation culminated in charges being brought in 1970 against sixteen alleged Basque subversives, including two women and two Roman Catholic priests. In the trial that followed in Burgos, six of the defendants were sentenced to death and all but one of the remainder received sentences ranging from twelve to seventy years. The court referred to ETA as a 'separatist Marxist terrorist organization . . . whose purposes were to . . . destroy by violence the organization of the state, dismember a part of the national territory by subversive actions, terrorism, armed warfare and social revolution'. This was not bad for a group that had done practically nothing for eleven years; it displayed to the outside world not so much a communist threat as a thirty-year-old fascist society suffering from incipient paranoia.

ETA hammered the point home during the trial by abducting Eugen Beihl, the West German honorary counsel and representative of several German industrial concerns in Spain, and then freeing him before sentence was passed, 'to show first our people, then the world, that ETA is not an irresponsible, fanatical and bloodthirsty band'. Beihl was later quoted as considering himself a friend of the Basques.

Even before Franco commuted the death sentences, the contrast in styles had already been clearly demonstrated. ETA went on in the next three years to broaden their appeal with two actions which, in their daring and romance, evoked memories of the early Tupamaros and comparisons with the then contemporary Red Brigades in Italy. In January 1972 an industrialist was kidnapped near Bilbao. His release after three days was secured only after his company had agreed to rehire 120 dismissed employees, increase the wages of their workforce and grant a measure of worker participation in the management of the company. Another short kidnap in January 1973 had a similar effect at the factories of the victim; this time the deal included the return of workers dismissed for having gone on strike, a large pay rise, better sick pay and a guaranteed annual vacation of one month for the employees. Throughout this phase of their activity ETA killed no more than a handful of people, and their most notorious assassination did more perhaps than any other single event to make a return to democracy possible in Spain. This was the blowing-up in December 1973 of the man whom Franco had chosen as his successor, Admiral Luis Carrero Blanco. The seventy-year-old Prime Minister, one of the few fully-fledged fascists of the old school left in Spain, was not a well-liked figure, and ETA gained immeasurably from the popular perception that what they were against (Franco) mattered more than what they were killing for (a Basque homeland).

The fact that the organization depended for its appeal on the nature of its enemy rather than on the strength of its ideas made it paradoxically reliant on the continuance of fascism in Spain. With Franco's death in November 1975, however, the country began a remarkable move towards democracy. The new king, Juan Carlos, was not the figurehead the fascist establishment had hoped he would be (and might have been, at least for a while, had it not been for the death of Carrero Blanco). On the contrary, he deftly managed the old order so as to bring about its voluntary extinction. Reform proposals were put before the Cortes as early as April 1976. The following December the democratic initiative which they had outlined was overwhelmingly endorsed in a national referendum, and the sure-footed holding of free elections the following year confirmed the success of this unprecedented (because peaceful) dismantling of a fascist state.

The arrival of democracy had immediate and profound implications for the Basque country. Many of the political prisoners held by Franco were released without delay and by October 1977 every single ETA detainee, regardless of his or her crime, was at liberty (though a few convicted of very serious offences were compelled to leave the country). Even more importantly, the new political climate involved a restructuring of central government so as to give better expression to regional aspirations. In the context of the Basque provinces this meant, first, the creation in late 1977 of a Basque General Council to act as a consultative body, and second, the enactment (followed by a referendum giving local approval) of a statute of autonomy for the region in 1979. This law gave the Basques control over their own police force, certain powers in relation to taxation and a general say on, among other matters, energy, planning and industrial and economic policy. In a ceremony to mark the radical change, the leader of the old Basque government returned from France to hand over to the new regional authorities the powers notionally held by his long-exiled administration; after forty years, 'the democrat had outlived the dictator'.[3]

During the period, therefore, ETA were presented with almost everything for which they had been fighting. Like the Tamil Tigers and the Sikh extremists after them, however, the organization could not recognize victory even when it seemed unavoidable. Unlike the Tigers, ETA could maintain their bellicosity only at the price of internal cohesion. The history of the organization after the death of Franco is one that involves the peeling away of layer upon layer of political veneers, so as eventually to reach, by the end of the 1980s, the original and unadulterated militarists below. There had always been tension within ETA between left-wingers with an emphasis on political activism and nationalists with a more straightforwardly violent approach, and this division was brought to the surface by the onset of the democratic process.

One faction, ETApm, looked to the building of an alliance between the armed struggle and the workers. Significantly, its goals included not only Basque freedom but also democratic centralism and the achievement of a truly socialist society. Politically, it was composed of radicals rather than Basque chauvinists, and it accepted the need to work within the bourgeois liberal structures which were then being erected. Thus it was perfectly logical that this group should fight the 1977 elections in a coalition with other left-leaning parties, and that it should campaign for the approval of the autonomy reforms of 1979. By the same process of development, ETApm came eventually to reject political violence as a method of achieving change.

Such compromises were anathema to the second major faction, ETAm. It was less politically left-wing than its rival splinter group, but was unhesitatingly committed to Basque freedom and the armed struggle it was convinced was necessary to achieve it. ETAm rejected not only autonomy for the region but also the whole edifice of democratic government in Spain, believing that the reconciliation practised by the new administration was an even greater threat to the realization of its ideals than Franco had ever been. With the onset of democracy, therefore, the militarists availed themselves of the new freedom in the country to step up their campaigns of violence. A number of assassinations occurred in 1976 and 1977, but the major escalation came in 1978, when the autonomy proposals were being discussed. During that year and the following two, a total of over 220 people died in ETA-related violence. The campaign has been continued throughout the 1980s, with the result that, by the end of the decade, some 600 people had died since ETA first took up arms. There are, inevitably, bloody punctuation marks along the way: the 1986 bomb in a Madrid bus which killed ten guardia civil and wounded forty-three people; and the 1987 explosion in a supermarket car park in Barcelona which caused twenty-one fatalities. The group's category of 'legitimate' targets has expanded over the years, and when the attacks on economic targets (to harm the tourist industry), the kidnapping of wholly innocent civilians and the inevitable mistakes are taken into account, it is clear that ETAm violence has now reached that point of indiscriminateness where much of it can be confidently classed as truly terrorist.

The message behind the violence is more imponderable than the killing. ETAm refused to participate in the 1977 elections, but shortly afterwards a party was formed which was closely linked to it. Ever since its foundation Herri Batasuna has consistently refused to condemn ETAm violence, while sharing its absolutist position on Basque freedom. Despite this ambiguity on the military question, the party won a handful of seats at the 1979 national elections (which it refused to take up), and in the municipal elections which followed shortly afterwards, its candidates won more seats than ETApm, finishing second only to the old, respectable PNV in the battle for the Basque vote. Throughout the violence of the 1980s, election results have time after time indicated that there is a reliable Herri Batasuna vote of between 15 and 20 per cent despite the level of violence engaged in by ETAm. In one sense, these figures are disturbing for ETAm opponents; in another, they demonstrate the cul-de-sac into which they have led their supporters, for it now looks inherently unlikely that the idea of Basque sovereignty achieved through military action will ever command the support of even a quarter, much less a majority, of the Basque people.

Far from assisting ETAm, Herri Batasuna has exploded the fantasy of their popular appeal. So there is nowhere else for ETAm to go. The future points only to more killing and bombing as a means of achieving the pointless communication of an already rejected message. It is not an attractive prospect and has led factions within ETAm to push for negotiation with the government. Preliminary talks began in Algeria in 1987, but these stalled after an ETAm-inspired car bomb explosion killed eleven people, and then broke down completely when ETAm kidnapped a leading Spanish industrialist.

It seemed as though the ultramilitarists were stating their position in the language they knew best. But what is there to talk about? Once ETAm give up violence they become unimportant, since their political message is in disfavour and they have little else to say. When Herri Batasuna decided to end their boycott of the Cortes in 1989, their four representatives caused uproar at the opening session by refusing voluntarily to pledge allegiance to the Spanish constitution. That evening the four were attacked while dining in a Madrid restaurant and one of their number was shot dead. In its ambiguity, its bloodiness and above all its pointlessness, the day stands as a summary of ETA's thirty-year campaign.

8   The IRA

The similarities between ETA and the Northern Irish subversive group, the IRA, are more apparent than real. The Basque region is for all practical purposes united. There is no movement similar to ETA in France, and there has been no real push within even the extremist organizations for the inclusion within their imagined nation of the two Basque provinces not presently part of Spain. Matching this geographic unity has been a uniformity of outlook. The Basque people originate from the same racial background and support a common local language. The overwhelming majority subscribe to the Catholic faith and the Basque people as a whole share cultural values and interests which may distinguish them from other Spaniards but not from one another. Since the successful achievement of local autonomy in 1979, varieties of Basque nationalism have spread themselves peacefully across the traditional political spectrum, with Herri Batasuna lurking, confused and useless, just off the end at one extreme. To the extent that the Basque region has had a problem, it has been one of too much homogeneity. Northern Ireland, in contrast, has been cursed by a surfeit of separateness. Like Sri Lanka and Lebanon, though not nearly so disastrously as in either of those countries, there are too many diverse groups jostling with one another in search of total political victory, within a very small geographical space, burdened by too much history.

Versions of Ireland

The past continues to bewitch and confuse the Irish problem, with the IRA being but the latest militant manifestation of its tight grip on the political imagination. The voices of history are many, and each community in Northern Ireland has chosen a version tailor-made to its own prejudice. The nationalist rendering views Ireland as Britain's first, its perennial and its final colonial problem. It looks at the conquest of the country in ancient times and laments the gradual reduction in status of the native Irish from the proud people of old to the subjugated dependants of a foreign power. In this version English control of the country was wholly bad, epitomized by such disasters as the penal laws against Catholics, the famines of 1845–50 and the economic exploitation of the countryside for the benefit of absentee British landowners. It was right and natural for the Irish to fight for their freedom against such alien domination and, moreover, it did not matter so much whether this was done constitutionally, through astute nationalist voting in the House of Commons, or unconstitutionally, through support for underground revolutionary movements like the IRB and its successor, the IRA.

Nationalist history points proudly to the key moments of the 'colonial' struggle which eventually brought freedom to three-quarters of the island: the Home Rule movement of Charles Stewart Parnell; the Gaelic revival of the 1890s; the magnificent symbolism of Pearse's Easter Rising in 1916; the Sinn Fein popular rebellion of 1919–21, which culminated in the creation of a new nation, the Irish Free State, in 1922; and the transformation of that country into an independent republic, outside the Commonwealth, in April 1949. This is the country, Ireland, which is a member of the United Nations, participates as an equal in the European Community and revels in its status as a self-governing nation, all the more precious for having been so long denied.

And yet nationalist triumphalism is tempered by a sense of incompleteness. There remains within the United Kingdom six counties in the north, 'the fourth green field', that are not yet part of the happy southern family. In the context of the historical development just outlined, the continuing division of Ireland appears illogical and out of date. The world has seen many examples of colonial liberation and the departing imperial powers have not as a rule sought to preserve part of their old hegemony through the devious device of partition. Why then should not Ireland be united, in accordance with the principles of self-determination universally respected across the world?

Answering this question involves positing a second view of the facts. For Ireland is and always was far more than the merely colonized territory that simplistic comparisons with other places would suggest. Even at the purely legalistic level, the whole country was an integral part of the United Kingdom for over 100 years, and politically, the proximity of the interconnections between the two islands have made the colonial model inappropriate since at least the end of the eighteenth century. But the main way in which Ireland is different lies in the depth and range of the British settlement of the country, which in terms of commitment and permanence could not be further from what is suggested by at least some colonial analogies.

English power found its first full expression between the period from 1550 to 1650, when there occurred the systematic and wholesale 'plantation' of British subjects on land formerly possessed or owned by the native Irish. The first of these plantations took place in the Irish midlands in the middle of the sixteenth century. The southern province of Munster followed in 1586. In neither place did the new policy cause the total estrangement between the planter and the native that might have been expected. In Munster particularly, the policy was characterized by relatively unstructured social relations between the classes and this, together with the fact that the province already enjoyed close and regular communications with England, meant that the newcomers did not perceive themselves to be under threat from the natives. By the same token, the receptivity of the planters to Irish ways and the fact that at least some land remained with the locals prevented catastrophic alienation. None of this applied to the northern part of the country, the province known as Ulster. The leaders of a serious Irish revolt at the end of the reign of Elizabeth I had hailed from this part of the country and, after their defeat in 1601 and the flight of many of them from the country some six years later, revenge was exacted in the form of a comprehensive plantation of the province.

The effect of the implementation of this policy in 1609–10 was disastrous for the indigenous Irish. They were expelled to the less productive land, a trend that was exacerbated by later demographic developments. Those few who kept any property did so through the payment of high rents and without any security of tenure. On to the good land of Ulster came not the sober planters hoped for by the authorities but rather Englishmen who were 'generally "plain country gentlemen", tight-fisted and easily scared away' and Scots who were 'too ready to use natives to supply their wants and to let land to them'.[1] Segregation was the aim in theory, but it proved impossible in practice; the expelled native always remained close at hand, hard-up and resentful. This fuelled the insecurities and fears already latent in the new arrivals and their vulnerability led them to define their status and their difference with especial, almost anxious, clarity. Religion was as important here as national background: the Protestantism of the settler was a useful assertion of identity in the face of the native Catholic hordes all around. Sometimes these insecurities were given tangible expression through the erection of impressive defences, like the walls of Londonderry, completed in 1618, or the creation of English-style boroughs across the province, where the settlers could achieve safety in numbers while re-creating the atmosphere of home.

The nationalist version of history sees these people arriving and settling (the 'Brits' coming to milk the land), but it has never quite managed to acknowledge their descendants. The kith and kin of the first Ulster settlers have remained separate, treasuring their Britishness as an alternative to the embarrassment of their Irishness. With the political fusion of the two countries in 1800, they seized upon the maintenance of the Union as a further manifestation of their distinctiveness. The self-interested loyalism that was thereby contrived was enough to see them through various nineteenth-century crises involving the prospect of Dublin rule, and in 1885 the Conservative Party was won over to the cause, an important ally which they were not to lose for a century. Immeasurably strengthened by this alliance, in 1912–14 they defeated the most serious proposal yet for Irish autonomy, through a combination of intransigence ('Ulster will fight and Ulster will be right') and good fortune (the intervention of the First World War). The great conflict of 1914–18 shook up Ireland and set it spinning off in various extremist directions. When its shock waves died away, it was apparent that the vast majority in the country now wanted rather more than the 'glorified local government'[2] that had been on offer earlier, while the intense (and much advertised) patriotism of the Ulster Protestant in the trenches made it politically essential that he should not be thanked for defending his country by being summarily ejected from it.

The Unionist Ascendancy

The decision to solve these problems by partitioning Ireland, put into effect in the early 1920s, gave Ulster Protestantism the best of all possible worlds: continued membership of the United Kingdom, with MPs at Westminster and all the other trappings of Britishness, plus their very own parliament in Belfast. The new arrangements were greeted with widespread violence across the north; in 1922 alone, over 200 people died and 1,000 were injured. This was hardly surprising. The borders of the new substate were determined not by history, tradition or geography, but by the imperatives of sectarian demography. In a process similar to that indulged in by the Christian Maronites in Lebanon two decades later, the territory was structured so as to retain Protestant power over the maximum amount of land. This territorial imperialism merely compounded Protestant feelings of neurosis and insecurity, since the assertion of control over large numbers of Catholics in the western part of the province greatly reduced the size of their own majority. In the end 'Northern Ireland' turned out to have six counties; three Ulster ones which were overwhelmingly Catholic were jettisoned while two (Fermanagh and Tyrone) with narrow Catholic majorities were retained. The overall head count gave the Protestants a 56:44 per cent advantage, but despite this relatively narrow divide, there was no doubt from the start that Northern Ireland's legislature regarded itself as a 'Protestant parliament for a Protestant people'. It removed itself to Stormont, a provincial delusion of legislative grandeur. The system of voting was quickly changed, by abolishing proportional representation, so as to guarantee unionism a perpetual hold on power. In places with a preponderance of Catholics, the electoral boundaries were contorted so as to produce magically constructed Protestant majorities on local councils in what were patently nationalist areas. The settlers of the seventeenth century had finally come into their own.

Within this new unit the Catholic nationalists were not so much neighbours, much less potential partners in government, as the quintessential enemy within. 'Race and religion were inextricably intertwined in Ulster unionist consciousness. Unionists could not rely on the criterion of colour, for the Catholics lacked the imagination to go off-white, nor on the criterion of language, for the Catholics had unsportingly abandoned their own. It was therefore imperative to sustain Protestantism as the symbol of racial superiority.'[3]

Like most insecure people and nations (Israel and Lebanon among them), this unionist state got its retaliation in first. An armed special constabulary was formed (the B-Specials) and many of its recruits were drawn from loyalist paramilitary groups. Together with the also overwhelmingly Protestant Royal Ulster Constabulary (RUC), and with the assistance of draconian security legislation, it kept a stern and stifling peace. In all aspects of life in the Province, the Catholics found themselves marginalized:

Lack of senior positions in the civil service and the judiciary proportionate to their numbers simply highlighted the much broader range of discrimination in the patronage system of public bodies, high and low. Catholics were excluded from power, their political representatives were rendered impotent, their votes were nullified, their children were disadvantaged despite the extra financial sacrifices their parents were called upon to make for their education, and the community was then mocked for not having sufficient qualifications for positions of importance.[4]

On one occasion, the Northern Irish Prime Minister, Lord Craigavon, stiffly warned his Australian counterpart that he needed to 'watch' his Catholic population since 'they breed like bloody rabbits'.[5] On another, the Minister for Home Affairs, Sir Richard Dawson Bates, stopped using his telephone to conduct important business when he learned 'with a great deal of surprise' that a Roman Catholic telephonist had been appointed to Stormont.[6]

The politics of bigotry practised in Northern Ireland for forty-five years were connived in by the Westminster authorities. Nothing was done to interfere with even the wilder excesses of the parliament within its jurisdiction; on the contrary, its leaders were showered with royal honours and even its extraordinary Stormont buildings were dignified with a state opening by the Prince of Wales. Things finally began to fall apart in 1968. In autumn that year the emerging Northern Ireland Civil Rights Association drew deliberate and indignant attention to examples of petty religious apartheid. The flashpoint became the allocation of council homes to single Protestants ahead of large Catholic families. When protest demonstrations about such matters provoked extremely violent responses from the police and B-Specials, affairs quickly drifted out of control. One exceptionally nasty confrontation, between protesters on a march and the extreme Protestants and B-Specials who ambushed them at Burntollet Bridge in January 1969, gave the world television pictures which showed how deep the bitterness now went.

In August of that year the disturbances, which had been sporadic until then, came to a head in vicious rioting in Londonderry and Belfast. At least seven people were killed, over 1,600 were injured and property damage in Belfast alone came to £8 million. Thousands of families were forced to abandon their homes to the mobs and flee to safety. Significantly, the vast majority of these families were Catholic and there is little doubt that for a few crucial days that summer the full fury of Protestant mobs, aided and abetted by the B-Specials, was vented on innocent and undefended Catholic communities.

The Provisional IRA

The law and order situation was chaotically grave by the time the British Prime Minister, Harold Wilson, ordered UK troops on to the streets of Northern Ireland on 14 August 1969. They came primarily to protect the Catholics and were initially received with open arms by those whom they had come to save. Like the marines in Beirut and the Indians in Sri Lanka in later years, however, they soon found that the welcome they enjoyed did not endure for long. For in the mêlée of that summer's violence, another protector, this time an indigenous one, had begun to insinuate itself after many years of moribundity.

The IRA was a small group which claimed to be the true successor to the revolutionary army that had fought the British in the Anglo-Irish war of 1919–21. It had remained true to the cause of a united Ireland, for which it had been proscribed in the South and constantly hunted in the North. Having mounted the occasional desultory attack since partition, the last being the border campaign of 1956–62, it had by the end of the 1960s lapsed into lassitudinous left-wing politics. This was not the way to prepare for the dramas of 1969: class consensus and a delicate social conscience proved to be no defence against rioting Protestant mobs, and the IRA's inactivity irretrievably disgraced it in nationalist eyes. The movement split in two, with the 'Official' IRA taking the route into mainstream left-wing politics that ETApm were to follow some five years later, and the Provisional IRA remaining behind to fight the old enemy in the traditional republican way, without the clutter of a confusing modern ideology.

In the crucial two years after August 1969, it now seems clear that the best recruiting officer the Provisionals had were the British army. A series of appallingly inept military operations (the deaths of unarmed Catholics during the suppression of civil disorder; house searches; disproportionate aggressiveness and hostility to local people) gave them the foothold in their community which the mainstream IRA had lost two years before, and they were never to relinquish it. In 1970 a bomb killed two RUC officers. In the first two months of 1971 the girlfriends of British soldiers were tarred and feathered, a Stormont minister was shot seventeen times (incredibly he survived the attack) and the first British soldiers were killed by the IRA.

The new military campaign had begun and has continued ever since, with only the occasional abatement. In their first twenty years the 'troubles', as they are euphemistically called, have been responsible for over 2,700 deaths. Of these, about one-third were members of the security forces, over one-half were civilians and the rest have been from one or other of the paramilitary groups that multiplied in the Province in the early 1970s. The death rate was most severe in the years 1972–6, when an average of 285 people lost their lives every year. Since then the annual toll has levelled out at rather less than 100. These figures are far less than for either India or Sri Lanka, a point that should be dwelt upon by those who believe that the

Northern Irish problem could not get any worse. Nevertheless, the cost has been severe, £410 million every year, according to a recent estimate,[7] and references to greater bloodshed elsewhere should not be allowed to obscure the debilitating impact subversive violence has had not only on Northern Ireland but on the Republic to the south and on the British Isles as a whole.

The Provisional IRA is the most consistent, imaginative and difficult to control of all contemporary subversive groups. It has always been delighted to welcome popular support and is the first to capitalize on any blunders the authorities send its way, such as the internment of innocent Catholics in 1971, the killing by the army of thirteen men, many of them teenagers, in Londonderry in 1972 or the Thatcher government's overemotional response to the provocation of IRA hunger strikers in 1981. But the group does not need such support. Its cell structure, borrowed from the Tupamaros, and its commitment to a long war of attrition, reminiscent of Mao, mean that its campaign is built to last and is not dependent on the vagaries of public opinion.

Ordinary politicians may practise the 'politics of the last atrocity' but the IRA has no need to. Furthermore, the organization has been able over the years to attract foreign support from a variety of sources. Of course, there has always been the Republic of Ireland, not foreign in any meaningful sense, but a country with a long contiguous border and, in the early days at least, a not unsympathetic local population. The huge Irish-American community has also provided financial support, and rather more than that on occasion. The first Armalites were shipped over in 1970 and as recently as August 1990 an Irishman and three US citizens were sentenced to jail by the Boston Federal Court for conspiracy to supply the IRA with parts for sophisticated surface-to-air missiles, detonators for bombs and other weaponry. Most seriously, there has been an important input by General Gadaffi's Libya, whose shipments of arms to the IRA transformed the strength of the organization in the latter half of the 1980s. Police sources estimate that 113 tonnes of firearms and explosives, including between 2 and 4 tonnes of Semtex explosive, parts of twelve SAM-7 missiles, anti-aircraft machine guns, 1,000 assault rifles and a million rounds of ammunition and a huge variety of other weapons and accessories entered Ireland via this route between August 1985 and September 1986.[8] (The General may have had it in mind to punish Mrs Thatcher, first for her decision to close the Libyan People's Bureau after the killing of a policewoman outside it in April 1984, and second for the fact that the 1986

US bombing raid on Tripoli was effected by planes taking off from bases in Britain.)

IRA tactics

Unlike the Tupamaros, the Red Brigades or ETA, the IRA have not shown a trend towards greater brutality as time has gone by. The massive atrocities of earlier years happen less frequently now, but not so rarely that they have disappeared altogether from the IRA arsenal. All one can say is that the organization has moved beyond the phase of angry revolt and now approaches its task with the self-conscious professionalism of career civil servants. The key to their operational success has been the lack of any clear pattern to their subversion. The motives behind it have been as varied as their choice of targets, but four broad categories of violence, reflecting separate but overlapping motivations, are discernible.

First, a consistent thread has been the use of violence to polarize the two communities of Northern Ireland. The theory here is to increase the atmosphere of violence to the point where law and order in the Province breaks down completely, after which, at the point of maximum instability, political victory can be extracted by the strongest extremist group. We have already seen the desperate consequences of such a strategy in Sri Lanka and the Punjab. It is by far the bloodiest of all terror tactics, since the wholesale slaughter of innocents is essential in order to reach that level of tension at which the opportunity for action reveals itself.

Undoubtedly, the tactic has been more enthusiastically embraced by loyalist gunmen than by the IRA, though both have colluded in what, in this context, is a common aim. The appalling rioting and house-burning of summer 1969 may be categorized in this way (in so far as it had any purpose at all other than pure hatred). More calculating was the death of fifteen Catholics in a bomb attack on McGurk's bar in Belfast in December 1971. Many of the 122 assassinations that took place the following year were purely sectarian in intent, and the explosions in the Abercorn restaurant (two dead, 130 injured) and in Belfast on 'Bloody Friday' (twenty IRA bombs, nine dead) were the high points in this deliberate raising of community tension. Sectarian atrocities punctuated the 1970s: the murder of three members of the Miami Showband in a loyalist attack in 1975; the killing of five Catholics in two separate incidents in Whitecross in January 1976, followed the next day by the retaliatory murder of ten Protestants at Kingsmill in south Armagh; the IRA bombing of the La Mon House Hotel in February 1978, which left twelve dead and twenty-three injured. The 1980s have not escaped, with atrocities at the Droppin' Well (seventeen killed in a bomb explosion at a disco) and Darkley (a machine-gun attack on a Protestant church service, three dead) introducing a new extremist faction into the equation: the Irish National Liberation Army (INLA). This group had claims to be the most brutal of them all until it predictably consumed itself in a murderous civil war in 1987. That same year the IRA's bomb at a remembrance day ceremony in Enniskillen (eleven dead, sixty-three injured) was a reminder that the INLA did not have a monopoly on mindless sectarianism.

Despite this terrible catalogue of death and destruction, however, killing the innocent in order to raise tensions has not been the favoured or prevalent tactic in Northern Ireland. This is the simple reason why the death toll in the Province is so far behind that achieved by the Tigers and the Sikh extremists. A second motivation underpins the deliberate pogroms already described, and also explains other actions in which the IRA have engaged. This is the well-known strategy of provocation, first seen in relation to the South American groups in the 1960s and which has been practised with varying degrees of success by subversive groups ever since. From 1979 on, the IRA have engaged in a variation of it in their deliberate and highly personal campaign to use their violence to unsettle the mind of Mrs Thatcher to the point where she overreacts with some extravagant military move – such as the introduction of internment or military law, both of which would drive all moderate nationalist opinion into the IRA camp. They are looking for the Irish equivalent of the storming of the Golden Temple. The slaughter of British troops on a large scale, such as at Warrenpoint in 1979 (eighteen dead) or Bessbrook in 1981 (five killed), is not only a morale booster; it is done in the knowledge that Mrs Thatcher has strong and emotional feelings about the death of young squaddies.

At a more personal level, her close friends and advisers on Ireland, Airey Neave and Ian Gow, have both been killed, the first by an INLA car bomb which exploded within the precincts of the House of Commons, the second by a similar device which exploded while he was reversing his car out of the driveway at his country home. Attempts on the lives of other colleagues such as Lord Armstrong and Lord McAlpine have been made, and the IRA's most dramatic attack of all was the explosion at the Grand Hotel Brighton in 1984, which caused the death of five people and so nearly killed Mrs Thatcher herself, as well as half her cabinet. The organization has been quite explicit about this aspect of its military operations. One of their spokesmen described Mrs Thatcher in the following terms in the course of an interview with David McKittrick of the *Independent*:

In personal terms she has obviously suffered quite a lot since 1984, and I don't think she's all that rational in dealing with IRA operations. She was almost killed, and I think that our words after Brighton still haunt her – 'Today we were unlucky. But remember, we only have to be lucky once. You will have to be lucky always.'

At her age you should be looking forward to retirement, sitting back on her laurels. It'll be very hard to enjoy your retirement with a permanent bodyguard.[9]

To her credit, the Prime Minister has not delivered the ridiculous repression which the IRA so clearly wants, though after a particularly bad attack on young soldiers in August 1988, when eight of them died in a bus explosion at Ballygawley in County Tyrone, it is said that Downing Street was close to giving in to insistent demands from unionist opinion for a reintroduction of internment.

Provocation was also one of the motives behind the bombing campaign on the British mainland in the early 1970s. In February 1972 an explosion at the Aldershot army base 35 miles from London killed five waitresses, a gardener and an army chaplain. In 1973 there were eighty-six explosions on mainland Britain, involving one fatality and 380 other casualties. In February 1974 eleven died and fourteen were injured when a huge bomb blew up a bus full of British service personnel and their families as they were travelling through Yorkshire. The dead included an entire family: a soldier, his wife and their two children. By the middle of November that year, there had already been further fatalities and over 100 injuries. Then came the bombs in two public houses in Birmingham on 21 November. The explosives were left in the pubs by members of the organization who pretended to be ordinary casual drinkers. An inadequate warning was telephoned too late to allow for any action by the authorities. The bombs blew the pubs apart, and with them went many of those inside. Twenty-one people were killed and 162 injured, some of them horribly maimed. The first police officers on the scene were confronted with nightmarish visions of fragmented bodies and dying dismembered torsos. Neither the pubs nor the people inside them had any connections with British security forces operating in Northern Ireland. These places were chosen for the simplest of reasons: they were located in England and this made it likely that their clientele would be English. The bombings showed that, like the PFLP and Carlos Marighela before them, the IRA had reached the point where the enemy had expanded to include the whole population.

These atrocities revealed a third motive behind IRA strategy, and it is this that makes them – and later, similar attacks such as the one in Knightsbridge in 1983 (when five died in a car bomb attack on Harrods) – fit into the category of pure acts of terror. For the prime purpose of such indiscriminate killing on the British 'mainland' is to communicate the IRA's message to the British people that they should get their troops and themselves out of Ireland. If it were said by a nationalist in west Belfast, no one would listen. It is arbitrary murder in Britain that makes the point audible, thereby fulfilling a key element in any definition of terror: namely, that the violence employed should be symbolic.

The IRA has greatly reduced such actions in recent years, particularly after the Knightsbridge bomb, which was considered by the organization to have been a major public-relations reverse. After many years of quiescence, however, a resurgence of this tactic was clearly detectable in summer 1990. The London stock exchange, the Conservative Carlton Club and a young adults' party at a Territorial army headquarters were bombed, and any one of these actions could have caused civilian casualties on a scale reminiscent of the 1970s, a fact which must have been known to those planting the explosives.

The IRA would say that these 1990 attacks were on 'legitimate targets' and were part of a quasi-guerrilla war that they are waging on the British. This leads to the fourth objective of their campaign, and the one that is most frequently in evidence. This is to make the cost of sustaining a presence in Ireland too high for the British authorities to bear. At some point, the IRA analysis goes, the UK government will have had enough of the bloodshed and will pack its bags and quietly leave Northern Ireland. Victory over the British army is not being sought, so in a sense each action continues to define its importance in terms of the message it sends rather than the strategic military goal that it achieves.

So violence under this head retains a symbolic dimension. To assess if it is also genuinely terrorist, we need to consider whether the targets are indiscriminately chosen, and this leads us back to further examination of the IRA's assertion that they are attacking legitimate targets in the course of a guerrilla-style conflict; on its validity hinges their claim to subversive respectability. Occasionally the war analysis fits the facts well, as when in 1985 the IRA killed nine RUC officers in a mortar attack on a police station in Newry, and had eight of their own men killed by the SAS in a similar assault at Loughgall two years later. These events were exceptional. More often employed in their war are covert devices like the booby-trapped land-mine which killed three RUC men in one explosion in Lurgan in October 1982, and four members of the local army regiment the UDR in a similar way a year later. The car bomb fits into this category, and a devastating example was the 1,000-lb explosion in a van which killed four RUC officers in Bessbrook in April 1979.

But the IRA does not restrict itself to assaults on law enforcement officers on duty. Their reach also extends to the officer who is off duty, or retired, or a part-time UDR reservist working alone on his farm in a remote part of the countryside. Typical in this regard were the blowing up in June 1990 of a pensioner who had been a police reservist three years previously, and the IRA's first triumph of that year, an RUC inspector who was shot dead while in his kitchen making a cup of tea for his wife. The unglamorous, almost banal, killing of such undefended individuals is the hallmark of the IRA's campaign against the security services. A similar point can be made about subversive attacks on the army. Six soldiers participating in a 'fun run' in June 1988 were killed by a bomb. The IRA's successes in Britain include the blowing-up of army bandsmen while they were playing music in Regent's Park; a bomb attack on the Royal Marine School of Music at Deal which killed eleven; and the shooting of three soldiers, one fatally, on a crowded platform at Lichfield railway station while they waited for a train at the start of a weekend's leave.

This attack mirrored the method favoured by the IRA in its aggressive campaign against British army personnel stationed on NATO duty in continental Europe. Among the casualties have been a soldier wounded while jogging, a corporal shot and killed in a restaurant in Wildenrath, West Germany, and an RAF man, machine-gunned to death while sitting in his car with two colleagues after an evening out in Roermond, the Netherlands.

This covert killing is hardly resonant with the images of a fairly fought war, but the IRA would be expected to argue that, like General Giap in Vietnam or Hezbollah in Lebanon, they should not be required to conduct their military campaign so as to facilitate their easy extermination by the opposition. And this is what would happen if they suddenly began to make heroic assaults on the army's headquarters in Newry or the RUC's central offices in Belfast. They fight their enemy in the way they know they can, not in a way their enemy chooses for them. In addition, the IRA have long regarded their 'legitimate targets' as extending well beyond security service personnel.

The common link shared by these various victims has been vulnerability rather than culpability. Lord Mountbatten was blown up in his boat off the coast of Ireland in 1979, and the unionist politicans Robert Bradford, Edgar Graham and Sir Norman Stronge have also been assassinated. So have a number of judges, including William Doyle, shot dead as he left a Catholic Church, and Lord Justice Gibson, blown up with his wife when returning by car from a holiday abroad. Many prison officers have been killed, two of the most distinguished being the deputy governor of Belfast prison in 1978 and the assistant governor of the Maze prison, who was shot outside his home in 1984. Building contractors have been threatened and regularly shot for doing work for the army or the RUC. The Dublin–Belfast rail link is famously almost as often disrupted as it is late on a bomb-free day. Economic targets have included hotels, shops, energy pylons, a coal boat (sunk off the Donegal coast in 1981) and, on occasion, whole towns (as in November 1978, when the IRA set off bombs and explosives in fourteen towns and villages on the same day).

Those who associate with 'legitimate targets' are also targets. This accounts for the civilians who died in the INLA bombing of the Droppin' Well pub disco, since it was a place that was known to be frequented by soldiers. Presumably, it also explains the death of Mrs Gibson, as well as that of Mary Travers, killed in an IRA attack on her father, a magistrate, when they were leaving Mass together. The local boy fourteen-year-old Paul Maxwell, blown up with Lord Mountbatten, should have refused to go to sea with this obvious enemy of Ireland. The wife of a British soldier, shot dead by the IRA in Dortmund in 1989, should not have married her husband; nor should the six-month-old baby killed with her RAF father the same year have been born. The IRA expressed 'profound regret' at this latter incident.

When do 'mistakes' become the inevitable consequence of carelessly planned and cavalierly executed attacks? In 1988 a 1,000-lb bomb intended for Mr Justice Higgins merely killed Robert and Maureen Hanna and their son David. A land mine in 1990 killed three members of the RUC, but also a thirty-seven-year-old Catholic nun. Earlier the same year an IRA bomb exploded at the wrong time during a march and killed a teenager from the Bogside area of Londonderry. In Holland in May 1990 an IRA unit saw two couples with a British-registered car and shot dead the two men in the party. They turned out to be Australians based in London on a brief holiday abroad; IRA protestations that they had been mistaken for soldiers would have been more convincing if there had been the slightest shred of evidence to that effect.

This is only a selection of recent events. There are many more 'mistakes' that the IRA have calmly regretted in between the killing. We are forced to conclude that because the category of 'legitimate' targets is so broad, and the killing of those included so recklessly executed, the IRA campaign is for all practical purposes indiscriminate in its effect. Therefore, because the violence is also symbolic, it is appropriate to regard much of the IRA's subversion as purely terrorist in its execution.

The Politics of the Provisionals

We may ask the same question as was posed in relation to ETA: what has the campaign of killing and destruction achieved? The IRA point to the collapse of the Stormont government in 1972. It is possible that without subversive violence there would have been no anxiety about Northern Ireland in London. The Anglo–Irish Agreement in 1985, in particular, represents an attempt to address the constitutional structure of the Province and it may owe its existence at least partly to IRA actions. The accord gave the Republic of Ireland a consultative role in the administration of Northern Ireland, and it was and is championed by non-violent nationalist political opinion in the Province, though the republican movement rejects it, just as ETAm turned away from the more dramatic autonomy proposals of the Madrid government.

One senior figure has described it as an attempt 'to isolate and draw popular support away from the Republican struggle, while putting a diplomatic veneer on Dublin rule, injecting a credibility into establishment 'nationalism' so that British rule and the interests it represents can be stabilized in the long-term, and insulating the British from international criticism of their involvement in Irish affairs'.[10]

It seems that the IRA need an unyielding Mrs Thatcher just as much as the ETA militants needed Franco. Like the latter group, the IRA has a political counterpart, Provisional Sinn Fein, and the two have worked in tandem since 1981, following a strategy famously described by Danny Morrison, then editor of the movement's newspaper, *An Phoblacht*, in the form of a chilling question, addressed to Sinn Fein's annual conference in November 1981: 'Is there anyone here who objects to taking power in Ireland with a ballot paper in one hand and an Armalite in the other?'[11]

The answer was an enthusiastic no, and in its early days this tactic of seeking popular support for violent subversion seemed certain to be a brilliant success. Buoyed by the death of imprisoned IRA hunger strikers in 1981, and assisted by an astute emphasis on social and 'working-class' issues reminiscent of the tactics of Lenin's Bolsheviks in Tsarist Russia, Provisional Sinn Fein received 35 per cent of the nationalist vote at Province-wide elections held in 1982. The following year their share of this vote went up to 43 per cent, and the robustly republican community of west Belfast returned the President of Sinn Fein, Gerry Adams, to the House of Commons. He did not take his seat, but the Party allowed participation in local government, with the result that a large sprinkling of Sinn Fein councillors began to appear in district councils, preaching their sermons about equality and justice under cover of their comrades' Armalites. As much as IRA violence, it was the fear that Sinn Fein would soon command majority support among nationalists that lead the British government to conclude the Anglo-Irish Agreement. Whether or not because of this initiative, the surge in Sinn Fein's vote has ceased, and by 1990 their support had levelled off at about one-third of the nationalist community. This was increasingly concentrated in specific areas of deprivation in Northern Ireland, where the party's radical stand is appealing and where they are the only group perceived to be on the side of the isolated and neglected locals. In the Republic, in contrast, the Party's invitation for popular support has led to its electoral obliteration. As with Herri Batasuna in Spain, though from a higher base, Sinn Fein seem to have reached a plateau of support from which it is unlikely they will slip (the electorate remaining with them would appear to be safely 'atrocity-proof') but to ascend beyond which seems impossible – unless the authorities come to the rescue with some grievously miscalculated overreaction. One astute commentator has neatly summed up the party's status:

Sinn Fein's identity is inseparable from its relationship with the IRA. Without that relationship, it is little more than a left-leaning, essentially working-class party with a limited constituency and of limited consequence. With that relationship, it exacts an impact on events out of all proportion to popular support for its policies. The power of the movement comes out of the barrel of a gun.[12]

With all the elections and executions, the IRA has not thought much about what it is fighting for. Yet the question is an important one, not least because they have been shooting and bombing now for over twenty years, and that is a long time, even for Mao's 'long war'. The organization comes back again and again to the simple fact that it has survived. Indeed, in recent years its whole personality has tended to be defined by its ghettoized mentality, by its sense of being surrounded by enemies on all sides: the UK government, the security forces and the unionists, of course, but also the

Catholic Church, moderate nationalists, the Dublin government and mainstream Irish-American opinion, typified by such notables as Senator Edward Kennedy and the former Speaker, Tip O'Neill. These feelings of isolation give added weight to their militancy, and the fact that the communities from which they come share their sense of quarantine guarantees them their bedrock of support. The insecurity that fosters IRA violence seems in this way ironically to mirror that of the neurotic Protestant settlers of an earlier age. Apart from survival, Sinn Fein and the IRA are both immensely proud of the fact that, as they put it, 'We cannot be beaten.' Reference is regularly made to an army assessment of their military capacity which draws this conclusion, but the obvious follow-up question, 'Can we ever win?', is rarely on their lips.

The IRA are unable to think about victory because they have no genuine idea how to define it. Any long-term vision or set of final goals that they may have had in the early days has all but disappeared. The dream of a thirty-two-county, united Ireland has vanished from the Republic's political agenda. In its place is a new Europeanism so intoxicatingly cosmopolitan and above all so unEnglish that the Irish no longer want to be reminded of any embarrassing nationalist dodos in the North. Yet without the South, IRA ambitions for a united Ireland are antediluvian rather than threatening; and the Sinn Fein-sponsored celebrations of Irish culture in their communities merely advertize their provincialism rather than their pan-Irishness.

The overall impression the IRA and Sinn Fein leave us with is one of a painful backwardness. The world, including Ireland, has moved on, leaving this tiny parochial band of pseudo-warriors wedded to a goal that everybody else has long forgotten and committed to a campaign of killing so meaningless that it celebrates military stalemate as a triumph. The proto-politicians among them can make no progress because of the violence; but the militarists cannot up the ante of violence because of the politicians. The IRA campaign ends up as work experience for the British army, a tragedy for the unlucky victims and a massive inconvenience for the whole country. It is a sad waste of talent and human life, more pitiable than despicable.

Conclusion

We have been careful up to now not to mix together the IRA and these various other examples of separatist groups within relatively free societies. It is possible, however, to identify a few trends that are common to all of them, without doing an injustice to any of their specific contexts. First, in relation to these 'pseudo-colonial' situations, it seems important to point out that each subversive group usually starts with a strong base of support on account of the existence of genuine injustice. They are popular because they are meeting a need within their community. This was certainly true of the IRA and ETA in the early days and seems to remain the case with the Tigers today. It is less obviously true in relation to the Sikh extremists, whose success has hinged much more on the mishandling of their subversion by successive Indian governments.

Second, each successful subversive group of this sort has had a foreign country from which it could draw at least passive support. The Tigers had India, ETA had France, the IRA had Ireland and the Sikh extremists had Pakistan. Cross-border cooperation has had an effect in Spain and Northern Ireland, has not been tried well in the Punjab and has been catastrophic in Sri Lanka, where the assistance offered by New Delhi turned out to be in effect an invasion.

Third, the effect of separatist violence has usually been the political advancement of moderate opinion, riding to success on the back of the government's concern to wean popular support away from the rebels. In Northern Ireland the IRA may have been right about the 'Armalite and the ballot box', but it was John Hume's peaceful nationalism that gained, not them. Similarly, in Spain the old Basque party enjoys power in its homeland which would not now be so complete had it not been for the fear of ETA. In the Punjab the moderate Sikhs' agreement with the New Delhi authorities would have worked had it not been for further insensitivities on Rajiv Gandhi's part. Only the Tigers seem to benefit from their own fighting, though, as has been shown, they are as much a traditional guerrilla army as a subversive group. It is relevant, however, that none of the four groups has achieved any of its primary aims.

Finally, the evidence points to the fact that no political solution will ever obliterate the militant factions altogether. There are too many complex additional factors, such as psychological maladjustment, daring 'macho' personalities, criminal tendencies or the pursuit of material gain, which can interpose themselves between at least certain subversives and the acceptance of even a totally generous political solution. The authorities need to conciliate the middle ground with imaginative proposals, but they must not expect violence to disappear overnight, or even to disappear. These groups will remain with us as grim reminders of a time when national sovereignty was something enjoyed in its totality or not enjoyed at all. The world has moved on from this position, and shared authority and partnership are now the accepted norms in international affairs, as evidenced by such groups as NATO, the EC and the other multinational blocs outside the West. The 'pseudo-colonials' fight in pursuit of a total power which even sovereignty – if it were achieved – could no longer guarantee. They are violent anachronisms in a changing political world.

9   The Price of Victory

Having surveyed the types of political subversion that afflict contemporary liberal societies, we are now in a position to turn to one of the most important issues in the whole sphere of 'terrorism': namely, the nature of the state's reaction to the challenge that terrorism poses to its established authority. Although clearly governments cannot afford to take a relaxed approach to such violence, it has to be said that few governments can be reproached for adopting a laid-back attitude to subversion; authority, even when it is democratic, is acutely alert to the need for its own survival. The risks lie in the other direction. Once they are fully mustered, the forces of even the puniest nation will inevitably dwarf in both breadth and impact all the energetic subversion that its rebellious opponents will have managed to contrive in years of hectic lawlessness.

In a situation that combines a tendency to panic in governmental circles with the ready availability of great military strength, the danger of an overreaction by officials will always be high, and we have already seen examples of serious misjudgement in earlier chapters: the conduct of the army in Northern Ireland in 1969–71; the storming of the Golden Temple by Mrs Gandhi's forces in 1984; and, most disastrously of all, the dismantling of the entire framework of free government in Uruguay in the early 1970s. The key challenge for any democratic state, therefore, is to get the balance right between the control of subversive violence and the maintenance of respect for freedom and equality which morally distinguishes it from its opponents.

The Middle East

To express the problem in terms of a balance between democracy and civil liberties serves to remind us of the importance of defining the sort of subversion we have in mind. In the context of the Middle East, the depth and variety of violence is such that it not only destroys the usefulness of the

131

notion of 'terrorism' but also makes any consequential discussion of the correct response to it inherently meaningless. The counter-terrorism represented by the US raid on Libya and Israel's bombing assaults on Syria, Tunisia and Lebanon merely remind us of how politically loaded this subject has become.

This is not to say, of course, that democratic countries in Europe and elsewhere should not protect themselves against international violence spilling over from the Levantine theatre. Airports should be made secure; diplomats should be well protected; border security should be comprehensive in the right places and at the right times; the intelligence services should be abreast of the subtleties of Middle Eastern dissent; and there should be international agreement against such unequivocal mischiefs as hijacking and assassination. Such apolitical, security-oriented measures as these should be, and are being, taken. It would be gratifying if the same energy could be brought to bear in analysing the reasons behind political violence in the region and in halting the atrocities committed by the friends of the West. However, these pious aspirations should not be allowed to distract from the obvious need to protect innocent civilians from the terrorism of disgruntled Palestinian subversives, no matter how heinously they have been treated. To understand the context of political violence is not to condone it.

The Disaffected

The most successful counter-terrorist policies to date have been those employed against the ideological subversives of Western Europe, and it is worth glancing at the backgrounds of these organizations in order to appreciate the effectiveness of the measures eventually adopted to defeat them. The radical left-wing groups which mushroomed around the democratic world at the start of the 1970s were small fry, but the hostile nature of their message and the fact that they derived their membership from the middle classes and the intelligentsia ensured that they were treated at the time with an anxious earnestness which their deeds (rather than their words) hardly deserved. Names like the Angry Brigade, the Red Army Faction and the Red Brigades revealed a plagiaristic attachment to the military structures of the reviled enemy, but an understanding of other titles could sometimes require an awareness of such 1960s 'obscuranta' as the works of Bob Dylan ('Weather Underground') and the transient philosophical kitsch of the period ('Symbionese Liberation Army'). By far the most troublesome of this band of rebellious dilettantes were in Italy and West Germany.

The Red Brigades (BR), based in northern Italy, were formed in the late 1960s by three students, Renato Curcio, Mara Cagol and Alberto Franceschini. Also involved was a millionaire publisher, Giangiacomo Feltrinelli, who was later to blow himself up trying to lay explosives under an electricity pylon. In its early days the group drew support not only from within the universities but also from among the radical workers in the factories of Milan and Turin. Their ideological baggage resembled in its rhetoric of violence the outbursts of the nineteenth-century Russian revolutionaries, except that now it was Marxist–Leninism rather than anarchism that was the rallying cry. (Neither Marx nor Lenin would have approved.) Their short period as the height of fashion, however, owed more to the schoolboyish cheek of their subversion than to the persuasiveness of their philosophy, which was a mixed bag of pro-proletarian and extremist theories. In 1970 they set fire to the cars of Pirelli executives, as a way of punishing the company for having made redundancies. In 1972 they kidnapped a company director for thirty minutes, during which time they photographed him under their adopted logo with a gun pointed to his head and a placard tied around his neck which declared that he was a 'fascist tried by the BR . . . The working classes have taken up arms; for the bosses it is the beginning of the end.'[1] Similar humiliation followed for an Alfa Romeo 'boss' the following year, and in December 1973 BR's capture of a senior Fiat executive led to the distribution of propaganda leaflets and the reinstatement of sacked workers, as the price of his release.[2]

This rather harmless (comparatively speaking) revolutionary prankstering took an inevitable turn towards the serious in 1974. The organization killed for the first time, and many of its members were arrested by the authorities. One of its founders, Mara Cagol, died in a shoot-out with the police. In subsequent years the level of violence increased markedly. There were more kidnappings and punishment shootings and an ever-widening range of persons found themselves cast in the now invariably fatal role of 'enemy of the people'. These included a public prosecutor, a judge, a lawyer and a journalist before the BR achieved the high point of their obscure war with the kidnap and subsequent murder, after fifty-five days in captivity, of the President of the Christian Democratic Party and former Prime Minister of Italy, Aldo Moro. The inability of the police to find him, and the apparent callousness and effortlessness with which the BR used his misery to propagate their message of revolution, created an atmosphere of panic in Italy. In the final years of the 1970s it seemed that the democratic framework of the country had been hijacked by a faceless gang of intellectual hoodlums who took out their bitterness on innocent victims. Their radical critique of the corruption of Italian society was made all the more disturbing because it was being communicated at a time of unprecedented stress within the body politic, arising out of the electoral strength of the Communist Party and the fear held by many on the right, and shared by Italy's NATO allies, that the country would soon be governed by a left-leaning coalition.

The Red Army Faction (RAF) in West Germany had much in common with the BR, though it was based more firmly in the universities; the RAF had little connection with the proletariat other than wild enthusiasm for them. It grew out of the hippie life of the drop-out student of the late 1960s, and, as countless painstaking studies have established, had an uncanny knack of attracting to its ranks shallowly intelligent middle-class people with unhappy family backgrounds and academic careers that were going nowhere. Its ideas were a lampoonable hotch-potch of every transient notion that appeared on the radical student agenda of the period, but its tactics were more serious, since its leaders had studied Marighela and the Tupamaros, and looked with affection on the concept of the urban guerrilla.

The group gained momentum when Gudrun Ensslin and Andreas Baader jumped bail and went underground while awaiting trail for having set fire to a Frankfürt department store in 1968. There followed a bombing campaign throughout 1969, the targets of which included US and Israeli properties and installations. Baader was rearrested in 1970, but was dramatically rescued by a well-known journalist turned revolutionary, Ulrike Meinhof, acting with the assistance of a former lawyer, Horst Mahler. After a short while robbing banks to raise cash, they began in 1972 to attack 'imperialist' targets and to assassinate selected officials of whom they disapproved. There were no more than a handful of fatalities before most of the gang was rounded up and jailed.

Just as in Italy, this gave rise to a second generation of like-minded subversives, whose ideology was now subsumed within the earthy ambition of securing the release of their revered leaders. The second wave of RAF militancy was more serious than the first, and involved, apart from the occasional assassination, a siege of the West German embassy in Stockholm, during which two officials died, and the kidnap of a senior Christian Democratic politician, in return for whose release the authorities freed five

RAF prisoners. The high point was reached in 1977 with the abduction and subsequent murder of the businessman Hans-Martin Schleyer. It was clear that the government had refused to negotiate, and shortly afterwards Baader and Ensslin were reported to have committed suicide in prison. Meinhof had already taken her own life, but the loss of their leaders did not deter those who were still at large and violent acts of subversion continued to occur sporadically during the rest of the decade. The 'balance sheet' for the period 1969–79 was sixty-nine attacks on people, with twenty-five fatalities. During the same period, seven RAF members were killed while being pursued, four lost their lives on a mission and seven died in prison.[3]

Neither these figures, nor those for the Red Brigades, bear comparison with those clocked up by ETA and the IRA, much less the Palestinian groups of the 1968–74 period, but their effect should not be underestimated on that account. Like the Red Brigades, the RAF's violence was an open affront to an insecure society. Its message was an apparently ominous one for a West Germany which was only then beginning to come to terms with its Nazi past and with the post-war partition to which it had been subjected.

Ideologically motivated political violence has continued to exert a mildly destructive influence in Europe since reaching its peak in Italy and West Germany in 1977–8. After maintaining the tempo of violence in the years 1979–81, the BR drifted into an almost entirely quiescent mode, and their last successful killing (of a senator) occurred in April 1988. In Belgium a small group calling itself the Fighting Communist Cells (CCC) set off a few explosions. Action Directe contributed a French dimension with a short flurry of death and damage, before its leaders were rounded up by the police and sentenced to long terms of imprisonment for the murder of Georges Besse, the chairman of Renault, in 1986.

These French and Belgian organizations caused a *frisson* of excitement among the more impressionable terrorologists with their announcement in 1985 that they were teaming up with the RAF to form a new united terrorist front. Nothing much came of this alliance, but the RAF has lingered on in West Germany, in a much reduced state and without the sanctuary in the GDR that it is now apparent many of its leaders had formerly enjoyed. An occasional attack is essayed as a sporadic reminder of its existence. Since 1985 three military personnel, a chauffeur, a diplomat and three businessmen have been killed, the most recent fatality being the head of Deutsche Bank, Alfred Herrhausen, who was blown up by a roadside bomb in November 1989. After a failed murder attempt in June 1990, the RAF announced that their intention now was to forge a 'longer-term struggle against the newly created greater Germany/West European superpower'. They accused the authorities in Bonn and East Germany, 'by taking steps towards greater Germany, of having the same aims and imperial plans as the Nazi fascists'.

Countering the Disaffected

It remains to be seen whether these recent declarations presage an escalation of their ersatz war or whether they amount to no more than the empty rhetoric of a 'busted flush', as one commentator graphically put it.[4] For the present, however, it seems safe to say that the European authorities have, largely speaking, defeated these subversive groups, and have managed this without sacrificing the essential characteristics that make them democratic nations.

It is worth pausing, therefore, to reflect upon how this has been achieved. First, it is significant that the RAF's failed attack in June 1990 was on Hans Neusel, State Secretary at the Interior Ministry, and a leading figure in the TREVI group. This organization was set up in 1975, after a suggestion by the then British Prime Minister, Harold Wilson. Its purpose was to provide a base for cooperation between EC countries in their handling of European subversion of all shapes and sizes. Under its aegis meetings are held between Community interior and justice ministers and senior police officers. It provides for the pooling and exchange of information and has, by all accounts, been remarkably successful. It is of obvious importance that such liaison should continue, just as it is equally clear that significant events like the conclusion of the Schengen Treaty (under which border controls between five EC countries are brought to an end) and the introduction of a common European market in 1992 should occur against a background of awareness on the part of policy-makers of the threat posed by domestic subversion. But TREVI and other similar bodies will continue to work well only if they are mindful of keeping a sense of proportion about the threat which they are seeking to combat. 'Counter-terrorism' must never become the Trojan horse by which totalitarian habits are smuggled into a democratic system. The challenge here is to develop structures of openness and accountability with which to harness and render democratic the powerful new Community bodies that are fast emerging. At a broad level, this involves tackling the problem of the 'democratic deficit' presently evident in the structures of the EC. More specifically, the hope of getting the balance right between counter-terrorism and liberty at Community level depends on such reform.

Second, in addition to the sort of international cooperation epitomized by TREVI, the European authorities concerned with ideological subversion have never lost sight of the political dimension to their opponents' crimes, and have turned this to good effect. The second- and third-generation militants of the post-romantic era rarely if ever enjoy any popular support for their activities. Unlike the pseudo-colonialists of ETA and the IRA, they had no local hinterland in which to rest and recharge their energies. Their rebellious sacrifices win them no respect anywhere outside their tiny cell of comrades. It is a lonely, isolated world, surrounded by the failure of others who have taken the same Sisyphean route to revolution and ended up in ignominious retreat. Not only is there no support from 'the people' on whose behalf the subversives believe themselves to be killing but there is downright and pervasive hostility. The authorities have been content with the development of this widespread perception that the subversives challenge the way of life of all the people, not just the rich, the police or the decision-makers at the top. As a result, the European public has generally been prepared to tolerate harsh laws as a temporary price worth paying for their elimination. Thus legislation passed in the second half of the 1970s gave the police forces of both West Germany and Italy new and sweeping powers to curb domestic terrorism. On top of this was a massive commitment of more police time and greater expenditure. Novel technological systems and psychological techniques were brought to bear on the isolation and discovery of underground groups. The resources devoted to their defeat were remarkable, and ultimately largely successful.

To give an example, the West German authorities had for many years been anxious to capture an obscure and tiny subversive group, Red Zora, the women's branch of an organization called Revolutionary Cells which had made a nuisance of itself. Red Zora had never been betrayed and had proved impossible to penetrate. The group never attacked people but had successfully carried out numerous bombings against buildings and property. They always used as a timer for the explosions a miniature alarm clock of a type made only by a single company, Amos Ltd. With the force of each explosion the clock was destroyed, but investigators found that one tiny component always survived. The police then went to Amos and bought up their entire supply of alarm clocks, all 900 of them then in production. They marked the components in each clock and put their own agents into the shops that sold them. Psychologists were called in and provided a profile of the terrorist buyer: she would be aged between twenty-five and forty, would have an 'intellectual appearance' and would ask specifically for 'an Amos clock'. All buyers were photographed by hidden cameras and those who fitted the profile were followed by police agents. Large numbers of police were involved. Dozens of houses were searched. The editor of a woman's weekly magazine became a prime suspect; she fitted the profile exactly. A search of her home revealed the bombing equipment that the authorities were looking for and included in the pile of weaponry was the incriminating, innocent-looking alarm clock. The Red Zora group was finished.

Third, apart from international cooperation and publicly supported national police work, the authorities have developed an additional way of countering ideological terrorism which has proved highly effective. After capture and conviction comes reconciliation. Once again the key to the process is the political content of the offences that the subversives have committed. Many of those imprisoned for their activities were in no ordinary sense criminals. Without an allegiance to the cause of revolt they would not have drifted beyond the law, and for many convicted subversives the ideology that underpinned their criminal actions does not survive the critical evaluation that they bring to bear on it during the long hours of their captivity. In West Germany, the authorities have assisted this process of reassessment by initiating dialogue with such prisoners with the express purpose of encouraging them to confront their past. The ultimate aim is to give them the option of escaping from the cul-de-sac into which their early militancy has driven them, thereby effecting their reintegration into society. It has proved an attractive opportunity for a number of ex-RAF operatives, who have eschewed terrorism and begun to rebuild their lives as free people.

The Italians have taken the process a stage further and cleverly turned the doubts and uncertainties of the captured Red Brigadists into a way of debilitating their organization even further. Two legal initiatives, the penitence law (1982) and the dissociation law (1987), encourage voluntary collaboration and the disavowal of the aims and methods of violent subversion. A leading writer on Italian terrorism has described their effect in the following way:

In order to benefit from the penitence law, which ran for one year, there were two basic requirements: firstly, the *pentito* had to make a full confession of all crimes committed, and secondly he or she had to make an active contribution towards the prevention of further acts of terrorism. It was then up to the court of law to decide on the relevance of the evidence provided, how much a prison sentence could be reduced. Those intending to avail themselves of the dissociation law had to make their intentions known within one month of the law appearing on the statute book, and fulfil three requirements: the confession of all their terrorist activities, the formal abjuration of violence as a means of political struggle, and the demonstration in prison of behaviour corresponding to a renunciation of the beliefs and principles of the armed struggle. In return, with the exception of convictions for *'strage'* or massacre, sentences were reduced from 'life' to thirty years; crimes of bloodshed involving direct responsibility by a quarter; for associative crimes by half and all other crimes by a third.[5]

The penitence law was a key part of the successful counter-terrorism strategy followed by the Italian authorities in the 1980s.

Separatist Subversion

The problems posed by separatist movements are far graver for democratic authorities than the irritations caused by the distorted idealism of the 'Euro-terrorists'. Far from being the Achilles' heel that it is with the RAF and the BR, the political dimension is in this context a great strength. As we have seen, both ETA and the IRA enjoy reasonably firm local support. Additionally, there is a wider group within each community which shares their political objectives without necessarily supporting their means. Both organizations can draw upon a long historical and cultural tradition supportive of their militancy, and each can claim – by referring to liberated countries across the world – to be surrounded by successful precedents. The validity of such assertions matters less than the fact that they can be made. Both Britain and Spain have recognized that the subversion of ETA and the IRA has to be tackled politically. Each country has engaged in sophisticated attempts to wean separatist communities away from support for the militants, through Basque autonomy and the Anglo–Irish Agreement respectively.

The authorities have also sought to emulate West German and Italian success in relation to winning the hearts and minds of convicted subversives, though this is much more difficult here since the violence is far more entrenched in popular culture than it ever was in either of those countries. However, despite the obstacles, Spain has had some success with its commitment to the 'social reinsertion' of suitable ETAm members, and the

Northern Irish authorities have recently embarked upon a brave policy of releasing back into the community prisoners who have been given life sentences for subversive crimes, mostly murder. A total of around 180 such convicts had been freed by the end of September 1990, the vast majority in the previous three years. They know they are liable to be peremptorily rearrested if they return to militancy, and the early indications are that this has rarely if ever occurred.

Neither political nor penal initiatives are enough in themselves to counter subversion. There must also be a policing or criminal dimension. With regard to ideologically motivated violence, the support the public at large give to the authorities means that law and order can be quite easily separated from politics. The police and the security forces apply the rule of law in their impartial pursuit of lawbreakers, who may be politically motivated but who are unequivocally criminal none the less.

With separatist violence, the situation is not so simple. Law and order and policing policies have inevitable political implications in themselves, encapsulated in the sensitive question invariably posed by the communities being policed: whose rule of law is being applied? If it is perceived to be that of the central authorities, unsympathetic to local feeling, then separatist pressures may well increase; if it is thought to be fair and impartial, then the militants' arguments about oppression lose much of their force. Thus the rule of law not only tackles the subversive manifestations of separatist feeling but also, depending on how it is applied, either exacerbates tensions or becomes part of the solution. This has been recognized in Spain, where an early decision was taken by the new democratic authorities to involve the Basque people in their own policing. Similar considerations led the pro-Tamil Indian army into Sri Lanka. It is, as ever, more complicated in the divided community of Northern Ireland, where one of the main sources of IRA support in the early days was the nationalist view that the 'rule of law' and 'law and order' were transparently partisan devices through which the unionists repressed their cultural identity and deprived them of the opportunity to protest.

Terrorism and the Rule of Law in Northern Ireland

There was undoubted truth in allegations about the operation of a biased rule of law in the early years of the disturbances in the Province. We have already examined the damage that was done both by the obvious alliance between the police and the Protestant mobs, and by the apparent antinationalist bent of the army in 1969–71. The most extreme example of the politicization of law and order was the decision, taken by the then still-existing unionist government in Stormont, to introduce internment in August 1971. Never was the rule of law more blatantly turned to the advantage of one community over another. The consequences of the move, codenamed Operation Demetrius, were well described in an important article written by David McKittrick at a time when the reintroduction of internment was reported to be under serious consideration in Downing Street:

The first Operation Demetrius swoop in the early hours of 9 August 1971 netted more innocent men than IRA activists. The files of the RUC Special Branch, it soon became obvious, were obsolete and inaccurate. Within hours street disorders were widespread. Hostility between the security forces and much of the Catholic community reached a new pitch, and polarization between the communities deteriorated dramatically. Those released told tales of casual brutality in the interrogation centres.

Internationally the image of British justice was considerably harmed – particularly in America, where the IRA benefited from a new wave of support. The dollars rolled in. Anglo-Irish relations plummeted: the Republic accused Britain of torture. Years later, the European Court of Human Rights found the UK guilty of inflicting 'inhuman and degrading treatment' on a number of internees.

Internment triggered off the bloodiest days of the troubles. Gun battles became nightly occurrences. Until 9 August, thirty people had died violently. In the remainder of 1971, 143 were killed. The following year, by far the worst of the troubles, 467 died.[6]

Coming after two years of inept army behaviour, this crass military response to subversion was the single most important breakthrough in terms of broadening their appeal, that the IRA has ever had.

The authorities learned the hard way that such draconian security operations created more problems than they solved. With the phasing out of internment in the mid-1970s, the control of subversion in Northern Ireland entered a new phase. The emphasis now switched to a policy of criminalization. No longer were suspected subversives grabbed by the army and bundled into indefinite detention. Instead, they were treated, in theory at least, in exactly the same way as ordinary criminals. The new vogue was for 'police primacy' and the supremacy of the 'rule of law'. Suspects found themselves being arrested by the police, interrogated and, if the evidence was sufficient, charged and tried in court with serious but, in an important sense, ordinary offences. Once incarcerated in jail, it followed that no extra privileges could be accorded to them, and it was over the denial of 'special status' that IRA men were eventually to starve themselves to death in 1981. The advantages the United Kingdom gained from this new approach were manifold. Instead of having to treat the subversives like military opponents, with all the embarrassment that that involved internationally, there was this powerful propaganda point that the IRA were 'no more than a bunch of criminals', committing murder, robbery and other acts of destruction under cover of a spurious veneer which had permitted them to pose as liberation fighters for far too long.

This message was aimed not only at the international audience but also at the nationalist communities. To be effective it was obvious that the rule of law and the legal system that was being applied needed not only to be but also to be seen to be impartial. This was always going to be a difficult task, given the suspicions that had built up over the years of unionist hegemony. In fact, it has proved to be impossible and the designation 'criminal' has been purchased at a very high price. Looking back over the fifteen years during which this policy has been in operation, the cumulative impact of all the changes, modifications and departures from the rule of law that have been deemed necessary by the authorities is indeed striking. The alterations have affected basic liberties in a number of fundamental ways. To start with, the rule of law that governs Northern Ireland has been transformed by the need to accommodate the IRA within its remit. In the early years, on account of alleged widespread intimidation, trial by jury was abolished for a broad range of crimes. It is now the norm to have serious cases heard by a judge alone, with a right of appeal to a three-judge court. A large number of trials before such tribunals have nothing to do with terrorism, but the government has been very slow to utilize an available procedure to bring the jury back into the equation. It is more convenient to operate without one, and a high proportion of defendants are now proceeded against in this way.

It would seem that this quiet jettisoning of a fundamental legal principle quickly became part of the accepted legal landscape. The same may be true of a more recent, and equally fundamental, change. The entitlement of a person not to incriminate himself or herself, manifested in a right to silence when under police suspicion of having committed a crime, has long been regarded as an essential feature of English common law. Traditionally the prosecution has had to prove the case and cannot rely on the accused inculpating himself or herself out of his or her own mouth. This no longer applies in Northern Ireland. Citing the way terrorists cleverly use silence to foil police interrogations and investigations, in 1988 the government ended this right in three broadly defined situations. To summarize a difficult provision, suspects failing to mention something when they are being questioned, or omitting to explain 'any object, substance or mark' on their person, or simply refusing to tell the police why they are in a certain place at a certain time may find the judge at their later trial prepared to infer guilt from their reluctance to cooperate. In place of the traditional police caution about the right to silence, there are now a variety of complicated and ominous messages, one of which may be given by way of illustration:

You do not have to say anything unless you wish to do so but I must warn you that if you fail to mention any fact which you rely on in your defence in court, your failure to take this opportunity to mention it may be treated in court as supporting any relevant evidence against you. If you wish to say anything, what you say may be given in evidence.

The change in the right to silence is in direct conflict with one of the provisons of the US Bill of Rights, as is the media ban on certain unacceptable political parties and points of view, introduced by the authorities in the same year. The effect of this new restriction on Provisional Sinn Fein and the IRA in particular is to prevent the British television and radio networks from broadcasting 'any matter which consists of or includes any words spoken, whether in the course of an interview or discussion or otherwise, by a person' who represents either group or who is expressing opinions which 'support or solicit or invite support' for either of them. The IRA are already a banned organization, though Provisional Sinn Fein remain a legal political party and, indeed, have a member of parliament at Westminster and numerous councillors scattered around the country.

The government said it needed the ban because the subversives were drawing support and sustenance from their access to the media and were using both television and radio to issue indirect threats. The clinching argument as far as the authorities were concerned, however, was the fact that the opinions being expressed were causing offence. This was the main reason why they were banished from the airwaves, a reaction that might be thought by some to be curiously disproportionate in a democracy. Since the introduction of the ban, interviews involving the discussion of Irish issues have been cancelled by nervous executives at the first sign of a suggestion that they might drift into the censored areas. Before the freeing of the Guildford Four, relatives campaigning for their release were sometimes prevented from appearing on radio, and a pop song by the Pogues declaring their innocence was denied air time. The political campaign for the removal of British troops from Northern Ireland has been reduced to media invisibility as a result of the fact that its goal is shared by Provisional Sinn Fein. An area of political cogitation unattractive to the government has been effectively cordoned off.

These changes to the right to silence, the entitlement to a jury and freedom of expression are by no means the end of the story. Special legislation gives a plethora of extraordinary powers to the authorities and more than compensates for the disadvantages that theoretically flow from their being constrained to apply an objective rule of law. Foremost among these has been the Prevention of Terrorism legislation, in place throughout the United Kingdom since 1974. Three of its provisions may be given by way of illustration of its impact on British civil liberties.

First, it creates the criminal offence of belonging to certain 'proscribed' organizations, including INLA and the IRA. It is not seriously argued that this law has substantially impeded the operational efficiency of any subversive groups. Public disgust at their activity lies behind the pro-scriptions – an emotionally understandable but dangerously broad basis for such a major qualification on the freedom of association. Second, the Prevention of Terrorism Act allows the authorities to exclude United Kingdom citizens from Britain and restrict them to Northern Ireland if they decide that such persons have 'been concerned in the commission, preparation, or instigation of acts of terrorism connected with Northern Ireland'. No court is involved in the making of this decision, and the authorities do not have to give any reasons for such banishments. The victims of this secret administrative process may make representations to government advisers (chosen by the authorities), but not being told the reasons for their expulsion narrows the options for even the most loquacious of advocates. Finally, the law since 1974 has allowed the detention without charge of 'suspected terrorists' for up to seven days. For the first forty-eight hours of this period all access to outsiders and lawyers may in certain circumstances be denied. When in 1989 the European Court of Human Rights condemned this provision as an infringement of basic freedom, the government simply declared that a 'public emergency threatening the life of the nation' warranted its continuance and proceeded to retain it despite the decision of the court.

It would seem that the rule of law is applied only when it is convenient. But quite apart from these structural alterations, national concern about its partial implementation by the authorities has continued unabated over the years. The police force remains overwhelmingly Protestant. Allegations of low-level harassment by the security forces and physical ill-treatment of suspects continue to surface. The damage done by rigorous house searches by the army causes far more offence than is officially acknowledged. And casting its ugly shadow over the whole administration of law in the Province since the early 1980s has been the 'shoot to kill' controversy. In a five-and-a-half-year period in the middle of the decade, forty-nine people died at the hands of the RUC and the army. In nineteen of the thirty-two incidents identified, the victims (the vast majority of whom were Catholic) were unarmed. Later incidents, such as the shooting of three unarmed IRA members by the SAS in Gibraltar in 1988, and the killing of a gang of robbers by an undercover security team in West Belfast in early 1990 have kept the issue on the boil.

Trials of security officers occur infrequently, and when they do they seem to lead inexorably to acquittals. In the years since 1969, only one conviction has been obtained in respect of a killing caused by the use of a firearm while on duty, and in that case the prisoner (a private in the army) was freed after three-and-a-half years, despite having been sentenced to life imprisonment for murder. Where there is no trial, the law does not even require the security officer who caused the death to give evidence at any subsequent coroner's inquest into the fatality. And perhaps most disturbing of all have been recent revelations of close connections between certain elements within the police and the UDR and loyalist paramilitary groups, whereby intelligence information on suspects has been fed to subversives less squeamish about murder than the officers collecting the data. The analogy between this relationship and the notorious death squads of Central and South America should be too close for comfort.

Conclusion

The great number of changes in the rule of law in Northern Ireland has occurred because of the anxiety of government ministers both to limit the activities of the IRA and to secure as many convictions as possible through the ordinary courts. Both are laudable objectives, but if the tactics employed to achieve them undermine the perceived impartiality of the legal process, then the whole approach quickly becomes self-defeating. The rule of law has a vital role in fostering a culture of reconciliation in the Province by being demonstrably fair, even-handed and responsive to the community in which it is applied. On the other hand, a policy of criminalization which separates 'law and order' and security issues from politics, and changes the law to suit its ends, hinders the ending of sectarian divisions by appearing to confirm the partisanship of British law. In such circumstances, measures aimed at tackling subversion in fact compound it.

Conclusion

Having ranged widely in our survey of political terror, placing the conflicts we have examined in their historical and regional context and – as far as possible – deducing from them lessons of general relevance to our subject, it should be clear that statements and assertions about the abstract problems of 'terrorism' and 'international terrorism' must be treated with caution. In particular, there has never been a set of objective criteria, the existence of which triggers the onset of this form of violence. Nor is it possible to predict the imminence of terror by pointing to an increase in regional tension somewhere in the world. The resort of subversive groups to terror tactics hinges on a complex interplay of many different factors and is not an automatic consequence of political disaffection. Nowhere is this more clearly borne out than by reference to one of the bloodiest subversive groups of recent times, the Sendero Luminoso of Peru.

The Paradox of Peru

In the nine years 1980–8, conservative estimates put the number killed as a direct result of political violence in Peru at over 11,000. Less than one-tenth of these were military or police personnel, the rest being evenly divided between civilian and subversive casualties.[1] In 1989 alone, over 1,600 political fatalities were reported, 420 of them in the five weeks preceding the municipal elections of that year. Indeed, so great was the tension that the authorities had to end the practice of dipping the fingers of voters in dye (as a safeguard against multiple visits to the ballot box), on account of the threat from subversives that they would mutilate those with the tell-tale mark of democracy on their hands. By the end of the decade, half the Peruvian population lived under various states of emergency and the tourist and commercial wealth of the nation had been ravaged.[2] Even the capital Lima had suffered the indignity of frequent losses of electricity, orchestrated by recalcitrant yet seemingly all-powerful guerrillas stalking freely in the hills above.

The subversive group responsible for much of this continuing decay is Sendero Luminoso. Their curious, almost religious-sounding name – Shining Path in English – is a delphic reference to Jose Carlos Mariategui, the founder and leader of the Peruvian Communist Party of the late 1920s.[3] The organization is certainly left-wing, but its communism seems in the light of the changes in Europe in 1989 to be extraordinarily antediluvian and rigid. Mao remains their paradigm, with regard both to policy and to practice. As a result, reformist tendencies in China and the USSR have been dismissed as in each case little more than a 'counter-revolution' aimed at the 'restoration of a more unbridled capitalism'.[4] However, Sendero craftily lace their communism with local ideas about native agrarian communities and this gives them a dimension of 'militant Messianism that is uniquely Peruvian'.[5] The support which flows from this is drawn mainly from the marginalized and the poor, and particularly from amongst the Indian population in certain provinces. But we should not be mislead by this into easy explanations of Sendero as no more than a consequence of inequality between rich and poor, particularly in relation to property ownership. On the contrary, Peru has had more land reform than almost any other country in the region. The military government that ruled from 1969–79 engaged in radical change of this sort deliberately in order to achieve (or so they thought) 'the inoculation of the Peruvian countryside against revolutionary violence'.[6] Over the decade, an estimated 370,000 families benefited from their reforms and 8.6 million hectares of land were transferred to peasant households.[7] If land reform were the sole issue in Peru, then the whole continent would be in bloody revolt.

The reasons for the emergence of Sendero lie not so much in economic or political theory as in the pervasive influence of one man, Dr Abimael Guzman, who in the 1960s was Professor of Philosophy in the education department of Ayacucho University. He was always a radical and regularly sent his students to work with the neglected and maligned Indian underclass. In 1980, his thinking developed to the point where he and his followers went into hiding and commenced the armed struggle for the overthrow of the State, with which Sendero Luminoso are now identified.

The strategy initially was to build up a rural following by taking over villages, eliminating the government's authority in selected areas and imposing their own ideology. This provoked a strong reaction from Peru's military and the alienation amongst the general population that this led to added to Sendero's appeal. Their rural base has continued to grow during the decade and has gained strength from a close liaison with drug barons faced with the same enemy, albeit for very different reasons. In the mid 1980s, the organization felt strong enough to expand its reach into the cities, where since then it has combined subversive violence with political campaigning on left-wing issues.

The methods employed by Sendero have been both guerrilla and terrorist, though the latter has been untypically prominent for such a primarily rural insurgency. The breadth of the victims of their retribution, ranging from government officials to aid workers and disobedient local peasants, indicates their determination to exercise sole authority in the areas they control. But it also reflects a heavy reliance on terror, of which Mao would have disapproved. This dependency on intimidation and petrifying violence has gone some way towards undermining their popular support, and Sendero has yet to push its revolt to the point where its threat to destroy Peru's infrastructure and government could be described as imminent.

As ever with such subversive groups, they continue to pin their strategy on provoking an overreaction from the authorities. This has indeed occurred. A massacre by the military in 1986 killed 270 inmates in Lima jail – many of the dead were suspected of terrorist activities. According to Amnesty International, 'disappearances' in Peru in the last three years of the decade were higher than in any other country in the world, and the suspicion remains that right-wing death squads have grown up to do the job that elements within the army believe is being denied them for reasons of political squeamishness.

But the harshest of this counter-terrorism has not, and will not, lead to Sendero success, despite their hopes and plans. Marighela's theories are as wrong now as when they were first developed two decades before. Instead, all that the uninvolved people of Peru have now and can expect in the future is an ongoing bloody stalemate. Sendero may eventually be defeated, but the risk is that it will be at the price of the already fragile and weak democratic structure of government.

Judging Terror

With its old-fashioned Maoism, its mystic religiosity, its hybrid guerrilla/ terrorist strategy, and above all with the viciousness of the reaction to it from the democratic authorities, Sendero Luminoso stand as a symbol of the complexity of our subject. None of the usual rules apply to these mysterious guerrillas, yet they thrive with ominous confidence all the same.

With this warning against glib generalizations in mind, let us turn now to recap some of the salient points that have emerged from this survey of political terror. The use of terror in its pure sense reached its height in the 1968–74 period. There had been similar subversive before – such as the Assassins, the Zealots and the nineteenth-century anarchists in Russia – but none of them had encompassed all the ingredients that came together in such a potent mix at the end of the 1960s. What made these peak years dramatic was the fact that political terror was simultaneously adopted by a wide range of groups acting separately in their various quarrels around the world. The PLO and other factions associated with their brand of violent Palestinian nationalism may have been most closely identified with the method, because of the international reach of their campaign of hijackings and shootings, but the IRA, ETA and assorted ideological groups also burst upon the scene at the same time.

It was an extraordinary coincidence of tactics and timing, facilitated by various changes in Western society, particularly those which made travel easier and communication via the new and burgeoning media industry more attractive. The label that emerged to describe this novel set of mischiefs was terrorism; by the middle of the 1970s, it was possible to state with reasonable accuracy what the word covered. However, since that time the word's meaning has been subject to constant change and contortion, as governments and groups alike have fought propaganda wars to affix the damning imprint on their opponents.

In order to avoid the pitfalls of this war over words, this book deals with the more general and neutral topic of violent subversion as opposed to terrorism, placing the various conflicts which are said to involve terrorist action in their political and geographic context. Thus the analysis of the Middle East led to the conclusion that the breadth of the conflict there made it inappropriate to concentrate on only that particular strand which we could with confidence designate as terrorist. Such an approach would inherently have supported the status quo in the region, since it would have ignored the state violence which explains (though it may not excuse) Palestinian militancy.

Without this broader picture, it would have seemed as though terrorist subversion was a mysterious pathology afflicting unstable extremists in the Middle East (always Palestinian and other Arabs), whereas in reality the violence there, being rooted in history and in hate, and being practised by armies as well as by rebels, is far worse and more extensive than this. The situation is clearer in relation to the other types of violent subversion examined – the pseudo-colonial extremism of the separatists and the ideological militants referred to in Chapters 7, 8 and 9 – though even here precise definitions of political terror do not always fit as easily as might have been expected.

Indeed, this narrative raises the fundamental question of whether the terrorist label has any utility in any context. Have we now reached the point where it should be dispensed with altogether, its meaning having been irredeemably compromised by the wide variety of uses to which it has been put. Whatever the attractions of this course, it is not practically possible. The word is too embedded in the parlance of politicians and in the psychology of the population. What we are entitled to call for, on the other hand, is greater discipline in the way that it is employed. Thus, at the very least, it should be restricted to the use of violence by substate groups.

There is no point in declaring Saddam Hussein a 'terrorist' for invading Kuwait; we have many other words available to capture the essence of such warmongering. Similarly, calling General Gadaffi, the Ayatalloh Khomeini, President Assad and others 'state terrorists' may have been accurate to the extent that they facilitated the commission of terror acts by substate groups acting within democratic countries, but the effect of such name-calling was to turn the definition of terrorism into a subset of US foreign policy, and no other development during the 1980s did more damage to the integrity of the word than this unhappy appropriation of it by diplomats and politicians. Furthermore, it should be possible to restrict the meaning of terrorism not only to substate groups but also solely to the violence in which they engage that has a political end. Mere criminality or thuggery should not be enough. Nor should injury motivated by anti-Semitism or racism. The fact that we abhor such terrible hate should not drive us to reach for the 'terrorist' stigma. We must find other words to encapsulate and convey our distaste.

These qualifications and restrictions leave us with a meaning of terrorism that is indelibly linked to the idea of violent political subversion by substate groups. This is a breakthrough of sorts, and at least removes terrorism from the realm of haphazardly formulated insults, but it remains deeply unsatisfactory, because it is still far too wide. In particular, it stigmatizes as terrorist not a particular method of violent subversion but rather the simple fact of subversion itself. No dimension of terror is involved and the context of the violence plays no part in the decision as to whether it falls within the definition. If this were the true meaning of terrorism, then all violent subversion would be terrorist. A political scientist who regards such a descriptive label as non-judgemental might be perfectly happy with this, and be prepared to proceed to an analysis of whether, and if so in what circumstances, such terrorism is ever justified. However, it is difficult for many of us who instinctively condemn all terrorism to keep this sense of detachment. If we accept that the word is value-laden in the sense that it carries with it overtones of moral opprobrium (and we have argued throughout that this is the case), the equation of terrorism with violent subversion can be logically made only by those who hold one or other of the two following views: first, that no governmental authority should ever have been or be overthrown by force from within its borders; or second, that (whatever happened in the past) no political system existing anywhere in the world today should be challenged by domestic violent action of any kind.

Both of these positions are perfectly respectable moral lines to take and each is typical of a pacifist perspective on political affairs. But non-pacifists arguing for the first would have to be prepared to castigate the founding fathers of the United States as well as the subversive cells of today; and similarly, proponents of the second view would have to maintain that it is illegitimate to challenge by force not only Western democracies but also Israeli control of the occupied territories and military oppression in Central and South America. Persuasive cases may no doubt be made for all these positions. But the vital point is that allowing the definition of terrorism to embrace all violent subversion leads the non-pacifist who is aware of the condemnatory ring to the word into a moral corner in which he or she might not be keen to remain: namely, the situation in which all authority is upheld (no matter how vicious) and all violent dissent condemned (no matter how justified, excusable or restrained in its execution).

So, if this linkage between terrorism and violent subversion is too general, how can we achieve greater specificity without risking the elimination of certain conduct which we would want to regard as terrorist? We have already seen how attempts to define the word quickly become vague as a result of this very desire not to omit anything. The answer to the difficulty lies in the bold step of rejecting altogether the search for a comprehensive definition and replacing it with the idea of a spectrum of behaviour, at the core of which lie those activities which are unequivocally terrorist, but on the fringes of which are scattered subversive acts which are more ambiguous in their impact. We have prepared the way for this analysis in Chapter 1 by examining what we there considered to be the essential elements in true terrorist acts. As we saw, these included such factors as the deliberate or reckless infliction of death or serious injury; indiscriminateness in the choice of victim; a strategy of provocation; the use of violence as a symbolic form of communication, aimed at an audience wider than that immediately present; and the systematic use of such violence so as to cause terror in the society affected by it. The greater the number of these variables present, the clearer it is that the subversive conduct under examination is purely terrorist in its methodology. By the same token, the fewer there are, or the less clearly they appear, the less terrorist the behaviour is likely to be. And at the outer edges of the range of conduct, where the subversive activity has none of these characteristics, the terrorist dimension will have disappeared altogether.

The organization of subversion along these lines with core acts of terror at the centre and other forms of violence occupying points in the penumbra beyond, is more than merely analytically convenient. Of course, there will inevitably be grey areas, but in general it leads us to the point where we can successfully bring together the meaning of terrorism with our realization that to call something terrorist is to condemn it. For one of the lessons that can be drawn from the many incidents of core terrorism discussed in this book is that such conduct is never acceptable, and this is true regardless of both the political context in which it occurs and the nature of the opponent against which it is employed. State violence may or may not be wrong but political terror is always wrong, everywhere. This is as true of such acts in South America and the Middle East as it is in Europe.

The unacceptability of the behaviour is clear on two levels. First, there is the ethical objection that it is always wrong to kill the innocent, and the victim of harsh and unjust treatment in the past does not on that account buy immunity from this simple moral rule; it is no solution to injustice to increase its presence in the world. Second, apart from ethics, there are obvious pragmatic objections to political terror, encapsulated in the observation, based on the experience of the groups examined here, that it simply does not work. The strategy of provocation, for example, has never amounted to more than a series of wildly brutal but (from the point of view of the terrorist) optimistic assumptions about the likely response of indigenous communities to state counter-terror. The support for the subversive that is supposed to follow such governmental action has never been more than an intellectual hypothesis, but the counter-terror provoked has been real enough, and has routinely obliterated the terrorist group in question – and countless innocent civilians as well. The evidence would suggest that acts of terror generally lead to increased state repression. Indeed, they both stimulate and are made to justify what are often quite unnecessarily severe measures. But even aided by such draconian official interventions, terror has never produced that dramatic rise in the terrorists' popularity which would make their assumption of power more than a distant possibility. Deprived of any hope of achieving their ultimate goals through terror, such groups invariably split between those who desire to enter the political mainsteam and those who stay behind to fight. For the first group, their terror background can be expected to dog them for the rest of their political careers; for the second, all that remains is a continuing downward spiral into ever more futile brutality. Both remain, united for ever by failure.

As we move across the spectrum, however, away from pure acts of terror, and towards rebellious violence, which is broader and vaguer in its definition, these generalizations become less apposite, and a new emphasis on context necessarily emerges. Here it is best not to refer to 'terrorism' at all but rather to describe the conduct under scrutiny as violent subversion, since this rightly focuses on the two key questions: namely, what kind of (non-terror) violence is being employed; and what is it that is being subverted? If the answer to the second of these is a democratic framework of government containing a mechanism whereby change can be peacefully brought about by popular decision, it would appear that such conduct is not morally justifiable. If the system that is being challenged is a totalitarian, authoritarian or racist one, and if the defiance takes the form of carefully calculated and restrained subversion, the question of its ethical correctness may be a much more open one, involving consideration of complex local and historical issues. Of course, there will be grey areas between terror and other forms of subversive violence. But we will be going a long way towards winning our war over words if we recognize this distinction and apply it with an awareness of history and context always in mind.

Notes

Introduction

1 T. Clarke, *By Blood and Fire: The Attack on the King David Hotel*.
2 T. P. Coogan, *The IRA*.
3 B. Netanyahu (ed.), *Terrorism: How the West Can Win*.
4 C. Dobson and R. Payne, *Terror!: The West Fights Back*.
5 N. Livingstone, *The War Against Terrorism*.
6 D. Rapoport (ed.), *Inside Terrorist Organizations*.
7 U. Ra'anan, R. L. Pfaltzgraff, R. H. Shultz, E. Halperin and I. Lukes, *Hydra of Carnage*.

1 The Trance of Terror

1 Quoted in D. Hirst, *The Gun and the Olive Branch*, p. 304.
2 Ibid., p. 311.
3 W. Laqueur, *The Age of Terrorism*.
4 B. M. Jenkins, 'The Study of Terrorism: Definitional Problems', pp. 2–3.
5 P. Wilkinson, *Terrorism and the Liberal State*, p. 51.
6 G. Wardlaw, *Political Terrorism*, p. 50.
7 W. Laqueur, op. cit., p. 144.
8 Quoted by R. Thackrah, 'Terrorism: A Definitional Problem', in P. Wilkinson and A. M. Stewart (eds.), *Contemporary Research on Terrorism*, p. 27.

2 Sparks

1 R. Clutterbuck, *Guerrillas and Terrorists*, p. 25.
2 W. Laqueur, *Guerrilla*, pp. 29–49.
3 Josephus, *The Jewish War*, p. 139.
4 B. Lewis, 'Islamic Terrorism?', in B. Netanyahu (ed.), *Terrorism: How the West Can Win*, p. 68.
5 Quoted in N. Hampson, 'From Regeneration to Terror: The Ideology of the French Revolution', in N. O'Sullivan (ed.), *Terrorism, Ideology, and Revolution*, p. 63.
6 Ibid., p. 64.
7 G. Wardlaw, *Political Terrorism*, p. 15.
8 C. Townshend, *Political Violence in Ireland*, pp. 161–2, 166. See also C. Townshend, 'The Process of Terror in Irish Politics', in N. O'Sullivan (ed.), *Terrorism, Ideology, and Revolution*, pp. 88–111.
9 A complication here is that the assassins thought they were killing other, even more senior, representatives of British rule, but my point is not invalidated by this.
10 W. Laqueur, *The Age of Terrorism*, p. 65.
11 C. Townshend, 'The Process of Terror in Irish Politics', in N. O'Sullivan (ed.), op. cit., p. 98.
12 Quoted in W. Laqueur and Y. Alexander (eds.), *The Terrorism Reader*, p. 65.
13 Ibid., pp. 68, 69.

14 Ibid., p. 75.
15 F. L. Ford, 'Reflections on Political Murder: Europe in the Nineteenth and Twentieth Centuries', in W. Mommsen and G. Hirschfeld (eds.), *Social Protest, Violence and Terror in Nineteenth- and Twentieth-century Europe*, p. 4.
16 Quoted in W. Laqueur, *The Age of Terrorism*, op. cit., p. 40.
17 F. L. Ford, op.cit., p. 7.

3 The Spiral of Brutality

1 B. Jenkins, 'International Terrorism: The Other World War', p. 8.
2 See R. Clutterbuck, *Guerrillas and Terrorists*, pp. 33–47.
3 See generally E. Guevara, *Guerrilla Warfare*.
4 W. Laqueur, *Guerrilla*, p. 332.
5 E. Guevara, quoted by G. Wardlaw, *Political Terrorism*, p. 47.
6 Ibid.
7 See R. Gott, *Guerrilla Movements in Latin America*.
8 D. Hodges (ed.), *Philosophy of the Urban Guerrilla: The Revolutionary Writings of Abraham Guillen*.
9 Ibid., p. 240.
10 Ibid., pp. 240–41.
11 Ibid., p. 266.
12 Ibid.
13 Ibid., p. 267.
14 Ibid., p. 271.
15 Ibid., p. 241.
16 C. Marighela, *For the Liberation of Brazil*, pp. 94–5.
17 Ibid., quoted in W. Laqueur and Y. Alexander (eds.), *The Terrorism Reader*, pp. 161–2.
18 R. Gillespie, 'The Urban Guerrilla in Latin America', in N. O'Sullivan (ed.), *Terrorism, Ideology, and Revolution*, p. 163. See also by the same author, *Soldiers of Perón: Argentina's Montoneros*. In writing this short section on Argentina, I have drawn heavily upon Gillespie's work.

4 The Dispossesed

1 W. Khalidi, *From Haven to Conquest*, pp. 846–9, referred to in D. Hirst, *The Gun and the Olive Branch*, p. 93.
2 T. Clarke, *By Blood and Fire: The Attack on the King David Hotel*, passim.
3 Hirst, op. cit., pp. 142–3.
4 E. H. Hutchinson, *Violent Truce*, pp. 152–8, quoted by D. Hirst, op. cit., pp. 181–2.
5 Hirst, op. cit., p. 306.
6 Ibid., p. 302.
7 Ibid., p. 308.
8 Ibid., pp. 310–17.

5 A War with Words

1 D. Hirst, *The Gun and the Olive Branch*, pp. 321–2.
2 Ibid., p. 322.
3 Y. Alexander and J. Sinai, *Terrorism: The PLO Connection*, p. ix.
4 B. Netanyahu (ed.), *Terrorism: How the West can Win*, p. 93.

5 S. T. Francis, *The Soviet Strategy of Terror*; E. Luttwak, *The Grand Strategy of the Soviet Union*; U. Ra'anan, R. L. Pfaltzgraff, R. H. Shultz, E. Halperin and I. Lukes, *Hydra of Carnage*.
6 N. C. Livingstone, *The War Against Terrorism*, p. 1.
7 Netanyahu, op. cit., p. ix.
8 Ibid., p. 6.
9 Ibid., p. ix.
10 Figures given by United Nations High Commissioner for Refugees, Beirut, 19 May 1978, quoted in D. Gilmour, *Lebanon: The Fractured Country*, p. 150.
11 Figures given by the United Nations Press Section, New York, 23 March 1978, quoted ibid., p. 149.
12 Ibid., p. 149.
13 Ibid., p. 160.
14 Ibid., p. 166.
15 Hirst, op. cit., p. 426.

6 War with the Shadows

1 Quoted in G. M. Levitt, *Democracies Against Terror: The Western Response to State-supported Terrorism*, p. 2.
2 D. C. Martin and J. Walcott, *Best Laid Plans: The Inside Story of America's War Against Terrorism*, p. 102.
3 Ibid., p. 115.
4 R. Fisk, *Pity the Nation: Lebanon at War*, pp. 524–5.
5 Quoted in Martin and Walcott, op. cit., pp. 187–8.
6 Ibid., p. 190.
7 Ibid., p. 275.
8 G. Wardlaw, *Political Terrorism*, p. 177.
9 Ibid., p. 178.
10 Ibid., p. 176 (footnotes omitted).
11 M. Bles and R. Low, *The Kidnap Business*, p. 288.
12 J. Flint, 'Prisoners Tell of Brutal Regime in Torture Chamber of Khiam', *Observer*, 13 May 1990.
13 Bles and Low, op. cit., p. 292.
14 J. Flint, 'The Youngest Martyrs: Palestine's Davids', *Observer*, 15 July 1990.

7 The Pseudo-colonials

1 See C. Greenwood, 'Terrorism and Humanitarian Law – The Debate over Additional Protocol 1', in (1989) *Israel Yearbook on Human Rights*, p. 187.
2 Amnesty International, *Sri Lanka: Extrajudicial Executions, Disappearances and Torture, 1987–90*.
3 P. Janke, 'Spanish Separatism: ETA's threat to Basque Democracy', in W. Gutteridge (ed.), *The New Terrorism*, p. 156.

8 The IRA

1 R. Foster, *Modern Ireland 1600–1672*, p. 67.
2 F. S. L. Lyons, 'The Meaning of Independence', in B. Farrell (ed.), *The Irish Parliamentary Tradition*, p. 227.
3 J. Lee, *Ireland 1912–85*, pp. 2–3.
4 D. Harkness, *Northern Ireland since 1920*, p. 75, quoted by Foster, op. cit., p. 557.

5 Quoted in Foster, op. cit., p. 557. The Prime Minister in question, Joseph Lyons, was himself a Catholic.

6 Ibid., pp. 529–30. The telephonist did not last long after this.

7 D. McKittrick, ' "Troubles" Cost UK and Ireland £410 Million a Year, Report Says', *Independent*, 22 May 1990.

8 J. Cusack, 'Libyan Weapons Transformed the IRA Campaign', *Irish Times*, 28 July 1990.

9 D. McKittrick, 'The Men of War Promise Third Violent Decade', *Independent*, 29 September 1990.

10 G. Adams, MP, the President of Sinn Fein, quoted in P. O'Malley, 'Northern Ireland: Questions of Nuance', p. 35.

11 P. O'Malley, *The Uncivil Wars: Ireland Today*, p. 275.

12 P. O'Malley, 'Northern Ireland: Questions of Nuance', p. 37.

9 The Price of Victory

1 Quoted in A. Jamieson, *The Heart Attacked: Terrorism and Conflict in the Italian State*, p. 77.

2 Ibid., pp. 78–9.

3 K. Wasmund, 'The Political Socialization of West German Terrorists', in P. Merkl (ed.), *Political Violence and Terror: Motifs and Motivations*, p. 192.

4 P. Wilkinson, 'Terrorism: Learning from Europe', *Independent*, 9 August 1990.

5 A. Jamieson, *The Heart Attacked: Terrorism and Conflict in the Italian State*, pp. 193–4.

6 D. McKittrick, 'Will the Trauma Return?', *Independent*, 22 August 1988.

Conclusion

1 W. A. Hazleton and S. Woy-Hazleton, 'Terrorism and the Marxist Left: Peru's Struggle Against Sendero Luminoso', *Terrorism*, 11, 1988, p. 471.

2 W. A. Hazleton and S. Woy-Hazleton, 'Sendero Luminoso and the Future of Peruvian Democracy', *Third World Quarterly*, 12, 1990, p. 21.

3 T. D. Mason and J. Swartzfager, 'Land Reform and the Rise of Sendero Luminoso in Peru', *Terrorism and Political Violence*, 1989, p. 534.

4 See the interview with Abimael Guzman, extracts from which are quoted in the *Independent*, 26 July 1988.

5 Hazleton and Woy-Hazleton, *Terrorism*, op. cit., p. 480.

6 Mason and Swartzfager, op. cit., pp. 517.

7 Ibid.

Bibliography

Adams, J., *The Financing of Terror*, New English Library, London, 1986.

Alexander, Y. and J. Sinai, *Terrorism: The PLO Connection*, Crane Russak, New York, 1989.

Amnesty International, *Sri Lanka: Extrajudicial Executions, Disappearances and Torture 1987–90*, Amnesty International, London, 1990.

Arendt, H., *On Revolution*, Faber and Faber, London, 1963.

Arnold, T. E., *The Violence Formula: Why People Lend Sympathy and Support to Terrorism*, Lexington Books, Lexington, 1988.

Aust, S., *The Baader-Meinhof Group: The Inside Story of a Phenomenon*, The Bodley Head, London, 1987.

Becker, J., *The Soviet Connection: State Sponsorship of Terrorism*, Institute for European Defence and Strategic Studies, Occasional Paper No. 13, London, 1985.

Bles, M. and R. Low, *The Kidnap Business*, Star Books, London, 1988.

Bowyer Bell, J., *A Time of Terror: How Democratic Societies Respond to Revolutionary Violence*, Basic Books Inc., New York, 1978.

Boyle, K., T. Hadden and P. Hillyard, *Ten Years On in Northern Ireland: The Legal Control of Political Violence*, The Cobden Trust, London, 1980.

Brogan, P., *World Conflicts: Why and Where They Are Happening*, Bloomsbury Publishing Ltd, London, 1990.

Burton, A. M., *Urban Terrorism: Theory, Practice and Response*, Leo Cooper, London, 1975.

– *Revolutionary Violence: The Theories*, Leo Cooper, London, 1977.

Campbell, K., 'Prospects for Terrorism in South Africa', *South Africa International*, 14, 1983, pp. 397–417.

Camus, A., *Resistance, Rebellion and Death*, Hamish Hamilton, London, 1961.

Cassese, A., *Terrorism, Politics and Law: The* Achille Lauro *Affair*, Polity Press, Cambridge, 1989.

Chaliand, G., *Terrorism: From Popular Struggle to Media Spectacle*, Saqi Books, London, 1987.

Chomsky, N., *The Fateful Triangle: The United States, Israel and the Palestinians*, Pluto Press, London, 1983.

– *The Culture of Terrorism*, Pluto Press, London, 1988.

Clark, R. P., *The Basque Insurgents: ETA, 1952–80*, University of Wisconsin Press, Madison, 1984.

Clarke, T., *By Blood and Fire: The Attack on the King David Hotel*, Hutchinson, London, 1981.

Cline, R. S. and Y. Alexander, *Terrorism: The Soviet Connection*, Crane Russak, published in cooperation with the Center for Strategic and International Studies, Georgetown University, Washington, DC, 1984.

Clutterbuck, R., *Guerrillas and Terrorists*, Faber and Faber, London, 1977.

– *The Media and Political Violence*, The Macmillan Press, London, 1981.

Cohen, M. J., *Palestine to Israel: From Mandate to Independence*, Frank Cass, London, 1988.

Coogan, T. P., *The IRA* (second edn), Fontana Paperbacks, London, 1980.

Cusack, J., 'Libyan Weapons Transformed the IRA Campaign', *Irish Times*, 28 July 1990.

Dobson, C. and R. Payne, *Terror!: The West Fights Back*, The Macmillan Press, London, 1982.

– *War Without End: The Terrorists – an Intelligence Dossier*, Harrap, London, 1986.

Ehrenfeld, R., *Narco-Terrorism: The Kremlin Connection*, The Heritage Foundation, Washington, DC, 1987.

Evans, R. E., 'Terrorism and Subversion of the State: Italian Legal Responses', *Terrorism and Political Violence*, 1, 1989, p. 324.

Ewing, K. D. and C. A. Gearty, *Freedom Under Thatcher: Civil Liberties in Modern Britain*, Oxford University Press, Oxford, 1990.

Fisk, R., *Pity the Nation: Lebanon at War*, André Deutsch, London, 1990.

Flapan, S., *The Birth of Israel: Myths and Realities*, Pantheon Books, New York, 1987.

Flint, J., 'Prisoners Tell of Brutal Regime in Torture Chamber of Khiam', *Observer*, 13 May 1990.

– 'The Youngest Martyrs: Palestine's Davids', *Observer*, 15 July 1990.

Ford, F. L., 'Reflections on Political Murder: Europe in the Nineteenth and Twentieth Centuries', in W. J. Mommsen and G. Hirschfeld (eds.), *Social Protest, Violence and Terror in Nineteenth- and Twentieth-century Europe*, The Macmillan Press, London, 1982.

– *Political Murder: From Tyrannicide to Terrorism*, Harvard University Press, Cambridge, Mass., 1985.

Foster, R., *Modern Ireland 1600–1972*, Allen Lane, The Penguin Press, London, 1988.

Francis, S. T., *The Soviet Strategy of Terror*, The Heritage Foundation, Washington, DC, 1981.

Freedman, L., C. Hill, A. Roberts, R. J. Vincent, P. Wilkinson and P. Windsor, *Terrorism and International Order*, Routledge and Kegan Paul, London, 1986.

Friedlander, R. A., *Terror Violence: Aspects of Social Control*, Oceana Publications, London, 1983.

Gal-Or, N., *International Cooperation to Suppress Terrorism*, Croom Helm, London, 1985.

Gillespie, R., *Soldiers of Peron: Argentina's Montoneros*, Clarendon Press, Oxford, 1982.

– 'The Urban Guerrilla in Latin America', in N. O'Sullivan (ed.), *Terrorism, Ideology and Revolution*, Wheatsheaf Books, Brighton, 1986, p. 150.

Gilmour, D., *Lebanon: The Fractured Country*, Martin Robertson, Oxford, 1983.

Golan, G., 'The Soviet Attitude Towards the Use of Terror', in A. Kurz (ed.), *Contemporary Trends in World Terrorism*, Praeger, New York, 1987, p. 94.

Goren, R., *The Soviet Union and Terrorism*, George Allen and Unwin, London, 1984.

Gott, R., *Guerrilla Movements in Latin America*, Thomas Nelson and Sons, London, 1970.

Green, S., *Living by the Sword: America and Israel in the Middle East 1968–87*, Faber and Faber, London, 1988.

Greenwood, C., 'Terrorism and Humanitarian Law: The Debate over Additional Protocol 1', *Israel Yearbook on Human Rights*, 19, 1989, p. 187.

Guevara, E., *Guerrilla Warfare*, Penguin, Harmondsworth, 1969.

Gutteridge, W. (ed.), *The New Terrorism*, Mansell Publishing, London, 1986.

Halliday, F., *Iran: Dictatorship and Development* (second edn), Penguin, Harmondsworth, 1979.

Hampson, N., 'From Regeneration to Terror: The Ideology of the French Revolution', in N. O'Sullivan (ed.), *Terrorism, Ideology and Revolution*, Wheatsheaf Books, Brighton, 1986, p. 49.

Harkness, D., *Northern Ireland since 1920*, Helicon, Dublin, 1983.

Hazleton, W. A. and S. Woy-Hazleton, 'Terrorism and the Marxist Left: Peru's Struggle against Sendero Luminoso', *Terrorism*, 11, 1988, p. 471.

– 'Sendero Luminoso and the Future of Peruvian Democracy', *Third World Quarterly*, 12, 1990, p. 21.

Heiberg, M., *The Making of the Basque Nation*, Cambridge University Press, Cambridge, 1989.

Hirst, D., *The Gun and the Olive Branch: The Roots of Violence in the Middle East* (second edn), Faber and Faber, London, 1984.

Hobsbawm, E. J., *Nations and Nationalism since 1780: Programme, Myth, Reality*, Cambridge University Press, Cambridge, 1990.

BIBLIOGRAPHY

Hodges, D. C. (ed.), *Philosophy of the Urban Guerrilla: The Revolutionary Writings of Abraham Guillen*, William Morrow, New York, 1973.

Hoffman, B., *Recent Trends and Future Prospects of Terrorism in the United States*, Rand Corporation, Santa Monica, California, 1988.

Horchem, H. F., 'The Lost Revolution of West Germany's Terrorists', *Terrorism and Political Violence*, 1, 1989, p. 353.

Hussain, A., *Political Terrorism and the State in the Middle East*, Mansell Publishing, London, 1988.

Hutchinson, E. H., *Violent Truce*, Devin-Adair, New York, 1956.

Jamieson, A., *The Heart Attacked: Terrorism and Conflict in the Italian State*, Marion Boyars, London, 1989.

– 'Entry, Discipline and Exit in the Italian Red Brigades', *Terrorism and Political Violence*, 2, 1990, p. 1.

Janke, P., 'Spanish Separatism: ETA's Threat to Basque Democracy', in W. Gutteridge (ed.), *The New Terrorism*, Mansell Publishing, London, 1986, p. 135.

Jenkins, B., *New Modes of Conflict*, Rand Corporation, Santa Monica, California, 1983.

– *The Study of Terrorism: Definitional Problems*, Rand Corporation, Santa Monica, California, 1980.

– *Terrorism: Between Prudence and Paranoia*, Rand Corporation, Santa Monica, California, 1983.

– *Future Trends in International Terrorism*, Rand Corporation, Santa Monica, California, 1985.

– *International Terrorism: The Other World War*, Rand Corporation, Santa Monica, California, 1985.

Josephus, *The Jewish War*, Penguin, Harmondsworth, 1970.

Kennedy, P., *The Rise and Fall of the Great Powers*, Fontana Press, London, 1989.

Khalidi, W., *From Haven to Conquest*, Institute for Palestinian Studies, Beirut, 1971.

Kiernan, T., *Yasir Arafat: The Man and the Myth*, Abacus, London, 1976.

Kurz, A. (ed.), *Contemporary Trends in World Terrorism*, Praeger, New York, 1987.

Laqueur, W., *Guerrilla: A Historical and Critical Study*, Weidenfeld & Nicolson, London, 1977.

– *The Guerrilla Reader*, Wildwood House, London, 1978.

– *The Age of Terrorism*, Weidenfeld & Nicolson, London, 1987.

Laqueur, W. and Y. Alexander (eds.), *The Terrorism Reader*, NAL Penguin, New York, 1987.

Lee, J. J., *Ireland, 1912–1985: Politics and Society*, Cambridge University Press, Cambridge, 1989.

Levitt, G. M., *Democracies Against Terror: The Western Response to State-supported Terrorism*, Praeger, New York, 1988.

Lewis, B., *The Assassins*, Al Saqi Books, London, 1985.

– 'Islamic Terrorism?', in B. Netanyahu (ed.), *Terrorism: How the West Can Win*, Weidenfeld & Nicolson, London, 1986, p. 65.

Livingstone, N. C., *The War Against Terrorism*, Lexington Books, Lexington, 1982.

Lodge, J. (ed.), *The Threat of Terrorism*, Wheatsheaf Books, Brighton, 1988.

Luttwak, E., *The Grand Strategy of the Soviet Union*, Weidenfeld & Nicolson, London, 1983.

Lyons, F. S. L., 'The Meaning of Independence', in B. Farrell (ed.), *The Irish Parliamentary Tradition*, Gill and Macmillan, Dublin, 1973, p. 223.

McKee, G. and R. Franey, *Time Bomb: Irish Bombers, English Justice and the Guildford Four*, Bloomsbury Publishing Ltd, London, 1988.

McKittrick, D., 'Will the Trauma Return?', *Independent*, 22 August 1988.

– 'The Men of War Promise Third Violent Decade', *Independent*, 29 September 1990.

– '"Troubles" cost UK and Ireland £410 Million a Year, Report Says', *Independent*, 22 May 1990.

Marighela, C., *For the Liberation of Brazil*, Penguin, Harmondsworth, 1971.

161

Martin, D. C. and J. Walcott, *Best Laid Plans: The Inside Story of America's War Against Terrorism*, Harper and Row, New York, 1988.

Mason, T. D. and J. Swartzfager, 'Land Reform and the Rise of Sendero Luminoso in Peru', *Terrorism and Political Violence*, 1, 1989, p. 516.

Merkl, P. (ed.), *Political Violence and Terror: Motifs and Motivations*, University of California Press, Los Angeles, 1986.

Mickolus, E. F., *Transnational Terrorism: A Chronology of Events, 1968–1979*, Aldwych Press, London, 1980.

Mommsen, W. J. and G. Hirschfeld (eds.), *Social Protest, Violence and Terror in Nineteenth- and Twentieth-century Europe*, The Macmillan Press, London, 1982.

Morris, B., *The Birth of the Palestinian Refugee Problem, 1947–1949*, Cambridge University Press, Cambridge, 1987.

Morris, E. and A. Hoe, *Terrorism: Threat and Response*, The Macmillan Press, Basingstoke, 1987.

Mullin, C., *Error of Judgement: The Birmingham Bombings*, Chatto and Windus, London, 1986.

Naimark, N. M., 'Terrorism and the Fall of Imperial Russia', *Terrorism and Political Violence*, 2, 1990, p. 171.

Netanyahu, B. (ed.), *Terrorism: How the West Can Win*, Weidenfeld & Nicolson, London, 1986.

Niezing, J. (ed.), *Urban Guerrilla*, Rotterdam University Press, Rotterdam, 1974.

No Comment, Article 19, London, 1989.

O'Malley, P., *The Uncivil Wars: Ireland Today*, Blackstaff Press, Belfast, 1983.

– *Northern Ireland: Questions of Nuance*, The John W. McCormack Institute of Public Affairs, University of Massachusetts, Boston, 1990.

O'Sullivan N. (ed.), *Terrorism, Ideology and Revolution*, Wheatsheaf Books, Brighton, 1986.

Porzecanski, A. C., *Uruguay's Tupamaros: The Urban Guerrilla*, Praeger, New York, 1973.

Ra'anan, U., R. L. Pfaltzgraff, R. H. Shultz, E. Halperin and I. Lukes, *Hydra of Carnage*, Lexington Books, Lexington, 1986.

Rapoport, D. (ed.), *Inside Terrorist Organizations*, Frank Cass, London, 1988.

Rapoport, D. and Y. Alexander (eds.), *The Morality of Terrorism: Religious and Secular Justifications*, Pergamon Press, New York, 1982.

Reich, W. (ed.), *Origins of Terrorism: Psychologies, Ideologies, Theologies, States of Mind*, Woodrow Wilson International Centre for Scholars and Cambridge University Press, Cambridge, 1990.

Rosie, G., *The Directory of International Terrorism*, Mainstream Publishing, Edinburgh, 1986.

Said, E., 'Identity, Negation and Violence', *New Left Review*, 171, 1988, p. 46.

Said, E. and C. Hitchens (eds.), *Blaming the Victims: Spurious Scholarship and the Palestinian Question*, Verso, London, 1988.

Schlagheck, D. M., *International Terrorism: An Introduction to the Concepts and Actors*, Lexington Books, Lexington, 1988.

Schmid, A. P. and J. de Graaf, *Violence as Communication: Insurgent Terrorism and the Western News Media*, Sage Publications, London, 1982.

Schmid, A. P., A. J. Jongman *et al.*, *Political Terrorism*, North Holland Publishing Company, Amsterdam, 1988.

Serfaty, S., 'The Soviet Union in Africa: Realities and Limits', *South Africa International*, 14, 1983, p. 311.

Shlaim, A., *Collusion Across the Jordan: King Abdullah, the Zionist Movement and the Partition of Palestine*, Clarendon Press, Oxford, 1988.

Slater, R. O. and M. Stohl (eds.), *Current Perspectives on International Terrorism*, The Macmillan Press, London, 1988.

Sobel, L. A. (ed.), *Political Terrorism 1968–74*, Clio Press, Oxford, 1975.

BIBLIOGRAPHY

– *Political Terrorism 1974–8*, Clio Press, Oxford, 1978.

Stalker, J., *Stalker*, Harrap, London, 1988.

Sterling, C., *The Terror Network: The Secret War of International Terrorism*, Weidenfeld & Nicolson, London, 1981.

Stohl, M. (ed.), *The Politics of Terrorism* (third edn), Marcel Dekker, New York, 1988.

Stohl, M. and G. A. Lopez (eds.), *Government Violence and Repression: An Agenda for Research*, Greenwood Press, New York, 1986.

Thackrah, R., 'Terrorism: A Definitional Problem', in P. Wilkinson and A. M. Stewart (eds.), *Contemporary Research on Terrorism*, Aberdeen University Press, Aberdeen, 1987, p. 24.

Townsend, C., *Political Violence in Ireland: Government and Resistance Since 1848*, Clarendon Press, Oxford, 1983.

– 'The Process of Terror in Irish Politics', in N. O'Sullivan (ed.), *Terrorism, Ideology and Revolution*, Wheatsheaf Books, Brighton, 1986.

Tucker, H. H. (ed.), *Combating the Terrorists: Democratic Responses to Political Violence*, Facts on File, New York, 1988.

Walter, E. V., *Terror and Resistance: A Study of Political Violence*, Oxford University Press, New York, 1969.

Wardlaw, G., *Political Terrorism: Theories, Tactics and Counter-measures* (second edn), Cambridge University Press, Cambridge, 1989.

Wasmund, K., 'The Political Socialization of West German Terrorists', in P. Merkl (ed.), *Political Violence and Terror: Motifs and Motivations*, University of California Press, Los Angeles, 1986.

Weinberg, L. and P. Davis, *Introduction to Political Terrorism*, McGraw-Hill, New York, 1989.

Wilkinson, P., *Terrorism and the Liberal State* (second edn), The Macmillan Press, London, 1986.

– 'Terrorism: Learning from Europe', *Independent*, 9 August 1990.

Wilkinson, P. and A. M. Stewart, *Contemporary Research on Terrorism*, Aberdeen University Press, Aberdeen, 1987.

Wright, R., *Sacred Rage: The Crusade of Modern Islam*, André Deutsch, London, 1986.

Index

Abbas, Abu 95
Abercorn restaurant 120
Abu Dhabi 63
Achille Lauro 95
Action Directe 135
Adams, Gerry 127
Aden 33
Afghanistan 4
Agrippa 19
Air France 55, 62
Air India 104, 105
Akali Dal 103, 104, 105
Akka hospital 71
Al-Dawa 81, 90
'Al Fatah Organization-Iraqi Branch' 63
Aldershot 122
Aldunate, Wilson Ferreira 42
Alexander II, Tsar 23
Alexander, Yonah 64
Alfa Romeo 133
Algeria 33, 62
Algerian war 79
Algiers 61, 81
Amal 76–7, 81, 82, 88, 94
American Task Force on Combating
    Terrorism 15
American University in Beirut 87, 88
Amin, Idi 66
Amman 52, 63
Amnesty International 102, 149
Amos Ltd 137, 138
Amsterdam 61
ANC (African National Congress) 4, 98
Anderson, Terry 88, 90
Anglo-Iranian Oil Company 73
Anglo-Irish Agreement (1985) 126, 127,
    139
Angola 33, 98
Angry Brigade 132
Aoun, Michel 93
Arab League 59
Arab Liberation Front 61
Arab Revolt 46
Arab Revolutionary Army Palestine
    Command 61–2

Arab Revolutionary Cells 93
Arafat, Yasser 49, 50, 57–61, 64, 66, 67,
    71, 93
Arens, Moshe 64
Argentina 36, 43, 44
Arm of the Arab Revolution 62
Armstrong, Lord 121
Assad, President 76, 151
Assassins 20, 23, 150
Associated Press 88
Athens 12, 52, 53, 56, 81, 83
Auque, Roger 89, 91
Austria 62
Ayacucho University 148

B-Specials 116, 117
Baader, Andreas 134, 135
Baader-Meinhof gang 3
Baalbek 79, 80
Baghdad airport 63
Bakunin, Mikhail 23–4, 39
Ballygawley, County Tyrone 122
Bandaranaike, Solomon West Ridgeway 99
Bangkok 56
Barcelona 110
Basque General Council 109
Basque Nationalist Party (PNV) 107, 110
Basque region/Basques 2, 3, 97, 106–11,
    112, 129, 139, 140
Bates, Sir Richard Dawson 117
Batista, Fulgencio 34, 35
Battalions of the Lebanese Resistance (later
    Amal) 76
Beaufort Castle 69
Beersheba 46
Begin, Menachem 13, 47, 67, 68, 69, 71,
    76, 95
Beihl, Eugen 108
Beirut 56, 67–72, 76–81, 90, 92, 93–4, 118
Beirut University College 93
Bekaa valley 69
Belfast 115, 117, 120, 124, 125, 127, 145
Belgium 63, 135
Benghazi 85
Bernadotte, Count Folke 47

Berri, Nabih 76, 79, 81, 82, 88, 94
Bessbrook 121, 124
Besse, Georges 135
Bhindranwale, Sant Jarnail Singh 103, 104, 105
Bin Ghashir 85
Bir al-Abed 79, 80, 81, 88
Birmingham pub bombings (1974) 1, 2, 8, 14, 122
Bismarck, Otto von, Prince 25
Black June movement 63
Black September 1, 10, 54, 55, 56
Blanco, Hugo 35
Bloody Friday 120
Bolivia 35, 59
Bolsheviks 28, 29, 127
Bonn 53
Born, Jorge 43
Born, Juan 43
Boston Federal Court 119
BR see Red Brigades
Bradford, Robert 125
Bravo, Douglas 35
Brazil 36, 40, 41, 44
Brezhnev, Leonid 64
Brian, Michel 89
Brighton bombing 121–2
Britain
    abstains from UN vote censuring Israel 52; detainees released 53; and First World War 28; and hostage-taking 92; and Ireland 112–46; and Malaya 33; and Palestine 46–7; US attack on Libya launched from 89, 119–20
British Airways 56, 60, 61
Broad Front 42
Brussels 53
Buckley, William 88
Buenos Aires 36
Bulgaria 75
Burgos 107
Burke, T. H. 23
Burntollet Bridge 117
Bush, George 15, 95

Cagol, Mara 133
Cairo 53, 55, 60, 75, 83
Camp David Agreement 58
Campora, President 43
Carlos 66
Carlton Club 123
Carrero Blanco, Admiral Luis 108
Carton, Marcel 88, 92
Casey, William 65
Castro, Fidel 34, 35
Catholic Church 128

Cavendish, Lord Frederick 23
Central America 145, 152
Chad 83
Chatila 71, 77
Chile 40
China 2, 30, 148
CIA 15, 73, 78, 79, 88
Cicippio, Joseph 93
Clan na Gael 22
Clerkenwell jail 22
Clutterbuck, Richard 17
Collett, Alec 88, 90
Collins, Michael 13
Colombia 35
Colombo 99, 100
Colorado Party 42
Committee of Public Safety 21
Communist Party (Italy) 134
Conrad of Montferrat 20
Conservative Party 115
Contras 4, 93
Convention (French) 21
Coogan, T. P. 5
Cordes, Rudolf 89
Coudari, Marcel 89
Craigavon, Lord 117
Croatian TWA hijack 9–10, 11
Crusaders 20
Cuba 34, 35
Curcio, Renato 133
Cyprus 33

Damascus 53, 55, 56, 59, 63, 82
Damour 71
Darkley 121
Dawson's Field 53, 54
Deal, Kent 124
Debray, Regis 34, 44
Deir Yassin 48, 51
Deutsche Bank 135
Dodge, David 87, 88, 91
Dominican Republic 59
Donegal 125
Dortmund 125
Douglas, Leigh 89, 90
Doyle, William 125
Dresden 27
Droppin' Well pub 121, 125
Druse 78, 79
Dubai 60
Dublin 115
Dylan, Bob 132

East Germany (GDR) 135, 136
Easter Uprising 113
Egypt 51, 58, 83, 95

Egypt Air 83
Eid, Guy 56
El Al 52, 53, 62, 83, 85
Elbrick, C. Burke 40
Enniskillen 121
Ensslin, Gudrun 134, 135
Entebbe airport, Uganda 62, 64, 66
ETA (Euzkadi ta Askatasuna) 7, 13, 66, 98,
    106–12, 120, 126, 129, 135, 137, 139,
    150
ETAm 110, 111, 126, 140
ETApm 109, 110, 118
European Community (EC) 106, 113, 130,
    136, 137
European Court of Human Rights 141, 144

Fadlallah, Sheikh Mohammed Hussein 76–
    7, 79, 88
Fatah 13, 49, 50, 68, 94
Fatah Revolutionary Council 83, 94
Fedayeen 49, 50, 51, 57, 66, 69, 71, 94
Feltrinelli, Giangiacomo 133
Fiat 133
Fighting Communist Cells (CCC) 135
Fighting Organization 23
First World War 27, 28, 115
Fontaine, Marcel 88, 92
Formosa 43
France 4, 18, 78, 79, 80, 91–2, 129, 135
Franceschini, Alberto 133
Franco, General 107–10, 126
Frankfürt 134
Franz Ferdinand, Archduke 27
Free Lebanon 68, 69
French Revolution 18, 20, 21
French Terror (1793–4) 19, 20–21

Gadaffi, General 2, 61, 83–7, 119, 151
Galilee 46
Gandhi, Indira 99, 104, 105, 106, 131
Gandhi, Rajiv 105, 106, 129
Gaza 46
Gaza Strip 3, 96
Geagea, Samir 93
Gemayel, Amin 77, 79
Gemayel, Bashir 71, 77, 78
Geneva Conventions (1949) 97
Germany 27, 40, 136
    see also East Germany; West Germany
Giampetro, Caetano Pellegrini 41
Giap, General 32, 37, 50, 124
Gibraltar 145
Gibson, Lord Justice 125
Gibson, Mrs 125
Girondins 21
Gladstone, W. E. 22

Golden Temple, Amritsar 103, 104, 121,
    131
Gow, Ian 121
Graham, Edgar 125
Greece 56
Greenpeace 4
Grenada 79
Guernica 107
Guevara, Ernesto 'Che' 34–5, 36, 41, 44
Guildford Four 143–4
Guillen, Abraham 37–8, 39
Guinea-Bissau 33
Guzman, Dr Abimael 148

Habash, Dr George 10, 52, 61, 89
Habib, Philip 69
Haddad, Sa'ad 68, 69
Haganah 47
Hague, The 53
Haifa 51
Haig, Alexander 65, 75
Hamadei, Mohammed 91
Hammami, Said 63, 64
Hanna, David 125
Hanna, Maureen 125
Hanna, Robert 125
Harakah al-Tahrir al-Falastini see Fatah
Harrods 123
Hawatmeh, Nayif 57
Hebrew University of Jerusalem 51
Hebron 46
Herrhausen, Alfred 135
Herri Batasuna 3, 110, 111, 112, 127
Hezbollah 76–7, 81, 88, 89, 90, 92, 94,
    124
Higgins, Mr Justice 125
Hiroshima 27
Hirst, D. 54
Hitler, Adolf 4, 27, 28
Holocaust 45, 47
Home Rule (Irish) 22, 113
Hrawi, Elias 93
Hume, John 129
Hussein, King of Jordan 50, 51, 54, 59, 61,
    67
Hussein, Saddam 4, 151

Illia, President 36
India 103, 105, 118, 129
Intifada 96
Invincibles 23
IRA (Irish Republican Army) 1, 2–3, 5, 7,
    10, 21, 66, 97, 98, 106, 112, 113, 117–29,
    135, 137, 139–45, 150
Iran 4, 62, 72, 73, 74, 87, 92, 93
Iran, Shah of 73, 74

Irangate affair 93
Iranian Revolutionary Guards 76, 79
Iraq 4, 61, 63, 83, 95
Ireland 22, 112–15, 118, 119, 123, 126,
    128, 129, 141
Irgun Zvai Leumi 13, 47, 48
Irish Free State 113
Irish National Liberation Army (INLA)
    121, 125, 144
Irish Parliamentary Party 22
Irish Republican Brotherhood (IRB) 22,
    26, 113
Islamabad 63
Islamic Amal 76–7, 79
Islamic Holy War for the Liberation of
    Palestine 89
Islamic Jihad 78–82, 88–91, 93, 95
Ismaeli sect 20
Israel 3, 4, 5, 9, 10, 45–53, 57, 58, 59, 64,
    66–73, 76, 78, 81–2, 87, 92, 94, 95–6,
    116
Istanbul 62
Italy 78, 85, 133–4, 135, 137, 138–9

Jacobins 22
Jacobsen, David 88, 89, 92
Jaffna 99, 101, 102
Japan 27, 30, 40
Japanese Red Army 55, 56
Jenco, Father Laurence 88, 92
Jenkins, Brian 102
Jerusalem 20, 51
Jibril, Ahmad 61, 94
John Paul, Pope 75
Jonathan Institute 64, 66
Jordan 51, 53–4, 61, 63
Jordan, River 49, 50, 54
Josephus 19
Joubert, Christian 88
Juan Carlos, King 108
Jumblatt, Walid 78, 79
JVP 99, 101, 102

Kafr Qasem 49, 51
Kaithal 105
Kauffmann, Jean-Paul 88, 92
Keenan, Brian 89
Kennedy, Senator Edward 128
Kenya 33
Kenyatta, Jomo 13
Kerr, Malcolm 88
KGB 75
Khaddam, Abdel Halim 63
Khaled, Leila 53, 54
Khalistan 104, 106
Khan, Reza 73

Khartoum 56, 60
Khiam prison 91
Khomeini, Ayatollah 72, 74, 151
Kilburn, Peter 88, 90
King David Hotel, Jerusalem 5, 47
Kingsmill, South Armagh 120
Kiryat Shmona 57
Klinghoffer, Leon 95
KLM 61
Kuomintang 30, 33
Kuwait 4, 56, 63, 81, 82, 90, 95, 151

La Mon House Hotel 120–21
Lahore 104
Laporte, Pierre 8
Latin America 6, 35, 40–44, 89, 100
Law of Suspects 21
League of Nations 33, 46
Lebanon 51, 56, 57, 63, 65, 67–72, 76, 77,
    80, 87–94, 112, 116, 124
Lenin 6, 28–9, 30, 34, 44, 127, 133
Leningrad, Siege of 27
Levick, Brian 88
Levin, Jeremy 88
Lewis, Bernard 20
Liberation Tigers of Tamil Eelam
    see Tamil Tigers
Libya 4, 60, 61, 62, 75, 83–7, 119, 132
Libyan People's Bureau 119
Lichfield 124
Lima 147, 149
Litani, River 68
Livingstone, N. C. 65
Lockerbie 1, 2, 94
Lod International Airport 14, 54, 56
London 27, 63
London stock exchange 123
Londonderry 115, 117, 119, 125
Long March 30
Loughgall 123
Lufthansa 56, 62
Lurgan 124

Maalot 57
McAlpine, Lord 121
McCarthy, John 89
McCarthy, Senator 2
McGurk's bar, Belfast 120
Madrid 60, 110, 111
Mahler, Horst 134
Malaga 61
Malaya 33
Malta 83
Mao Tse-tung 6, 30–34, 37, 44, 50, 119,
    127, 148, 149

Maoism 32, 33, 34, 149
Mariategui, Jose Carlos 148
Marighela, Carlos 39–42, 100, 122, 134, 149
Maronite Christians 77, 115
Martyr Abou Mahmoud Squad 60
Marx, Karl 25, 133
Marxism 30, 36
Marxist-Leninism 29, 33, 34, 133
Maxwell, Paul 125
Maze prison 125
Meinhof, Ulrike 134, 135
Miami Showband 120
Milan 133
Mitrione, Dan 42
Mitterrand, François 92
MNF (multinational force) 77, 78
Mogadishu, Somalia 62, 66
Montagnards 21
Montevideo 36
Montoneros 43–4
Moore, George C. 56
Moro, Aldo 133
Morozov, Nikolai 24, 25
Morrison, Danny 126
Mossadeq, Mohammed 73
Mount Lebanon 77
Mountbatten, Lord 124–5
Movement of the Deprived 76
Moyne, Lord 47
Mozambique 33, 98
MR-8 40
Mugabe, Robert 13
Munich airport 53, 56
Munich Olympics (1974) 1, 2, 10, 12, 14, 55, 64
Munster 114
Mussawi, Hussein 76

Nagasaki 27
Napoleon Bonaparte 18, 25, 50
Narodnaya Volya 23, 29
Nash, Geoffrey 88
National Party (Uruguay) 42
NATO 124, 130, 134
Nazism 28, 135, 136
Neave, Airey 121
Nechaev, Sergei 24
Netanyahu, Jonathan 62
Neusel, Hans 136
New Jersey 79–80
Newry 123, 124
Nicaragua 4, 93
Nidhal, Abu 61, 63, 69, 83, 88, 94
Noel, Cleo 56
Normandin, Jean-Louis 91

Northern Ireland 2, 3, 9, 33, 106, 112, 116–23, 126, 129, 131, 139–45
Northern Ireland Civil Rights Association 117

Obeid, Sheikh 92
'Official' IRA 118
Oman 33
O'Neill, Tip 128
Ongania, General 36
OPEC 62
Operation Demetrius 141
Operation Peace in Galilee 69, 72, 94

Padfield, Philip 89, 90
Pahlavi dynasty 73, 74
Pakistan 63, 103, 104, 129
Palestine 19, 46, 47, 48, 59
Palestine Liberation Front (PLF) 95
Palestine Liberation Organization (PLO) 4, 45, 50–52, 57–71, 76, 83, 84, 94, 95, 96, 98, 150
Palestine Popular Struggle Front 53
Palestine Revolution Movement 63
Palestinian National Council 59
Palestinians 9, 45, 51, 53, 54, 59, 68, 69, 96
Pan Am flight 103 1, 94
Pando 41
Paris 57, 63, 91
Parnell, Charles Stewart 113
Partition Plan 48
Party of God see Hezbollah
Pearse, Patrick 113
People's Front of Liberation Tigers 101
People's War 31
Perón, Isabel 43
Perón, Juan Domingo 43
Peru 35, 147–9
Peruvian Communist Party 148
PFLP (Popular Front for the Liberation of Palestine) 9, 10, 52–6, 61, 62, 65, 89, 97, 122
PFLP-GC 57, 61, 94
PFLP-Special Operations 62
Phalangists 70, 71, 72, 77–80, 87
Phoenix Park, Dublin 23
Pirelli 133
PNV see Basque Nationalist Party
Pogues 144
Polhill, Robert 93
Popular Democratic Front for the Liberation of Palestine (PDFLP) 57
Prevention of Terrorism (Temporary Provisions) Act (1989) 15, 144
Provisional IRA 118, 119

Provisional Programme 59, 64
Provisional Sinn Fein 126, 127, 143
Puerto Rico 9
Punjab 103–6, 120, 129
Punta del Este 41

Qashfi, Daud 92
Qibya 48, 49, 51
Quebec 8

Rainbow Warrior 4
Rand Corporation 13–14, 102
Ras a-Shak 57
Reagan, Ronald 65, 75, 79, 80, 83, 84, 85,
    87, 90, 92, 93, 95
Red Army Faction (RAF) 7, 21, 62, 66,
    132, 134, 135–6, 138, 139
Red Brigades (BR) 3, 7, 21, 66, 108, 120,
    132, 133, 134, 135, 138, 139
Red Cross 52, 53, 70, 82
Red Zora 137, 138
Reed, Frank 93
Regent's Park, London 124
Regier, Frank 88
Renault 135
Revolutionary Cells 137
Revolutionary Communist Party of Brazil
    39
Revolutionary Justice Organization 89, 93
Rhodesia 33
Robespierre, Maximilien de 21, 28
Roermond, the Netherlands 124
Romania 4
Romans 19, 20
Rome 52, 55, 63, 81
Rome airport 12, 56, 60, 83
Rossa, O'Donovan 23
Royal Marine School of Music 124
Royal Ulster Constabulary (RUC) 116,
    118, 123, 124, 125, 141
Russia 18, 19, 23–5, 28, 29, 37, 127
Russian Revolution 28

Sabra 71, 77
Sadat, Anwar 61, 75
Sadr, Imam Mousa 76
Saint-Just, Louis de 21
Saiqa 94
SAS 123, 145
Saudi Arabia 4, 62
SAVAK 74
Save the Children 96
Schengen Treaty 136
Schiphol airport 56
Schleyer, Hans-Martin 135
Schmidt, Alfred 89, 90

Second World War 27, 45
Secretary of State for Northern Ireland 16
Sendero Luminoso 147, 148, 149
Sendic, Raul 41
Sergei Alexanderovich, Grand Duke 25
Seurat, Michel 88
Shamir, Yitzhak 13, 47, 95
Sharon, Ariel 70, 76
Sheikh Abdullah barracks, near Baalbek 79
Shia Muslims 20, 66–7, 68, 74, 76, 77, 81–
    2, 90, 91, 94
Shining Path *see* Sendero Luminoso
Sicarii 19–20, 23
Sidon 57, 69, 70
Sidra, Gulf of 84
Sikhs 7, 97, 103–6, 109, 121, 129
Sinai, Joshua 64
Singapore 56
Singh, V. P. 106
Sinn Fein 3, 113, 126, 127, 128
Sipiagin, Dmitrii 23
Six Day War 49, 52, 59
Skirmishers 22
Social Revolutionary Party 23, 29
Sontag, Camille 89
Souq al-Gharb 79
South Africa 3, 33
South America 3, 19, 35, 121, 145, 152,
    153
South Lebanon Army 91
South Moluccan separatists 9, 11
Soviet Union 2, 28, 64–5, 92, 148
Spain 18, 85, 106, 108, 110, 127, 129, 139,
    140
Sri Lanka 97, 98–102, 104, 106, 112, 118,
    120, 129, 140
Stalin, Joseph 2, 27, 28
Steen, Alann 93
Stern Gang 13, 47, 48
Stethem, Robert 81, 82
Stockholm 134
Stormont 116, 117, 118, 126, 141
Stronge, Sir Norman 125
Sunni Muslims 77
Switzerland 40, 53
Symbionese Liberation Army 132
Syria 4, 53, 56, 63, 70, 76, 82, 84–7, 94

al-Tal, Wasfi 54
Tal Zaatar refugee camp 71
Tamil Tigers 7, 97–104, 109, 121, 129
Tamils 98–103, 140
Tehran 91, 92
Tel Aviv 12, 48, 51, 52, 55
Territorial army HQ 123
Thailand 82

Thatcher, Margaret 90, 119, 121, 122, 126
Torres, Camilo 35
Townshend, Charles 22
Tracy, Edward 93
Travers, Mary 125
TREVI 136, 137
Trincomalee 100, 101
Triple A death squads 44
Tripoli 4, 85, 120
Tunis 60
Tupamaros 41–4, 100, 108, 119, 120, 134
Turin 133
Turner, Jesse Jonathan 93
TWA 9, 53, 81–2, 84, 90, 91
Twelver branch, Shia Islam 74
Tyre 57, 69, 70
Tyrol 18

Ulster 114, 115, 116
Ulster Defence Regiment (UDR) 124, 145
UNICEF 70
United Arab Emirates 63
United Nations 9, 47, 48, 52, 58, 59, 64, 68, 97–8, 113
United States 4, 9, 52, 59, 70, 72, 74–5, 78–82, 84–8, 90, 92, 93, 95, 119–20, 141, 152
US Bill of Rights 143
Uruguay 36, 41, 44, 131
Ustashi 9

Venezuela 35
Versailles, Treaty of (1919) 33
Vienna 62, 66, 83
Vienna, Congress of (1815) 18
Vietcong 32
Vietnam War 32–3, 75, 79, 124
Voice of the Palestinian Revolution 63
VPR 40

Waite, Terry 93
Wales, Charles, Prince of 117
Wardlaw, Professor Grant 86–7
Warrenpoint 121
Washington, George 4
Weir, Benjamin 88, 90, 92
Weitling, Wilhelm 23, 39
West Bank 49–50, 51, 96
West Berlin 84, 85
West Germany 53, 55, 56, 62, 90, 91, 133, 134–5, 137, 138, 139
Whitecross 120
Wildenrath, West Germany 124
William of Orange 4
Wilson, Harold 117, 136
Wright, Jonathan 88

Yugoslavia 9

Zealots 19, 20, 150
Zionism 47, 48, 51, 59, 60
Zurich 52